Low Lords

by

TR Pearson

BARKING MAD PRESS

DEEP DARK

1

I don't truly remember my first one, but that was by design. They take you down early to show you so you won't be rattled later. The last thing you want in the deep dark is some terrified fool with a blade.

We baptized my brother, Brody, on the week of his second birthday. Mom was already gone by then. That left me and my sister, Leigh Ann, Uncle Grady, Dad, and Beauty. The birthday boy was wearing the sheepskin ceremonial cloak. In The Great Book they call it a karstula, but it looks more like an apron. Ours smelled of cedar and bright leaf tobacco because we kept it in Granddaddy's trunk.

I'd accidentally busted our ceremonial ivory groper. After my sister, Leigh Ann, got baptized, I dropped it coming through the crease. It broke in four pieces that we tried to glue, but it would never quite stay together, so me and Dad made a replacement out of a broomstick and shovel steel.

We needn't have bothered. Brody was going through one of his phases. Everything he laid his hands on he threw. That groper didn't get close to the cavern. Brody had flung it away by the time we'd reached the cow lot.

The baptism ceremony is pretty antique. Thomas Jefferson wrote the words. The preamble called for Brody to eat an entire pilot biscuit while we kept him on his litter and waited in the barn for twilight. The cracker was stale, so naturally, Brody gave it a toss as well.

Leigh Ann pouted while we sat around. She was having a phase of her own. She groaned. She sighed. She whined a little.

"Why are doing this anyway?"

Even Uncle Grady, who usually enjoyed explaining the traditions and the customs, didn't bother to joust with Leigh Ann. She was far too sullen for that. If I'm honest, I was feeling a little exasperated myself. I was two months shy of my fourteenth birthday. Leigh Ann was twelve and a half. And we were having to deal with a little brother who'd only just turned two.

Brody was supposed to keep our parents from busting up for good. He was the remedy to their troubles that hadn't worked or taken — the wailing, pooping constant reminder that we were Low Lords with an asterisk. Our co-cap wasn't cavern lost. Our co-cap walked away.

Dad and Uncle Grady tried to sing the old songs as we carried Brody across the pasture, but they gave up long before we'd reached our cave. The cows and the sheep and the donkeys scattered at the sight of us. We staked one of them out about once a week as a sacrifice and token, and they'd decided in their livestock brains that was something best avoided.

We were supposed to be hauling Brody on a proper gamadan, an elaborate contraption with handles and a roof made of nightwood and cat tail stalks. Ours had been one of the grander specimens, passed down through generations.

There was even a drawing of it in the appendix of The Great Book.

Uncle Grady had loaned our sedan chair out to brethren up in Owensboro, and they'd yet to trouble themselves — three full years later — to bring it back. Consequently, we were carrying Brody on an old piece of quilt nailed to a couple of pickets — more of a jackleg stretcher than anything else.

Brody was supposed to crawl on his own from the mouth of our cave on down, but we could hardly expect a toddler to reach the bottleneck alone. It was too far in, and the route was plagued with guano pits and rocky constrictions. Instead, we strapped him into a rig we'd made for Beauty, and he rode down on her back.

Dad and Uncle Grady had a hard time setting our ritual fire knot alight. It was a fraud and a stand-in, of course, but the actual things are scarce and pricey. A genuine fire knot is a lumpy fatwood tumor that you can scour the uplands for weeks on end and never come across. They're easier to find down south where the forests are far more piney.

A pack of enterprising Georgia brethren offer fire knots on the gear list, but you'd need to be a raging ceremonial fool to consider paying their rate.

We kept a wire-bound lump of rags soaking in fuel oil in the back of Grady's shed. His roof leaked, and the bucket had no lid, so water got into the pail, which meant Dad and Uncle Grady weren't having much luck with their matches. I finally gathered a fistful of switchgrass and convinced them to light that instead.

It soon got going well enough to let them fire the torch off of it. All the while they were telling me (especially Uncle Grady) how that saw grass was a waste of time and wouldn't light a thing.

We'd gotten to be one of those families. It's hard to say when it finally happened, but we'd reached that point where we were gloomy in a general way and usually primed to discourage any glimmer of spontaneous ambition. Nothing was going to succeed. Precious little was worth trying. Whatever you thought was mistaken. Whatever you wanted you didn't need.

That's a hard way to live. It's a grinding obligation to feel like you have to let the air out of every stinking thing.

With the torch finally lit, Uncle Grady had us drop our heads and give him a few "Yes, brother"s as he spoke the entire prologue from memory. I thought the thing would never end. If there's ever been a man more capable than Thomas Jefferson of stringing resolves and therefores and nonthelesses together in a thicket of blubbery prose, I hope he's long since gone to bones and mulch and took his pencil with him.

Grady finally reached "As it is written," T.J.'s version of "Amen". Then we passed single file into our modest crease in the ground. The portal, for ceremonial purposes, but it's just a blowhole. You can feel it exhaling. There's a natural chimney on the west side of the slope.

Uncle Grady carried the torch in first. I went in after with our hot box. Then Beauty came through with the boy of the moment strapped onto her back. Leigh Ann came behind

Brody, too peeved to carry her groper. She was dragging it, and the blade was clanking and singing on the rocks.

Every quarter minute or so, Dad stirred himself to tell her, "Hey!"

Even under the best of conditions, it's a good quarter hour to the squeeze. To my mind, the best of conditions was me and Beauty under alone. That was in violation of by-laws, of course. Low Lords caved in pairs or stayed home, but part of what gave those trips a charge and a thrill was depending on a creature who'd go anywhere I went and do it without comment or objection. If I never came out, she wouldn't either. You can't find too many people like that.

This descent was slower than usual because Uncle Grady had aged out of duty. He participated in the rituals and the occasional show stunts, but he didn't take his turn with a head lamp and a groper anymore. Dad was having his own troubles. A bad knee. An arthritic shoulder. A bite wound that was a decade old but still flared up sometimes.

There was more palaver to mark our progress. We stopped at all the stations and opened each locker along the way. The helmets and the headlamps got blessed. We took turns sipping from the granite chalice. On the second plateau, Grady pulled our hurricane lamp off its hook and gave it a rhyming couplet. Brody was supposed to eat another pilot biscuit, but he wouldn't even take it in hand.

Beauty nosed them up first. She always does. She stopped and made her noise. It's somewhere between a growl and a warble, a blend of fight and fun.

9

Tradition calls for the child to lead down to the squeeze, but things have changed in the past few years, and that's not safe anymore. They don't live as deep as they used to. I've heard various theories why. The pull of the sun. Their raging appetites. Simple overcrowding. Then there's the global warming theory. That one holds sway with me. With the seas rising and the water pouring in holes it never reached before, the cavus ferinus have moved ever higher in a bid to stay undrowned and dry.

I reached the squeeze first with the hot box and my groper and opened the gate for the rest of them. Dad and Leigh Ann came close behind. Our alabastards were lurking just beyond the reach of our headlamps. We could hear their sinusy breathing. The scratch of their claws on stone. Beauty came down snarling with Brody on her back. Uncle Grady lingered to bring up the rear because he's who we'd send out first.

We all packed onto a flat rock terrace just big enough to hold us. That was the spot where the cave opened up into an authentic cavern. Beauty's tail had gone bushy. Her spine hairs were up. She growled with every breath.

Uncle Grady said, "We of the darkness," and we all switched off our lamps.

Grady had memorized one decisive paragraph, a scrap of catechism from The Great Book. The CFs were so close to topside anymore, we couldn't afford to sit unlit and hear the entire thing. They'd swarm us, and we'd be fighting a full blown rear guard all the way out, so Grady was as quick with the chatter as Grady ever got.

We waited for him to finally arrive at "We welcome you unto us." It seemed like an eternity. It was maybe twenty seconds. We all had our thumbs on our switches. Our lamps came on, and there they were.

On the walls and the cave roof. Thick upon on the floor. They adapt to fit their caverns, and ours was spacious in Virginia. Not like the cramped one we'd manned in Cumberland where our alabastards were only knee-high. This Virginia swarm was people sized. Incisors like curved spikes. Vaguely reptile heads. Coal black eyes. Swept back ears. Stray tufts of wiry hair on their clammy, pale skin. Scaly nose flaps. Amber talons extended. Their usual fungal/guano stink.

I directed the hotbox towards the three alabastards crowded closest. They retreated, but only a little. Two of them were on the ceiling. One of them on the wall. They stopped after maybe ten feet and showed us their teeth and nasty cleft tongues.

Beauty snarled. She never bothered with barking where it came to alabastards. She had a fine set of choppers herself that she revealed to the entire swarm. That bought us another three feet of buffer. Beauty was bound to have been a legend throughout the deep dark by then. She'd torn up enough CFs to rate a dragon rep.

Grady eased out first with Beauty and the baptized boy behind him. Then Dad. Then Leigh Ann with me after her. I'd volunteered for the rear guard work. Alabastards would charge and draw back. Roll up and retreat. It was more unsettling than dangerous. The sort of bluff bears get up to, though one careless juvenile got a little too close, and I jabbed him with my groper, a prick between bones that let a stream of fluid out. Blue-green. Iridescent. The stuff looks like antifreeze. He scooped up some guano for a poultice and slapped it onto the wound.

I allowed Leigh Ann to clear the pipe entirely before I passed her my groper and crawled backwards up the crease, the way you had to now. I kept the hotbox aimed towards the deep dark, but they hardly care about the heat like they used to. Time was you could show the swarm a live coal, and they'd vanish into the black. No more. They've grown bold, maybe desperate. You just about have to slice them to make them stop.

Dad and Grady helped me out. They grabbed me by the ankles and pulled me the last few feet. An intrepid alabastard had followed me all the way to the mouth of our cave. He stuck his pale, ugly head through the opening and snorted. It seemed less like a threat than a show of bravado and thoroughgoing disrespect.

Beauty snarled. Uncle Grady recited some choice colonial doggerel. Leigh Ann looked glum. Brody, however, reminded us what we were there for. He pointed at that alabastard and laughed.

2

We rotate like the Methodist clergy, just on a longer schedule. Every six or eight years, we pack up our stuff and head out to assume a fresh post. When I was born, we were in Cumberland, Tennessee, where the caves are cramped and sandstone. Our CFs there were more like an infestation of rodents than anything else.

One of them alone could do you the kind of damage a bobcat might get up to. Four or five could make you wish you were dead. A dozen could kill you outright, but the thinking went you'd deserve it if you got in such a fix.

In Tennessee, it was me and my parents, Granddaddy Hoyt, Uncle Grady and Jo Jo, his son, who was devotedly unindustrious and eight years older than me.

At first we were plagued by some nosy backwoods neighbors who kept coming around to hunt until Granddaddy Hoyt took pains to explain to them our faith. Granddaddy had concocted a theology for us that made us sound like Jewish Mormons with a Christian Science bent. There was a little Amish in there as well intended to account for our curious caving clothes and the fact that we lived, as best we could, apart.

Granddaddy Hoyt assured our neighbors that, in addition to eating stewed crows at Christmas, we often circumcised the odd hillbilly on a whim. It didn't matter if he'd been seen to before, according to Granddaddy Hoyt. He showed those boys a pair of sheep shears and said, "We've got our own ways of doing." I don't believe we saw any hunters after that.

Our compound had three houses and one communal kitchen off in a low-slung building by itself. It was only big enough for a run of countertop, two stoves, a sink, and a long plank table where we took all our meals. We had an AM radio to keep us informed, mostly about the weather. We didn't own a television, and in Cumberland at least, there wasn't any internet back then. We barely had phone service, and the power would kick off for six or eight hours in an ambitious breeze.

The clan that had left when we came in — they'd gone to Nevada or somewhere — had more abandoned that compound than moved out of it. They'd left the houses filthy and cluttered. A heap of tin cans in the side yard. A rusty truck engine suspended from a tree limb by the barn. Inside was a tractor with two flat tires and a bush hog with a rusted deck. The fences were all tumbledown, and the livestock left behind might well have strayed if they'd not been too frail and bony to wander.

Uncle Grady reported that clan first thing. He was big on rules of order and kept a stack of official Legion forms for lodging his complaints. He'd sit at the big plank table with his clicky pen from Cypress Gardens (he'd not been to Cypress Gardens; he'd just found it on the ground), and he'd select the appropriate sheet from his stack and tick the appropriate boxes. Then off it would go in the packet to Carlsbad, and he'd frequently see results. Not resounding, decisive results but just partial satisfaction, like the money order Grady got us for the cost of repairing one tractor tire.

Dad and Grady's sister, Marie, had died two years before I was born. For a long time, they let me think that she'd fallen in a chasm. I pictured her chased by alabastards, doing them mischief with her groper until they swarmed her and forced her off a ledge and down into the dark. My mom was the one who finally told me Marie had gassed herself in Granddaddy's Pontiac sedan on a sleety March afternoon.

"It's a hard life," Mom explained to me. "Your Aunt Marie left it the best way she could find." I couldn't know at the time my mother would also prove to be Aunt Marie-ish, only with less nerve and a better range of options.

I was officially named after Granddaddy Hoyt, but it never stuck and took. I was Little Hoyt for a year or three, and then L.H. until I was seven. After that everybody just called me Mack. I can't remember why. I'm told I got baptized in a lively Cumberland swarm up. I was two at the time, like Brody. I've got no memory of it at all, but I do recall my first groper. Dad made the blade. Granddaddy Hoyt carved the handle. An alabastard took it from me the day Jo Jo got dragged off.

The thing that most sticks in my head about our years in the Tennessee mountains is the memory of my mother wandering along the hilltop above our pasture. She'd always called them walks, but even as a boy I had a sense that they were more than that and worse.

We managed a solution cave in Cumberland, sculpted by drainage over the years. The guys who'd tended it before us hadn't done a thing to improve it. In fact, they'd so cluttered up the main channel with their junked equipment and trash that it was all you could do to crawl down to the squeeze. Granddaddy Hoyt was particularly indignant about the state of the cavern. Trash was for pits topside. Channels and passes should always be clean.

Granddaddy Hoyt let me and Jo Jo see to the clutter. He was from the dynamite generation. He enlarged the passage all by himself. Once he was done, I could have ridden on his shoulders to the squeeze.

Dad and Granddaddy welded up a gate out of solid pipe steel. It fit the choke so precisely you could hardly slip a groper blade past it, and it was stout enough to make us all wonder why we couldn't just bolt it shut and stay topside. Of course, Uncle Grady and Dad and Granddaddy had seen enough of alabastards to know we had to show the colors, serve as the armed and living evidence that there was a force arrayed against them determined to keep them where they were.

"Otherwise," Granddaddy Hoyt explained, "they're sure to get wolfy with us."

I believed him. I was that kind of kid. Jo Jo didn't because he was that sort. To his way of thinking, a stout steel gate suited him right down to the ground. It would free him to do as he pleased, which usually involved a bit of goat abuse and loads of aimless fiddling. Jo Jo was also a Magnus, Robot Fighter fan of the highest order, so he was content to read back issues for entire afternoons and tell anybody within earshot about the harm he'd rain on Talpa and Xyrkol given half a chance.

16

I can see now Jo Jo just wanted to be a kid, but that's not what we'd been born into. My Dad was always more honest about that with me than Grady ever was with Jo Jo.

In the ordinary way of things, me and Jo Jo never did duty together. We always went down with a grown up, and we were usually good for a half shift. But then the barn caught fire one morning, and the adults had to choose between two potential dangers. They settled on the barn and sent me and Jo Jo down to man the squeeze alone. I know now they thought we'd be on our own for an hour at the most, but when live coals drifted to the kitchen roof, the grownups didn't know the leisure to give us any thought. So me and Jo Jo stayed a while on the ledge on the deep side of the squeeze with the steel gate standing open behind us and our gropers leaning against a rock.

We were used to hearing the snorts and scuttling noises our alabastards made and expected to see one or two venture into the halo of our lamplight. Not close enough to be a threat but like fish rising for the briefest moment to the surface from the murky depths. We got quite a bit more than that but only after our second hour, once the alabastards could be certain that something peculiar was going on.

Parked at a choke point it's easy to believe that, since you're the sentinel, you're the one who's doing all the watching. What I learned that day with Jo Jo is that they're always watching back. Worse than that, they're calculating, plotting, probably seething too. Up to then, I'd imagined them like pale Jo Jo's, doing nothing much in the dark.

Jo Jo was bending my ear about Leeja Clane. She was Magnus, the Robot Fighter's main squeeze and future bride, and Jo Jo had tumbled for her in a fairly significant way. I'd just turned seven at the time while Jo Jo was nearly fifteen, so he should have been the one telling me that Leeja Clane was only ink on paper, but instead he was holding forth about the future he hoped to have with her. From the artwork I'd seen, it was chiefly a cleavage driven kind of love.

The only thing active about Jo Jo was his imagination, so he could hold forth at length about what he'd get up to with this comic book girl. There was some world travel on a hovercraft and quite a lot of dining out. Jo Jo described the bed they'd sleep in and the view that it would have, but he was mercifully reluctant to talk about any romantic particulars.

I was young enough to still be scared of females. I'd gone to the Rexall with my mother not long before and a girl there had punched me in the arm. She did it just because she wanted to and I happened to be handy, and I was informed in no uncertain terms that I couldn't punch her back. So I was all up in the air about females, but luckily Jo Jo had no specifics on the sorts of things that happened between dinner out and the sun rising on his spectacular view.

Leeja Clane distracted Jo Jo, and Jo Jo distracted me, while the threat by fire to our kitchen was occupying all the grown ups. For their part, the alabastards noticed. They organized. They struck.

It was a textbook swarm up. I know that now. They came in three waves, four across. We didn't see the first batch until they were on top us, and I mean attached to us with their talons and their teeth. They're greasy, and they smell like last month's socks. I'd never touched one before, but me and Jo Jo had to get up to some immediate and ferocious flailing.

One of them must have been charged with hauling our gropers into the dark. He made a fine job of it while we were busy fighting off the other three. Then six more came flanking in. Two of them kept me occupied – snarling and nipping and clawing –while the rest of them went at Jo Jo. Four more rushed in to cover him up. They knocked off his helmet and headlamp, tumbled him into the deep dark and dragged him into the bowels of the cave.

The pair I'd been fighting retreated, dropped off the ledge and disappeared, and suddenly it was just me at the squeeze, and Jo Jo's voice was faint already. He was calling out as pitifully as any human might.

"Mack!" I heard. Then "Help!" Then gurgling, and then nothing.

I'd like to say I went down after him because I felt duty-bound to do it. That I was fueled by indignation. I'd like to say that too. That I waded in among those beasts they way Magnus, The Robert Fighter would. The truth is, I was too shocked at first to do anything at all. I just stood there with my headlamp beam fixed on the last place I'd seen my cousin.

After a half minute or so I managed to call out, "Jo Jo!" twice.

I could barely hear him shouting back. They'd hauled him well into the deep dark.

The kitchen was saved by the time I got topside. Uncle Grady, in fact, was already making a sketch of the new barn they'd build and identifying the supplies and materials Carlsbad might agree to pay for.

I hadn't settled on just what I'd tell them, but it turned out they didn't need awfully much. One look at me bleeding from scratches and nips and they grabbed up their cave gear and lit out. It was gropers and hot boxes all around. My mom nocked a bolt in her ripper on the way. The things look like compact crossbows. They have a complicated system of sprung wood and pulleys. Her arrows, or bolts, were barbed and stubby, not the sort of thing even an alabastard could just grab by the shaft and yank out.

We all hustled down to the squeeze. In my panic, I'd left the steel gate standing open. They didn't even pause but plunged on into the inky chamber below the ledge. I followed, wasn't about to sit around and wait for them to get swallowed up to.

You can't bring enough light into a proper cavern to make it like anywhere else. The industrial lantern that causes your cellar to look like the Sahara at noon, is just starlight in the blackness once you've haul it underground. Where you're going is unlit, unknown. Where you've been has closed behind you. You're in a pocket of salvation that's batteries and bulbs and luck.

We had matches and candles in our pockets. We had packets of fuel-soaked rags, but they were all just a way of saying, "I'm giving up but not quite yet."

The sort of caving we were up to plays with your head. At seven years old, I was hardly equipped to be anything but frantic and rattled. That's why Granddaddy smacked me. I've done it to Brody since. One sharp blow across the jaw. I must have been whimpering or something. Or possibly Granddaddy had swung as a way heading the whimpering off. I just know I was stunned. Granddaddy wasn't the sort to hit a child, but that was the point, and I took it instinctively and straightaway. Everything was different where we were. I had to be different too.

Beyond the ledge, the cavern opened. We had twenty feet of domed roof across a chamber the size of a hotel ballroom. There were outlets — channels left and right and a big opening dead ahead. That was the one that looked most traveled. Alabastards leave residue. The slick up the rocks, darken and stain them. We could tell where they liked to go.

"There," was all Granddaddy Hoyt needed to say. He pointed with his groper. It was the one his own grandfather had made. The shaft was carved bone and had been palm oiled through the years. The blade looked like what you'd find on a scimitar.

We stopped at the mouth of the main channel on the far side of the chamber. It was dark behind us and dark before us, dead quiet except for what sounded at first like some sort of metallic squeak.

"Hold it in," Granddaddy told us. He meant our breath, and we all did. We stood there not moving. Stood there not breathing. The squeaking was regular, respirational. Granddaddy said, "Got to be him."

I couldn't help but notice that Dad and Uncle Grady had fallen in line down under the way they never did topside. Mom too. She was serving as our skirmisher and bringing up the rear, and from what I could see she was focused on that job alone without her usual hint of faraway sadness, her customary touch of despair. Mom's lifetime of training had taken hold. I knew if she could be pure warrior, I had to be that too.

Dad got sent on reconnaissance down the main passageway. There were cast-off cow bones here and there, scraps of raccoon and rabbit fur. Typical alabastard trash and leavings.

Mom caught a scout in the beam of her headlamp. He was so high up a far wall as to nearly be on the ceiling. He glistened in the light beam, froze and looked our way. Mom took aim, but Granddaddy stopped her. "Not yet," was all he said. The beast watched us pressed against the rock with a couple of talons shoved into a crevice. Mom kept a ripper bolt aimed at the hollow of his neck.

"Come on," Dad called, and in we went along the bone-strewn passage. I'd let the panic go by then and had my groper cocked and ready. I was having to use the spare we'd found in a back closet. It was dinged and mended, a makeshift mess.

"Poke. Don't swing," Grady told me because if I took a wild whack, he was the one I'd slice.

Dad was waiting for us up where the channel branched. We all stopped and held our breath again and listened.

"Hear him?" Granddad asked us.

We did. Jo Jo was wheezing. He had asthma, which made a cave about the worst place for him to be.

Then it became a matter of figuring out which channel led straight to him. Sound travels in a crazy way once you're deep into a cavern, so Dad got sent up the passage on the left while Grady eased up the one on the right.

"Up here," Grady said after he'd squatted for a bit and listened.

"You two," Granddaddy Hoyt told me and Mom and pointed where he wanted us to do our rear guarding from. He and Dad joined Grady on the passage to the right.

We heard their feet on the stone and the odd equipment clatter for a quarter minute or so and then didn't hear much of anything at all. A scrape in the dark across the chamber where we'd been. The sound of our breathing. I saw alabastards everywhere I looked, but once I blinked, they'd vanish. It was just ghosting from the mix of dark and light.

"They're eating him, aren't they?"

That's probably not the sort of question most mother's field about a nephew. Mine gave it some thought before she told me back, "Not yet."

"They came all at once," I told her. I was already working out a blameless account in my head. "Just boiled up on us."

"They'll do that," my mother said, but I could see she was only half listening and fixed on a point in the murky chamber, a spot on the high cavern roof.

"What?'

"Sssshhh."

I held my breath. I looked where my mother was looking. I thought I detected pale movement, but I'd been seeing that everywhere.

"Behind me," she said.

I didn't quarrel. I cowered.

"I see you." She barely whispered as she raised her weapon and fired.

By the time the steel tip had sparked against rock, she was nocking another arrow. You could hear them out there in the dark of the chamber snorting and clawing and racing around.

I flinched and kind of poked Mom with my groper.

"Easy," she said as she took aim again.

My eyes had adjusted enough to allow me to see them as well. They were thick on the ceiling and down the far wall. We had between us six more arrows and a groper, a depressive mother and a terrified child. There was a hot box somewhere unless they'd hauled it down the channel. I shifted around to locate it.

"Don't," my mother told me, "move."

We watched them. They watched us. Mom had settled on a spot and held her aim. I heard racket behind us and turned to see lamplight. Dad came out of the channel with Jo Jo close behind him. He was bleeding where they'd clawed him but seemed to have all his limbs and pieces. Grady and Granddaddy popped out as well.

"We ready?" Mom asked.

"Do it," Dad told her.

She let fly with an arrow. No spark this time but a squeaking shriek like a bat would make if it was the size of a canoe. The creature she'd hit fell to the cave floor and went into full alabastard spasm while the rest of them hissed and squealed.

"Go!" Granddaddy shouted, and we set out double-time across the chamber towards the ledge and the squeeze.

A few of those alabastards lunged in our direction. One of them took a grievous wound from Uncle Grady's groper and gushed fluid all over the place. The rest of the swarm turned on him and took him apart the way they do. The thing I'd been told from the very first, the nugget I'd been pressed to remember, was that the beasts below were hungry and that they would surely feed. It was only words before that moment and was a hell of a thing to see.

Dad had to all but drag me along. The gore and the frenzy were nearly hypnotic. I was still looking back when they pulled me up through the squeeze and shut and bolted the gate.

We got talked at, of course, and reprimanded. They sat me and Jo Jo down at the plank table in the kitchen. They brought in my sister, Leigh Ann, and made her get harangued as well. It didn't matter to them that she'd not even been there. This was a lesson that needed learning.

Granddaddy Hoyt and Uncle Grady teamed up to berate and instruct us, but it all amounted to little more than "Pay Attention!" in the end.

Me and Leigh Ann paid most of our attention to the scratch on Jo Jo's neck. Mom was cleaning it up in the kitchen while we were getting yelled at. It was a funny looking thing, a design etched in Jo Jo's flesh. I'd seen something similar in the Apocrypha at the tail end of The Great Book. The thing looked like the letter Q pitched on its side and wearing a pointy hat.

There was no agreement anywhere on what it meant exactly. Through the years, a handful of civilian cavers had gotten branded like that. Alabastards didn't generally show themselves to regular people. Unless, of course, they intended to haul them off and feast on them in time. But six or eight had emerged undamaged through the years except for the curious scratches on their necks.

Mom was bathing Jo Jo's seepy mark in peroxide. Alabastards had no venom to speak of, but they sure carried germs and mess. She got to me shortly thereafter and sluiced out all my scratches too. Then we both got balm, the special smelly stuff they still cooked in the old way.

Jo Jo looked defeated. Jo Jo seemed scared.

"It was dark," he told us. "They were all over the place. Snorting and scratching. Breathing on me."

Jo Jo laid around the house for a week after that. Leigh Ann said she caught him crying in the barn.

He simply wasn't up to the crusade. Everybody must have known it. We never really talked about it, but Uncle Grady sent forms in the packet to help Jo Jo land a gig at Carlsbad. Something safe at the institute where they processed requests and reviewed and tweaked Legion policy. Jo Jo was sure to be protected there but still moderately useful. I imagined him reading his father's forms with all their boxes ticked.

The day we drove Jo Jo to Oliver Springs and put him on the bus, the day he traded cavern duty for administration in New Mexico, was only a scant three months after he'd been grabbed and branded. We all talked like he was off for an internship, something temporary, but it was clear nobody expected Jo Jo back.

We said our goodbyes at the open bus door. I gave Jo Jo the comic I'd bought for him. It featured robot fighting and cleavage in just about equal parts. He slid open his window and waved as the bus rolled south towards the interstate.

I made a vow to myself as I watched him go that I'd always stay fit for the fight.

3

Central Virginia was a trouble spot when we graduated to it. Anybody could have managed Cumberland after our eight years there. In the wake of what happened to Jo Jo, the grown ups determined to do what it took to throttle the pluck and spirit out of our swarm. We no longer just sat at the squeeze but ventured deep with strategic intent.

I say we, but it was chiefly them. I got to hear dinner-table talk about the progress they were making. They would come in filthy and clawed up. It sounded like hard going at first. Uncle Grady kept up with the objectives and the metrics, mapped their progress in a ledger he updated twice a week. Since nobody else would sit still to let him talk it through, he presented it all to me and Leigh Ann, though she usually fell asleep.

They were mounting a sweep and driving all our alabastards before them, a custodial bit of business The Great Book recommended but Low Lords hardly ever did. It was enough of a chore to man the squeeze and maintain an imposing border while also keeping livestock and yard fowl, cultivating a vegetable garden, making a pass at schooling children and staying on decent terms with the locals.

Our calling was a universe of work, a full-time occupation, and we could usually put off our neighbors with Amish Christian Science for only a year or two. Eventually, the sheriff would roll up like the sheriff always did, and then people would come around to find out what exactly the law had wanted. Most humans are unashamedly nosy that way. They'd follow a police cruiser or a fire truck into the far back lot of Hades.

We got our law enforcement visit in the middle of the big Cumberland cavern push. A neighbor had lost a donkey, and the county sheriff swung by to alert us so we'd be on the lookout for it. That's what he told Granddaddy anyway. Granddaddy had a history with donkeys.

"Wandered off, did he?"

The sheriff nodded. There was so much of him he needed a good half minute to get out of his car.

"Probably after a coyote," Granddaddy Hoyt informed the guy. "They'll stomp one and chase him, but they always come back."

The sheriff hadn't much cared about donkeys coming in. It was all just a pretense for him. He dispensed with the creature altogether once he'd found the breath to speak.

"Where y'all from?"

"Texas." Granddaddy Hoyt always said we were from Texas. He wasn't. We weren't. He just liked Texas as a sprawling place to be from.

The sheriff nodded. He'd heard of Texas. "What brings you up here?"

"Cows and stuff."

"Peculiar bunch used to live back in here. Let everything go to hell."

Granddaddy could go along with that. He nodded and spat. "Wasn't much to look at. Got kind of a deal."

29

"What's that goat eating?" the sheriff asked.

Granddaddy had a glance. It was a chicken. The goat wasn't so much eating it as tossing it around the yard. "Hey," Granddaddy shouted my way. I was messing around on the porch. "Kick him."

"Yes sir," I said and did.

"Haven' t seen y'all in town," the sheriff said.

"We've been."

"Neighbors say you're Jews or something."

That worked well enough for Granddaddy. It was sort of like Texas. He nodded and spat, told the sheriff, "Yeah."

"People are funny around here. Nosy, you know?"

Granddaddy winced like his lunch was repeating on him. He nodded.

The sheriff waited to get talked at further, to get offered a cup of coffee or a slice of pie. Granddaddy didn't go in for that sort of thing. He was accomplished at standing by and saying nothing at all.

"Well." The sheriff was the one to yield. "You'll give a shout if that donkey comes around?"

"Won't ever see him," Granddaddy said. "Probably back in the field by now."

We watched the sheriff labor to fold himself and fit back in his car. "I'm going to say I was here, filled you in. People in these parts are funny. Don't see you around. Don't hear from you. Wonder what you're about."

Granddaddy nodded. He took the sheriff's meaning. That night at the supper table, he said to everyone, "It's time."

They knew what he meant, so I didn't need to.

We had the neighbors in for a kind of dinner on the ground. It was the traditional way, my mother explained, to defuse and satisfy them. Nobody was allowed to bring anything because of the customs of our faith. We served an ample but flavorless meal — we were religiously disposed against flavor — and everybody was made to dance to a record Granddaddy kept for Amish Christian Science purposes alone. The music on it sounded like a man calling his dog while he played a garden hoe with a boot. The dance itself was some spastic thing Granddaddy had put together over time.

Not too many neighbors stuck around for dessert. Burnt cookies with no sugar in them. We had a thing about sugar as well. Granddaddy had suspected he'd have to trot out his circumcising tools, but the food and the music proved enough to drive everybody away.

Once it was just us in the compound again, the grown-ups all had proper brandy from the jar Granddaddy kept on the coat closet shelf. Mom brought out the spiced nuts and the fudge.

"Curious for years," Granddaddy said by way of a toast. He made a show of checking his watch, an old scarred up Hamilton in his pocket. "Bored silly in two hours."

What I couldn't quite see then, I sure know now. We're always riding herd both topside and below. There's no leisure for robot fighting and cleavage, no time for socializing. We keep the nosy ones out and the greasy ones down. We've got livestock instead of friends.

Then Beauty showed up. She was far and away the best thing to come out of Tennessee. The road ended at the gate to our property, and there was a wide place where cars could turn around and where people of a certain sort could jettison their rubbish. The kind who'd never contemplate paying a dollar at the landfill when there were ditches and ravines close by where they could pitch their stuff for free.

We got beer boxes mostly, fast-food bags, spent motor oil in Prestone jugs, the odd TV and toaster oven. Six kittens once that Granddaddy took charge of. I don't know what exactly he did with them, but they didn't graduate to cats. Granddaddy's tender spot was for donkeys, and it was the only tender spot he had. So he would have sent Beauty where the kittens went if my Mom hadn't intervened.

We were coming back from the county co-op with a spool of barbed wire, corn for the chickens, assorted salt and mineral blocks for the cows. It was just me and Mom and Granddaddy in his ancient Pontiac. I got out to open the gate. It was one of the few jobs I was allowed just then, so I did it with more pride and care than unhooking a chain requires.

I walked the gate open. Jo Jo had been one to just push it and let it swing.

"Hard on the hinges. Hard on the post," Granddaddy would tell him only to have Jo Jo push it and swing it the next time they rolled up.

So I walked the gate and waited for the sedan to pass through. I was about to shut it fast and chain it when I spied in the weeds a creature so greasy and nasty I thought it was a baby possum. She was laying on a hamburger wrapper, all ribs and scabs. I still can't say exactly why I reached for her. There must have been something in the way she sized me up with her crusty near eye.

I remember saying out loud, "You're a dog, aren't you?"

I prefer to think she told me, "Like no other" back.

For Granddaddy, a dog wasn't any closer to a donkey than a cat. Most especially a scabbed up starving puppy infested with mites and fleas.

"Give it here," he said once we'd parked in the yard.

I must have looked at my mother the way Beauty had looked at me.

"Hoyt," she said and shook her head. She only called him Hoyt when she was determined to put him off or put him onto something.

"Emily," Granddaddy told her, but I could hear him retreating already. Mom always got what she asked for because she never asked for much.

Then we had that conversation parents have with their children about pets. If she lived, I'd groom her, I'd feed her, I'd train her. She'd drive cattle. War with goats. Kill yard fowl at her peril.

Uncle Grady got a look at her before I'd cleaned her up. She appeared diseased and smelled like rotten suet. "Ought to call her Beauty," he said and laughed.

"Yes sir," I told him, bristling. "I think I might."

Our people had owned terriers mostly. Back in the day, they were thought to be cave ready. You'd go down to the choke with a Jack Russell or two, and they'd nose up trouble coming well before it reached your light. The problem was you had to keep them tied because they were profoundly pigheaded. Anybody who's ever claimed to have trained a Jack Russell is trafficking in lies.

You can't depend on them to stay put. They're excitable to a fault. So the second one gets loose in a cave, he's in the deep dark and gone for good.

Dad and Uncle Grady had three of them. Curly and Jasper and Flo. They feature in a couple of snapshots of Dad and Grady as boys. The clan was in Indiana at the time, doing a stint at Wyandotte. Uncle Grady says Dad got careless with the leashes. Dad insists he never did. The way he tells it, the alabastards worked those dogs into a frenzy. They'd scratch around on the cave walls, grunting and snorting. They'd move up into sniffing range and then retreat.

"Backed out of their collars," is the way Dad tells it. "Off and gone, and that was that."

They found Flo's bones a couple of weeks later. They could tell from the leg she'd fractured. They brought her up and buried her and swore off dogs after that.

"She isn't a Jack," I said of Beauty. I was showing her off after I'd bathed her and fed her oatmeal and chicken entrails for a week. She was starting to look like a thing that might live.

Uncle Grady put in the needle. "I'll say," was all he told me.

We showed him, me and Beauty. I'd like to think she was the product of my exemplary training skills. That I was the one who taught her how to be calm and tactical. How to know what I wanted from just a look. How to understand in her dog brain that what alabastards did best of all was bait and then destroy most creatures like her.

Beauty cared as much as she had to about the rest of the family. She let them order her around and she'd nuzzle them enough to pass for an affectionate pet, but the truth was right there in the open for anybody to see. Beauty was mine, and I was hers. Everything else was for show.

I took her down to the squeeze her second week on the farm. We were treating her mites with a paste my dad had made up from kerosene, gear grease, and furniture wax, so she looked a long way from regal and smelled like a machine shop. I was by myself — a family violation — and intended just to carry her to the safe side of the gate.

We sat for a while there in the dark waiting for company to swarm up, but nothing came. They'll do that. They seem to know when you'd like to see them and make a point of hanging back in the dark. That's why you very rarely hear about an alabastard from a tourist. The ones who come out never saw them. The ones who saw them only rarely come out.

"Don't tell anybody," I instructed Beauty as I unlocked the gate, swung it open, and eased down towards the ledge.

I hadn't bothered to bring my groper. I had a headlamp and the old hotbox that we left in the cave and hardly used. It had a loop of rope for a handle and an old sheet of rusty tin for a reflector. My great granddaddy had knocked it together when Granddaddy Hoyt was a boy. I lit it, but I didn't even let it get warm, so it's no wonder those creatures came scrabbling up on us, thick on the walls and the cavern ceiling.

You always know when they're swarming teeth-first, with meat and gristle on their minds, because there's some kind of charge in the air. It's like vinegar on your tongue. But when they're making a feint or have just raced up for a look, it tastes like nothing and feels benign. I sampled the air. They'd only swarmed for a peek. I could feel it, could even see it somehow in their coal-black eyes.

There was this thing about alabastards that Grady's sort could never quite acknowledge, wouldn't allow themselves to accept. Those creatures weren't like animals topside. I didn't think of them as animals at all. They took some kind of long view on the world and appeared to have a purchase on the future. They could think a month or a year ahead, lay traps that only sprung in time. Imagine a cow doing something like that. You can't because it wouldn't.

Grady's sort preferred to believe we were caught up in a heroic struggle. It was our savvy against blind alabastard relentlessness. We had a Council of Elders, a bureaucracy, official paperwork. They ate bats and owls and sheep when we'd let them, gnawed on each other in a pinch. It wasn't a fair fight, just a long one. Grady's sort was smug.

My mother in particular thought differently. It was the root cause of her sadness. Mom had seen the same things Grady saw and had decided we couldn't win.

I raised my puppy over my head, held her up so they could all get a look.

"Her name's Beauty," I told them.

They made that noise in their necks they make when they're cogitating. Beauty studied them. They studied her.

"You ought to watch out," I said.

They lingered a bit and then withdrew, scrabbled back into the deep dark. I crawled outside the gate and shut it, paused for a moment to come to grips with the foolishness I'd been up to. Down to the squeeze with a cold hotbox, no groper, a head lamp, and a greasy puppy. That was a Jo Jo caliber exploit, and I felt lucky to have escaped untouched.

The thing was, I came away with both my hide and a worthwhile insight. Alabastards like a contest. Jack Russells only like a fight.

4

We lost Granddaddy Hoyt two months before we got rotated to Virginia. I was out in the pasture with him when he went. We were replacing the last of the lousy fence posts the previous clan had left us. They'd been the sorts to shove anything they had handy in the ground. Granddaddy Hoyt would only use black locust, which we harvested ourselves. Iron wood and beech and gum trees had been fine for the previous crew. That brand of fencing shiftlessness raised moral questions with Granddaddy Hoyt.

"Would you look at this," he'd usually say when we arrived at a rotted, trashwood fencepost. "What kind of man would stick that in the ground?"

I'd heard that question so many times that I should have had a reliable answer, but I traded off between telling him, "I don't know," and shrugging and shaking my head.

"What happens when a cow comes leaning?"

"Falls over."

"Doesn't take Nostradamus to see that."

"No sir."

Then Granddaddy would kick the offending post, and it would usually splinter and break, tip over as far as the barbed wire would allow.

"People," Granddaddy usually muttered, and somehow he always seemed freshly disappointed.

That was the thing about Granddaddy Hoyt. He never gave up on people, but they sure had a way of living down to his lowest expectations.

Working a day with Granddaddy Hoyt around the edges of the pasture afforded me the chance to get instructed by him in shorthand. He was not at all the type to circle a thing with palaver. He was somewhere between pithy and the dirt.

"Your Uncle Grady's a good man," he told me more than once, "but . . ." He'd shake his head. He'd sigh. It was Granddaddy Hoyt's way of saying a man can be decent and an officious twat.

"That sister of yours is girly. Look out for her in a while." I thought of that later when Leigh Ann snagged her first and only boyfriend in New York.

He had virtually nothing to say about my dad, which qualified as high praise, but he'd always raise concern about my mother. Since we were usually out in the pasture, he could point to where she walked.

"Don't like the look of it," Granddaddy told me. "Seen it before."

He had. Some of ours had abandoned us for the world. One of them had been Granddaddy's brother. I'd never heard his name spoken. He got edited out of the family history. Gassing yourself in a Pontiac can be shaped into a mishap. Walking away is only ever betrayal.

I remember trying once to talk to Granddaddy Hoyt about the alabastards. I had ideas there was more going on with them than the brain trust at Carlsbad allowed.

"They're in there," I told Granddaddy Hoyt. I can be pithy too.

"Not supposed to be," he said. He shook his head and added, "But . . ." That was as close as we ever came to a meeting of the minds.

Uncle Grady kept encouraging Granddaddy Hoyt to go emeritus. He'd get to take the bus around and serve as a draw at conclaves. Granddaddy would be one of Carlsbad's men on the ground. He'd give talks about Legion life, the hardships and the coping. Granddaddy wasn't much on the larger picture, but he could knock a decent hotbox together in a half hour, had a raft of strategies for keeping your neighbors both satisfied and scarce, and he was a man of unchecked passion where it came to livestock fencing. He could have been an asset to Carlsbad, but he didn't want to go.

In the end, he left us like he had to. Granddaddy was constitutionally incapable of dithering. He was improving a fence hole with a steel pike he'd made just for that purpose. He raised it and drove it into the hole, wiggled it around like usual. Then Granddaddy stopped and stood there doing nothing.

He finally told me, "Uh oh."

He went to his knees and then pitched over in the dirt. He gurgled a little and quit.

Dad and Uncle Grady agreed it was his heart, and that's all we had by way of a determination and an inquest. We didn't go to doctors in the usual course of things. We were sub rosa. We were off the map. So it wasn't like we were going to seek a certificate for a corpse, a form anyway beyond the one that

Grady sent to Carlsbad along with a snapshot of Granddaddy Hoyt, an old one that Granddaddy had particularly liked. He was standing out on a sun-drenched lawn in an undershirt with a hammer.

That snapshot got featured in the quarterly over a tribute to Granddaddy Hoyt. I could tell Uncle Grady had written the thing. All the right boxes were ticked.

We buried him ourselves. He'd made his own casket, a simple pine box that he'd nailed up a decade back when he was passing a kidney stone.

Uncle Grady spoke the prescribed words. Jo Jo had come home for the occasion. He had a severe haircut and a functionary's twill trousers that had probably been creased and tidy before he got onto the bus. Otherwise, he was still Jo Jo. A rolled-up comic in his pocket. Cleavage in his head.

We marked the grave with a rock you'd never notice unless you knew too, and Mom and Leigh Ann got together and laid out the kind of meal you have when people are dead. Leigh Ann had a way with field greens. A lot of pepper. A little fatty pork. Granddaddy had taught her his technique.

Mom and Dad quizzed Jo Jo about his duties in Carlsbad. He said he fetched stuff for people and pushed what sounded like a mail cart around.

"Where in Virginia are y'all headed?" Jo Jo asked his dad.

Albermarle County, as it turned out. Above a place called Mint Springs, which was little more than a swimming lake and an abandoned lumber mill. We inherited sheep and two serviceable houses. A barn, a junky ATV, a rebuilt lawn tractor, and a cavern that started out as hardly more than a crease in the ground.

We'd only been there four months before Mom had Brody. Dad had decided Brody would be the salvation of his marriage, and Mom had let him think that. She never told him different.

Brody was fourteen months old when Mom finally left us.

"She's taking a break," Dad told us on the day Mom went down to the hard top and caught a ride.

Dad seemed to think she'd come back that afternoon, and he stayed up by the house waiting for her while I did duty at the squeeze with Uncle Grady. Leigh Ann fed Brody saltines and rode him in the wheelbarrow so he wouldn't cry. It was well past dark before Dad came in off the porch.

Mom had been sinking since we left Tennessee. She said less to us all the time until she said hardly anything at all. It got to where she took almost all of her duty with Grady. New cave. New problems for Grady to game out now that Granddaddy Hoyt was gone. He'd talk to Mom about blasting and excavation he wanted done, barriers he wanted erected. Grady was usually good for an hour or two on Carlsbad politics. Changes he'd make if he were in charge. Traditions he'd ensure were honored. Efficiencies he'd introduce. Dead wood he'd cut away.

She didn't need to talk to him back. That was the curse and the charm of Grady. No matter how you preferred your chats, he did it all himself.

I think we believed, even me and Leigh Ann, that Mom would never leave Brody. We could see her walking away from us, certainly from Dad, but Brody was just a defenseless infant.

What mother could turn her back on that? Ours, I guess because that's just what she did. Worse still, she didn't tell us she was leaving. Mom threw a few things in a bag, not even a proper piece of luggage, and went down the driveway to the road. I was coming across the pasture as she was setting out. I can still see the look on her face when she passed me in the yard.

There was no sadness or resignation to it. Nothing human like that. She was finished with us and so looked more like a woman who didn't know me.

"Where you going?" I asked her since the driveway wasn't on her usual route.

She shifted her bag. Pointed with her nose. "Down there," was all she said.

I didn't think much of it until supper. Grady had made one of his casseroles. They were called that for the dish, not the contents. He never worked from a recipe and was only ever volume constrained. He'd fill our piece of crockery, sprinkle potato chip litter and shredded cheese on top, and then shove it in the oven until it was bubbly. Stewed compost as cuisine.

"Where's Mom?" Leigh Ann asked. She was almost twelve and deep in her inquisitive phase. So "Where's Mom?" was just another question in her general litany. She also wondered who'd thought up shoe strings and if you could make decent tea with thistles. Mom not at the supper table fit precisely in between.

That's when we got the only explanation we'd ever hear.

"She's taking a break," Dad told us.

"From what?" Leigh Ann wanted to know.

"Hmm," Grady said of the casserole by way of changing the subject. He poked the burned, cheesy scab on the thing with a regular dinner fork. Getting through to the beans and the mushroom soup and the tuna promised to be a challenge. "I burned this one a little," he said.

Brody gurgled from his high chair. He threw his sippy cup into the pantry closet. I think that was the moment his tossing phase began.

For my part, I'd seen just enough of our avocation to wonder why more of us didn't pack a bag and catch a ride on the road. I couldn't resent my mother for leaving, and I couldn't imagine she'd ever be back.

She called a week later but only talked to Dad, and he persevered in the fiction that her absence was temporary.

"People get tired," he told us. "People get fed up."

That wasn't a surprising thing to hear, so I didn't really press him. Leigh Ann might have if she hadn't had chicken fingers on the brain. Our Virginia place had come with satellite TV, which Dad let us watch a little over the strident objections of Uncle Grady who stood in reflexive opposition to all new-fangled stuff.

We'd never seen a commercial before. They especially grabbed Leigh Ann, most particularly the fast-food advertisements with fries and burgers and buckets of cola. Businesses that thrived without a casserole in sight. She was particularly seduced by chicken fingers dressed in honey mustard sauce.

On the day Leigh Ann turned twelve, Dad brought home a box of chicken fingers for her. She didn't just get the honey mustard dip but the ranch as well, and Leigh Ann had a feast while the rest of us shoved casserole around our plates and Brody threw his spoon and his rattle and his bowl and, finally, his pacifier.

Leigh Ann got quieter as she ate. It turned out the best way to break a child of her infatuation with chicken fingers was to bring some home and let her eat a few. Leigh Ann cried all night. We took turns holding her hair.

The entire culture for us was, more or less, chicken fingers writ large. We'd think we needed something we'd discovered in the world and then learn that we had no use much for it. Gadgets and clothes and delectable snacks, new tools for managing livestock, and all sorts of fancy gear for caving. We'd see it. We'd want it. Sometimes we'd even buy an item or three, but we always seemed to go back to the stuff we'd lived with all along.

I'm not saying it's better to stand apart and ignore updates and improvements, but sometimes the antique methods, the traditional wares, and your brain are all you need.

So there was something I could agree with Uncle Grady about, but he was full-time at it and static. I had caveats and conditions.

If Grady had been open to new thinking, our Virginia alabastards would have surely touched some off. They were quite a lot bigger than the Cumberland batch. Most of them were at least as tall as me, a few a good head higher, and the clan before us had worked out an accommodation with them, hardly the sort of thing you'd do if they were as wild as a pack of wolves.

They got a sheep a month. A herd elder was fine. “Them things,” the guy we’d replaced had told us, “don’t know from mutton.”

One sheep would get tied to a stake at the cave mouth. The alabastards would grab it and haul it down. In return, they’d stay below the squeeze and be (for their sort) docile. That’s why their swarm ups, like the one for Brody’s baptism, felt sort of like a pageant and a show. Menacing but not dangerous outright. Scrupulously true to form. Looking like a swarm up ought to look.

We kept to the agreement for probably a year. We’d inherited nearly sixty sheep, a mule, and three milk cows, and we had to make the usual house improvements and cultivate a garden. There’d been twelve people in the previous clan, and we were down to five. One of us was a toddler and another was a moody girl, so we had our hands full topside for a while.

It was clear to Dad and Uncle Grady probably right away and clear to me a little bit behind them that what the clan before us had thought of as an armistice was something far more devious and troublesome than that. Uncle Grady went through the ledger those folks had left. The duty books all stayed with the farms, and Grady noticed that the reconnaissance entries never came with any particulars or notes. Each foray lasted exactly an hour and, according to the ledger, nothing ever happened. I’d been around alabastards enough to know that couldn’t possibly be true.

“Looks like they haven’t been below the squeeze for thirty-four months,” Grady told us once he’d done the math.

"Not even for the annual?" Dad asked him. That was a Carlsbad sanctioned spring-cleaning push that we were all supposed to do.

Grady showed us the pertinent ledger pages. He shook his head and told us, "Nope."

It was precisely the kind of problem we were too short-handed to have, which is why Dad let Grady call in the Flex Corps from Dahlonega, Georgia. They were like fire jumpers. They'd roll in on a trouble spot and enter a cave in force. They'd been known to spend most of a week under ground, way down in the deep dark where the days and nights all blend together. They'd sweep CFs before them (they only ever called them that), and shove them as far down into the system as they could manage. Then they'd hook hoses to turbines and heat up the buffer to help buy the local clan some time.

In the wake of a Flex Corps visit, your alabastards were sure to be throttled and maybe even authentically meek for a while. But they were just as sure, in time, to be seized with primal rage.

That was the fundamental problem with handing off local upset to the Flex Corps. They'd leave just like they'd come in — all at once and in a hurry — so they never had to live with the consequences of their work. They bought you a little time and space but generated venom. When your alabastards boiled back up, and they always did, they'd be even more vicious and unruly than before.

Dad and Uncle Grady had previously dealt with Flex Corps residue, and they'd drawn entirely different lessons from it. They'd had leakage in their cavern up at Lost River in

Pennsylvania. Their swarm had found a vent they could slip out through anytime they liked. It was on the opposite side of the ridge from the mapped official cavern entrance, and the alabastards fairly pillaged the nearby countryside.

They grabbed cows and swine primarily but nabbed a pony too. One of them slipped into a farm house, and the widow who lived there dropped him with two blasts from her shotgun. She took off part of one shoulder and all of his head.

As freakish creatures go, that dead cavus ferinus proved acceptable tabloid fodder, but he wasn't in any condition to be of use to the regular news, most especially after Granddaddy Hoyt insisted in print that the thing was a feral pig. He'd seen it out in the woods not a week before. What the hell else could it be?

Granddaddy made enough noise to kill the story. Then they called in the Flex Corps to seal off the leak and drive the local swarm back into the deep dark.

"Three days under," Grady told me. "They lived on jerky and stuff."

"We had two easy months," Dad recalled. "Then they came roaring up. Couldn't hate on the Flex Corps. They weren't around. So they hated us instead."

"Well, what do you want to do?" It always seemed to come down to that very question with Uncle Grady. There was never any room to amend his plans. Either we did exactly what Uncle Grady wanted, or he got all shirty and asked us, "What do you want to do?"

"I want that sorry crew before us to come back and fix it," Dad told him.

"They got sent all the way out to Idaho, so they're over there screwing that up."

"You know what'll happen."

Uncle Grady nodded. "I think I'd rather have them mad than sneaky."

"I don't know," Dad said. That was his sign of giving up.

"Put in the request?"

"I guess."

Grady went directly to his paperwork drawer and fished out the proper form.

"How long before they come?"

"It's Tuesday? Friday probably."

"We owe them a sheep tomorrow."

"Give it," Grady said. "Wouldn't want to tip them off."

We had an old, weak ewe that me and Dad and Leigh Ann walked out of the pasture that night and down to the cleft rock that marked the entrance to our cavern. The previous crew had driven a pipe in the ground about ten yards back from the cave mouth, and that's where we tethered that sickly ewe who gave us a weary "What now?" look.

"Let's stick for a minute," Dad said, and me and Leigh Ann retired with him behind a hedgerow. "Have you ever stayed to watch?" he asked us.

"No sir," I told him. "Uncle Grady said don't." He'd passed on to me and Leigh Ann the instructions he'd gotten from the clan we replaced. Tie up a sheep and walk away. That's exactly what we'd been doing.

"This one time," Dad said, "let's just see."

We didn't have to wait long. I'd assumed that just a pair of them would come up. They'd haul the sheep in, and that would be that, but they came pouring out of that cleft in the rock like water. Twenty or thirty of them. Too many to count.

"I was afraid of this," Dad said more to himself than to me or Leigh Ann.

It wasn't like they were up to no good exactly. Most of them were simply fooling around in the open air except for the one that had the actual job of grabbing the sheep by its tether.

Leigh Ann was still young and inexperienced enough to ask Dad, "What's the problem?"

"Topside's ours," he told her. "Deep dark's for them." With that, Dad stepped out from behind the hedgerow and shouted towards the alabastards, "Hey!"

They all turned and looked at him. Looked at us.

"Go on!"

But they didn't. They stuck where they were in a way that was telling and peculiar. It'd be like clapping your hands at a bear and have him raise up on is rear legs and say, "What?"

They should have poured right back in through the cleft and shown some hurry up as they did it. Instead, they stayed where they were. They eyed Dad. Me and Leigh Ann too.

"Go!" Dad took an aggressive step forward. That swayed them enough to start their progress back into the cavern, but they sure weren't in a hurry and kind of dawdled as they went.

We stayed there until they were all back inside. Then Dad went over and had a look through the cleft, lingered until the last one had descended out of sight.

50

On the way across the pasture, Dad asked me, “Ever shot your mother’s ripper?”

I had once, but I wasn’t supposed to. I’d fired an arrow into a poplar tree where it had stuck and stayed.

“No sir,” I said.

“We’ll pull it out and tune it up,” he told me. “This might be just the time to start.”

5

The Flex Corps brass treated us little better than civilians. They brought everything they needed, even a tank truck with their own water. Leigh Ann made them cookies they wouldn't eat. Brody did service as the toddler they wouldn't acknowledge. Uncle Grady got to show them the cavern map the previous clan had left. The only attention directed Dad's way came from a beefy sergeant.

"Keep those sheep back," he shouted as he steered a truck through our pasture gate.

They sent three rangers down first thing to bring up a sample, they called it. Since alabastards across the map are so varied and changeable, grabbing a local specimen is always the first thing they do. They hauled out an adult male they'd caught in a steel net. They had a cage for him in our side yard. It was wired up to a generator.

"The thing'll cook you," we got warned. "You'll only touch it once."

That alabastard brushed against the bars, which resulted in spark and excitement enough to instruct and illuminate him. After that, he just squatted in his pan of wood shavings and glowered at us.

The Flex Corps brass didn't seem to care if we studied the creature as long as we stayed out of the way of their anthropology techs. One guy, one girl. They made notes and shot video, worked their calibrations from a remove. I don't know exactly what they came up with, but I can tell you what I saw.

No tail at all, not even the residual stub our dwarf swarm in Cumberland had. There were ears of a sort instead of only slits in the side of the head. The hands had regular fingers and claws that, like a cat's, retracted. The feet could have passed for human too, just slightly oversized and with cave calluses and the filth. No privates that I could see. They must have retracted as well. Given how those beasts bang around caverns in the dark, the less that sticks out or dangles the better.

The beast's lips covered his teeth just like mine did. The canines must have curled back or collapsed or something. His eyes were kind of slanty, so he looked like an old Asian man who lived in a windowless room, always went out under a parasol, never felt the sun. And that was without a scrap of clothing and with cave grime clinging to him. If he'd been wearing a shirt and pants and strolling through a teeming city, it would have taken a tuned in Low Lord to even look at him twice.

They'd put a tent up over his cage to shield him from the sun, but he was having trouble bearing topside brightness and kept balling up and hiding his head.

Leigh Ann fetched our copy of The Big Book of Beasts from the magazine caddy in the front room. It's a volume full of sketches and water colors by a guy named Rayburn Meade. He was a subterranean John J. Audubon and devoted his adult life to drawing "troglodytical fauna", he called them. Yes, there was the odd bat and the occasional blind fish, but alabastards were what he fixed on mostly, and The Big Book of Beasts is loaded with them — in life, in death, at war, in repose — and always in meticulous detail.

The first full plate is from 1784, a pen and ink rendering of a battle-scarred adult in full scuttle. It's coming at your across a cavern ceiling. I used to dream about that creature. It would wake me up at night. Groper scars. Bared teeth. Fully extended talons. Stiff tufts of feral hair. Muscle and sinew and a pocket of blue fluid seen through skin so pale that it almost seemed transparent.

For a long time, I thought Rayburn Meade was the bravest man who ever lived. I imagined him with his sketch pad and a candle in the deep dark, baiting his trogs to venture close and give him something to draw. Then I found out in a book about him, a tribute the wife of an Elder wrote, that he'd seen all the cave beasts he ever would on one trip to New Mexico. They were already preserving them back then in barrels and glass tankards, and Rayburn Meade had been given free range of the embalmed menagerie.

He ventured into an actual cavern once but complained of "nervosa" and suffered rank panic. It's easy to be claustrophobic when your enclosed space comes with talons and teeth.

Rayburn Meade's chief blessings were a lively imagination and an eye for anatomical detail. He talked at length to rangers and surveyors, demolition men and sentries, and populated their exploits with the cave beasts that he drew.

Leigh Ann flipped through our Rayburn Meade book looking for a likeness of the creature the Flex Corps had hauled up and caged in our yard. She thought she found it once or twice, but in truth, she wasn't close. Rayburn Meade had never seen our sort of alabastard. That was a measure of just how far they'd come in a couple of hundred years.

The opening sketch was revealing, the one from 1784. The creature was identified as "juvenile female" and was squatting on a rock. She looked like a medieval gargoyle. She had a tail with a spike on the end of it and nubs on her head that could pass for horns. Her teeth were fangs effectively and her feet were size of throw pillows. Put her in a hooded gown and loose her in a city, and the first civilian who came across her would chop her head off with an ax.

She was plainly an animal, either that or a minion of Lucifer. She wouldn't have squatted in a cage and looked at us. She would have lunged and fried on the bars.

The female Flex Corps tech poked the prisoner with a wooden rod. It looked like a bid to measure how little he cared for getting poked. But no matter how hard she prodded, she couldn't get much of a rise. That alabastard stayed balled up peeking at her with one eye until he finally got exercised enough to wrap his fingers around that dowel. He relieved her of it slowly, drew it into the cage.

He didn't do it in anger, didn't jerk the thing away from the girl with violence. She had it for a bit while she poked him, and then she didn't have it anymore.

"Nil plus," she told her colleague.

He nodded. "Nil plus." He made a notation on the sort of form that would have made Uncle Grady delirious. It had more subheads and bold lines and tick boxes than most documents could ever hope to hold.

"Our ones in Tennessee had tails and stuff," Leigh Ann said to the girl tech mostly.

She was wearing a tidy black uniform like the rest of them. Her name was sewn above her left breast pocket. Tuttle. "How long a tail?"

"Just nubs," I said. "They were maybe this high." I held my hand off the ground a little over a foot.

"Solution?"

She meant the cavern. I nodded.

"Where's his hair?" Leigh Ann asked.

Tuttle's colleague uncoiled an air hose and gave the nozzle to his partner. Then he glared at me and Leigh Ann. Bowen. He was officially something in the Flex Corps, and we were nothing but cave minders and kids. I could tell that fellow was well on his way to Uncle Grady's brand of officious twatdom.

Tuttle hit the alabastard with a blast of hot air. It shrank and snarled but failed to lunge. She aimed the nozzle again. Same result.

"Nil plus," she said.

Bowen ticked one of his many boxes. "Nil plus."

It looked like we were getting treated for a domestic infestation. A crew set up a kind of tent flush against the mouth of our cavern.

"For staging," Uncle Grady explained to us. He had a Flex Corps manual in among his books, so he knew the protocol, every phase, and exactly what to call it.

"They'll swelter it for twenty-four hours," he said. "Probe and then swelter it some more."

"D-80," Grady told us and pointed at a truck that was essentially a massive furnace on a flatbed. A crew was busy running duct work from it through the staging tent and into the mouth of the cave.

"The heat'll drive them back," Dad explained. "I hear sometimes that's enough."

Grady snorted. He had no use for optimism and hopefulness. Dire stuff happened. You ticked boxes. You filed reports.

The specimen they'd pulled out of our cave was in a vat come morning. I went out to feed the chickens and guineas and saw his cage was empty and collapsed. There was what looked like a big plastic rain barrel beside it. He was bobbing in chemicals with sutures up his back where they'd gone in and taken stuff out.

His eyes were open. His claws were extended. Nil plus, I thought to myself.

There was nobody topside but the mess crew and the maintenance grunts who were keeping the D-80 humming. Everybody else had gone under.

Dad and Leigh Ann joined me and Beauty while Grady babysat Brody. We drove the sheep deep into the pasture, over where the gates were all shut.

"What are they doing?" Leigh Ann asked as she pointed at the ground.

"Moving day probably," Dad told her, but we both let him know that wasn't enough.

He knew as much as Grady, maybe even a little more, since Dad had something Grady lacked – an imagination. So we made him describe the sort of battle raging underneath us. He was reluctant at first, like always, but he got in the spirit in time.

"They fill the cavern and push them back. The alabastards are probably drowsy from the heat.

"Just gropers?" Leigh Ann asked.

"Rippers too," Dad told her. "Net blasters and gas grenades. They'll spank them, make an example. A few alabastards might end up dead, but the job is to push them down."

"They killed the one in the cage."

Dad nodded. Leigh Ann whined.

"They always take a sample. Hard to keep up otherwise."

"What do we do different once they leave?"

"Patrols and regular duty."

"Not enough of us for that."

Dad nodded again. "Grady's already put in the paper for provisionals."

"How many?"

"He asked for four," Dad told me. "If we're lucky, we'll get one or two."

"For how long?"

"Why all the questions?" Dad wanted to know. "We'll make it work as best we can."

"These are a lot bigger than in Tennessee," Leigh Ann said.

"A lot smarter too," I added. "That one in the cage . . ." I started.

"How smart can he be," Dad asked me, "if he's dead?"

That was precisely the place where Dad and Grady intersected. They were never quite ready to allow that we could ever be outflanked. Topside was for the triumphant. The deep dark for the subjugated. Retractable claws, recoiled incisors, fleshy ears, and almost regular feet were hardly enough to change the balance. We'd stay up, and they'd stay down. The Flex Corps would see to hiccups. Carlsbad would keep things right.

Dad's faith wasn't quite as impervious as his brother's, but it was far stouter than anything I'd ever been able to manage myself. I had too much of my mother in me.

After three days, the troops all surfaced, and the staging tent was struck. One of the junior officers convened a Q-rap in our kitchen, which meant that he came in with tech Tuttle and walked us through the metrics.

"High activity, low saturation" was the prevailing verdict. Our alabastards were energetic but fell well short of cavern density standards.

"Thin swarm," the officer told us and allowed Tuttle to enlarge.

"Could be provision strain, inter-tribal fallout, or extended communication," she told us. I guess we didn't look enlightened. "There weren't nearly as many of them as we expected. We're not sure where they went."

The Flex Corps officer ran through the numbers the way a doctor runs through blood work. Each one meant something to him, I guess, but hardly anything to us. Even Grady was stymied. He quizzed the guy at first but gave up soon enough.

"I'll need a copy of that," Grady finally said.

"Three ought slash niner," the officer told him.

That was the number on the form Grady needed to submit.

"I've never even seen one of those," Grady announced in a tone that was touched with pure wonder.

The officer produced said form and handed it to Grady. He was lost in study of it for the remainder of the Q-rap, like a baby who's been given a keyring.

I can't say the 'metrics' were helpful in any practical way. Once that officer had run through all of his numbers, Dad asked him, "What should we do?"

He packed up his papers. "Observe regular order."

"We're just two adults, three kids."

"Where's your other co cap?" he asked Dad. The officer checked his cover printout. He laid his finger on the entry for our mother. "I'm showing an R-14."

Dad told him, "She's not coming back."

"Do a status update and put in for provisionals. Regular duty and tactical patrols for now."

He gathered his papers and stood up. He didn't salute exactly, but he made one of those stomping turns the Carlsbad regulars are prone to.

The trucks were packed by the time we got outside. The colonel rolled out first with a blast on his horn. The whole convoy was gone in a couple of minutes and left nothing behind but flattened grass and wheel ruts.

Grady and Leigh Ann policed the pasture while me and Dad headed down to the squeeze to see what the Flex Corps had wrought. Aside from the ground being packed and trampled at the mouth of the cave, there was little evidence that the Flex

Corps had paid a call. No trash in or out. One the way to the ledge, we found one broken ripper arrow shoved into a crevice. Somebody had oiled the hinges on our gate and replaced two screws on the throw bolt.

We'd hauled down our gropers and a hotbox. Dad had made me bring Mom's ripper.

"So you can get used to it," he told me, but I knew it wasn't just that. We didn't know what the Flex Corps had left, what level of fury and indignation, raw animal rage. Who could say what we'd find.

I'd had a glance at a photo while we were getting briefed on the 'metrics.' It was a snapshot sticking partly out of the file that I probably wasn't even supposed to see. A pile of dead alabastards heaped one on top of another.

We let the beams of our headlamps play across the main cavern chamber. No beasts alive or dead. Not even the usual crickets and bats. Nothing but barely relieved darkness. It was still unnaturally warm.

"I'm hot," I said to Dad.

"Him too."

With that, he pointed. One alabastard high up the far wall. Claws extended, clinging to the rock face like a climber. He was looking over his shoulder at us. We trained both our lights upon him. He made no attempt to shrink back into the darkness like they do.

He looked worthy of a Rayburn Meade sketch. Not because he was a throwback with a tail and horns and big puffy taloned feet but because he looked from where we sat like evolved perfection. He was big, probably six foot five from tip to tip, and he had more of a square chin and regular profile, a more manly face than we usually see. A couple of scars crossed on his back, up around his left shoulder socket. They made what looked like an X in puffy, glazed tissue. Otherwise, he was unblemished. A shimmering, mother-of-pearl white.

"Ever seen that one before?" Dad asked me.

"No, sir. You?"

He shook his head. "I'd remember." We watched him. He watched us.

"He doesn't look happy," I whispered.

"Doesn't exactly look mad."

He just clung to the rock and watched us. We stayed at the squeeze and watched him back.

"Want to go dark and see what comes up?" Dad reached for his switch as he said it.

"All right," I said, but I didn't exactly feel enthusiastic.

I hardly wanted our alabastards to visit their Flex Corps rage on me. Worse still, we'd left Beauty up in the pasture with Leigh Ann and Uncle Grady.

"A quarter minute," Dad told me. "Three, two . . ." Together we switched off our lights.

I couldn't help but notice we were quickish with our counting. We hit fifteen seconds in probably twelve and switched our lights back on. We both had our gropers up and ready, but the cavern was just as we'd left it. Empty before us clear to far wall where the beast we'd gone dark on still hung.

He hadn't needed light to see us and probably kept watching all along. There he was eyeing us over the shoulder with the shiny scar. They don't blink as a rule. They'll squint sometimes if you're swinging at their heads, but he kept his black eyes fully open and trained on me and Dad.

"Go on," Dad finally told him.

He didn't respond at first.

"Git." Dad shook his groper, and that beast came off the wall.

He uncurled and hung by his talons before he dropped to the cavern floor. He had the sort of build you'd call strapping if you were a maiden aunt. He didn't sag anywhere, was all taut flesh and muscle, and he had what looked like a strip of black cloth around one wrist.

"What's that?" Dad asked.

I had a feeling I knew. "Know if the Flex Corps lost anybody down here?"

Dad shook his head. "Grady might. He was talking to the brass."

That alabastard stepped our way enough to make us both tense up. It wasn't even a full stride. He just kind of turned to face us.

"Could be they ripped up a uniform," I said.

Dad was thinking the same thing. "Trophy."

It was hard not to notice how clean the beast was. They're moist as a rule, so the cave grime sticks to them. Dirt and guano and God knows what else. You almost never see a scoured one, even though they seem to resent the filth. I'd once watched four of the Cumberland swarm crawl out of that cave to stand in a downpour and rub some of their crust off. I remember them seeming as close to happy as I imagined alabastards get.

The one before us was astoundingly clean following what was sure to have been a lively encounter with the Flex Corps. As he turned towards the deep dark after one final glance, he looked almost noble. He wasn't the sort to scuttle. He walked into the gloom.

It didn't feel like a significant meeting at the time, just a bit unusual and unnerving. But looking back now, I know that moment marks the beginning of a battle I can't imagine the end of yet.

It was Uncle Grady who named him. It turned out he'd seen that creature himself. We described him at the supper table. The clean white skin, the upright gate, the puffy shoulder scar.

"Oh yeah," Grady told as he pushed butter beans around his plate with a chunk of cornbread. "The big chief, I'm guessing." He chewed. He swallowed. He told us, "Cracker Daddy."

6

Our first provisional showed up drunk. You always ran the risk of taking somebody else's trouble. His name was Kevin, but he had some sort of hip-hop handle he wanted us all to use. It had letters and numbers and dashes and stuff. We just called him "come on" instead or "wake up" or "let's go" or "use a coaster why don't you." He barely seemed worth acknowledging while we waited for his recall papers to go through.

Leigh Ann particularly detested him because he treated her like a fragile female. She was closing on fourteen but had hardly come to grips with growing into womanhood. Boys were topsiders you kicked around. She'd see them in town sometimes when it was her turn to ride along to the grocery store and the county co-op.

Leigh Ann had white blonde hair at that age that she wore in braids, and she was rangy and tough. It was hard to get her in and out of spots where civilians gathered without Leigh Ann finding cause to throw a punch or two.

Boys clearly liked the look of her, but she didn't care at all for them. Kevin made the mistake of telling Leigh Ann that she was going to be a fine looking woman, that she was just the sort of female Carlsbad would trumpet since most of the girls in the Legion looked like they had bird dogs in the woodpile.

"But you're pretty," Kevin told her, and Leigh Ann hit him with a chair.

Dad stitched him up, and they bought him a pint of vodka to pacify him, but Kevin kept whining for the full six weeks we had to tolerate him.

We all took turns doing cave duty with him, even Leigh Ann who accidentally poked him with her groper a time or six. A bleeding wound was enough to distract him, but you could never quite shut him up. Kevin, naturally, had served all over the country. Nowhere for very long. That was a measure of just how poor a provisional Kevin was. He had nerve enough. I saw how he handled himself on a few patrols, but Kevin was dim and full of raw contempt for alabastards.

"I say burn them." That was his favorite suggestion. Kevin had a fond dream of sluicing the caverns with gasoline, all of them everywhere at the same moment. "Then everybody throw in a fire knot." He'd make a noise to approximate the roar of the deep dark alight.

For Kevin, alabastards were a custodial problem, a messy bit of business he had to police and contain. He could do it slightly better or slightly worse, depending on how his luck was running and if he'd drained a pint completely or quit only halfway down. Kevin wasn't ever likely to learn a thing from the creatures he herded. One was just like another for him. They were something to shove around.

I don't know that Kevin changed his mind after tangling with Cracker Daddy. Most people would have, but Kevin was given to the brand of uninformed opinion that's three parts bile and one part mulishness.

We were on what Grady called a lancing probe. It was Dad and me and Kevin. We'd climbed down off the ledge at the squeeze and had crossed the main cavern chamber to a passage we planned to clear and then draw back out of straightaway. That was the probing and the lancing together. In short, we were just nosing around.

It was fine with me for us to stay in eyeshot of the ledge. I was still new to Mom's ripper and couldn't yet fire the thing with her sort of aim. I'd practiced with it plenty by then, out in the pasture away from the sheep where I'd nailed a square of plywood onto a locust tree.

I had good sessions and poor ones. That weapon was difficult to aim, and I had to deal with the sorts of breezes I wouldn't know down in the cavern. The arrows (or bolts) were short and erratically made. Standing thirty yards from my target, I was like a sniper firing a snub-nose pistol. My ammo went all over the place.

I'll admit at first I was having a spot of emotional trouble as well. That ripper smelled a little like my mother. There was the faintest hint about it of the lotion she used to use. Nothing fancy, some drugstore brand she could be sure to find all over, but it had a distinctive limey-lanolin aroma that still clung. So there was a twinge attached to that ripper that I was obliged to contend with in addition to the general difficulty of drawing a bead with the thing.

I practiced for probably three or four months, but I never really got better. I kept adjusting the site and tweaking the arrows, and there were days when I'd get homed in, but they'd be followed by days when I could hardly hit a thing.

Uncle Grady was the one who finally put me out of my misery. Grady had larded on a few pounds and was trying to slim down. He was a thick guy by nature, so it wasn't like he was hoping to get fit, but Grady wasn't about to go out and buy new trousers. So he started walking afternoons. He measured out a circuit and covered three miles what Grady would call briskly, but he was just strolling, and often we'd see him stop and scratch and think.

I was out practicing one afternoon when Grady veered through the pasture and paused to watch me shoot. One arrow hit the target on one of the outer rings. One arrow barely caught the plywood. One headed for the horizon.

"What in the world are you doing?" Grady asked me.

"Practicing."

"Practicing what?"

"You know. Aiming. Hitting stuff."

"No aiming to do down there. Practice loading or don't waste your time."

Then off he went. A half dozen ewes made a show of urinating. They'd taken against Grady from the moment we'd arrived. Whenever he'd step onto the front porch, they'd all glare at him and pee.

Grady was often wrong, and Grady was usually irritating, but I understood immediately that he was correct on this occasion. I'd been out in the pasture wasting my time. Our cavern was close quarters. The key was to be ready to fire. So I went to work mastering a technique for nocking arrows in a hurry. I got to where I could cock and load with one gesture in mere seconds. Then I'd shoot from my waste or my shoulder. It hardly mattered which. I just kept drawing close until I hit my target every time.

"I think I've got it," I finally announced one evening in the kitchen after I'd greased that ripper and hung it on the wall.

"It's time then," Uncle Grady said and acquainted us with lancing probes.

We were three months after the Flex Corps by then, and we still couldn't raise a swarm up.

"They'll come back up," Dad told Grady. "Why don't we wait for them to do it?"

Grady had a whole strategic spiel that he favored Dad with.

Kevin, of course, was against the whole idea of mounting patrols.

"That's not the job," he kept saying. "Anywhere they are down there's fine."

He had a point. We were duty bound to serve as the cork in the bottle, and that was technically about all we had to do, but we still had round-ups on our yearly schedule, bi-annual rolling insertions, and what Carlsbad called 'active reconnaissance' that was an every other quarter sort of thing. We would blunder into the deep dark and lay waste to whatever we found.

Nothing much we did seemed to help or matter in any lasting sense. The Flex Corps might have throttled and cowed our swarm, but it was bound to be temporary. Grady was too interested in standards and procedure to ever acknowledge that.

"Here's the directive," he said to Kevin and shoved a sheet of Carlsbad paperwork Kevin's way.

Kevin only glanced at it. “That’s not the job.”

“Is tomorrow,” Grady told him, and that was that.

Being a provisional, Kevin didn’t have any choice but to do what he was told unless he’d changed his mind about collecting his stipend and enjoying our hospitality. There were forms Grady could file, back pay he could take from Kevin, so all Kevin could do was grunt and mutter, and he did plenty of both.

I was junior clan, so I had even less sway than Kevin did. Dad only locked horns with Uncle Grady over what he considered the big stuff. That’s what he told me and Leigh Ann anyway, but we’d grown used to seeing him say nothing and go along. Occasionally Dad would persuade Grady to dispense with a demand or two, ease up on recon timing, adjust the duty schedule, but we did things Uncle Grady’s way. He’d well and truly taken over. He was Granddaddy Hoyt without the solid judgment and the folksy charm.

So me and Dad and Kevin undertook a lancing probe with Grady directing us from the mouth of the cave over the radio. Leigh Ann was topside with Brody and Beauty messing around in the yard.

Kevin let his earpiece dangle.“Not the job,” was all he’d say while me and Dad endured near endless instructive chatter from Grady.

He wanted temperature and humidity readings.

“Spore?” he asked every couple of minutes.

Kevin resented getting stuck with the hotbox. He complained for a while and then flung it down.

“Grab it, boy,” he told me.

I had an arrow nocked. I was maybe four feet from Kevin and didn't see how I could miss him. We'd use him for bait instead of a sheep, would eventually recon our way to his bones. It was enough of a vicious fantasy to satisfy and occupy me until Dad drew up short and Kevin stopped as well.

I heard Kevin say, "Good God" in a tone that sounded impressed, and Kevin was rarely impressed by anything.

It was him again, Cracker Daddy.

We'd come out in a room known as the flat grotto. The roof was low, maybe seven feet, and there was water trickling into a sink hole just off to our right. I'd only been in there once before. That was back when we'd first reached Virginia, and we were checking the map the clan had left us against the actual cave.

Cracker Daddy stood across the way with his wives or attendants or something. They were females mostly and three or four juveniles with no sex showing yet.

He was upright, standing erect just like we were. The rest of them were half crouched and shifty in the typical alabastard way. There were maybe twenty yards between us. They were all just in ripper range.

"Let one go," Kevin advised me.

Dad said, "Hold off."

Kevin shook and his head and muttered, "Not the job."

We all looked at each other. Us across at them, and all of them back across at us.

"Put the box out here," Dad told me.

"It's barely warm," I said.

"This ain't the job."

"Zip it," Dad said. He took a full stride forward.

A few of the females pulled back a half step, but most of them appeared to be drawing pluck directly from Cracker Daddy. He stayed planted right where we'd found him. Glaring at us. Sizing us up.

"Let's spread out and push," Dad told me and Kevin. He didn't sound confident exactly but more like a man who didn't want to answer to his brother for having retreated without even mounting a half-hearted thrust.

I flanked left.

"I'm good here," Kevin said.

Dad showed Kevin the shiny, honed blade of his groper. "You won't be for long."

Kevin groaned and muttered. He suddenly saw the wisdom in shifting right, and the three of us pressed towards those alabastards together. Not with any velocity. The idea was just to drive them away, send them back through whatever crack in the rock they'd passed through to get where they were.

Ordinarily, we could count on alabastards to shift before us and be herded. They'd chafe and fight occasionally. That's why we kept our gropers sharp. But as a rule, Low Lords and alabastards had reached an accommodation. We skirmished when we had to, but otherwise, they bent and yielded when we pushed.

Not this time, though. We advanced a few yards, our headlamp beams playing on what I counted as seven alabastards. The big chief was the only adult male among them, but the females had teeth and talons and disagreeable dispositions. It wasn't like there was any advantage to battling with them.

"You nocked?" Dad asked.

"Yes, sir."

"Fire when I say."

"Right."

"I ain't much on these probes," Kevin announced. "This ain't the job" was implied.

We'd long assumed they couldn't understand us, that we could strategize right in front of them, belittle them within earshot without any consequence. That changed in a hurry and on the spot once Kevin got too antsy to keep himself in check.

He made a bluff with his groper. He charged three or four feet ahead and whipped the thing back and forth to menace those creatures with his blade.

Cracker Daddy uncoiled — that's the best way I can describe it — and swatted Kevin's groper not just out of his hands but clean across the cavern. It clanged against the far cave wall and rattled to the floor. That would have been enough snare our attention, but Cracker Daddy shouted, "No!" as well.

It didn't sound like an animal's approximation of a word. Beauty would yip and yap on occasion in a fashion you might take for talking. This was regular commentary. This was an alabastard saying a thing.

I was astounded. An alabastard doing anything but grunting and skittering ran counter to The Great Book and every lesson I'd been taught. Kevin was plainly terrified. Dad, for his part, was something worse. Something deeper and more profound.

He flashed on the future, I have to think, or at the very least appeared ready to think we'd just left the past behind.

"Uh oh," he managed.

Our earpieces crackled. "Status?" Grady asked us. "Spore?"

"Contact," I told him back.

"Force?"

"Shut up," Dad suggested."

We got static followed by a noise that sounded like Beauty trying to talk. Dad fished his earpiece out to dangle. I did the same.

Kevin said, "Hell," which sounded like his version of "I quit," and he did the thing we all knew not to do with alabastards. It was in The Great Book. It was in the appendix. It was in the apocrypha too. You never ever turned your back on even a Cumberland alabastard. It was a known provocation, set down in scripture. It was kind of like poking a snake.

Surely Kevin had been warned and instructed through the years, but his worthless instincts took over, and he wheeled and headed for the passage we'd taken from the squeeze. Cracker Daddy made a noise in his sinuses or somewhere, and four females converged on Kevin.

Alabastards at full scramble are a terror to behold. They move like crabs or spiders but with no deliberation. They're fast and frantic and headlong. Kevin made the mistake of glancing back. He warbled for help as they reached him. They chuffed and snorted and clawed at Kevin until another noise from the big beast put them in retreat.

They were back beside him in a flash. Kevin rolled over and moaned. He was seeping a little from claw marks. His coveralls were in tatters. Our earpieces crackled.

"Status!?" Grady couldn't help himself.

Kevin turned out to be more pitiful than hurt. They could have laid him open and emptied him out. They had the weapons and the strength to do it, but they'd just scratched a mark on his neck, as it turned out. A sideways Q wearing a hat.

"Come on," I said and grabbed him by what was left of his coveralls collar. I picked up his helmet. "We'll come back for your groper."

"You maybe," he said.

I shielded Kevin as he plunged into the crease that we'd come out of.

I went in next. Dad followed. We eased back. They didn't pursue. We crossed to the ledge, climbed up and shut the gate. Eased up the pipe to the surface without a word.

Grady was waiting for us. He eyed Kevin's wounds. "Contact?"

I nodded.

"Spore?"

7

It was a brand new game. Dad and I knew it. Kevin must have known it too. He stayed with us another couple of weeks. I think mostly for the salve. Every day Uncle Grady mixed up a fresh batch of ointment for Kevin's neck.

Carlsbad had long tried to analyze cavus ferinus toxin, but none of their chemists had come up with anything to touch that ancient Great Book salve. There were roots and leaves and extractions in it. Three different boiled barks and a kind of red clay that you could only find in southern Idaho. Like the fire knots, and the hotbox pans, and the traditional groper oil, that clay was a pricey Low Lord gear list buy.

Kevin waited until his wounds had closed and his scabs had just about flaked off – hung around until he was well and truly branded – and then went to bed one night early enough to make us all suspicious, to cause Dad to take the ignition key out of the truck. Kevin didn't have much to pack. He'd come only with a grip and a groper. The latter was down in the cavern still, and the former he left behind. He departed with just the clothes he had on and that sideways Q on his cheek. He walked all the way out to the blacktop and hitched a ride.

"Just like Mom," Leigh Ann said.

I can't say I hadn't thought it.

Naturally, there was a form for a provisional leaving before his replacement showed up. Uncle Grady filled ours out, ticked all the proper boxes and supplied the requested enlargements. Carlsbad was obliged to seek Kevin's input, but the chances were good they'd never find him. Even still, we couldn't get a replacement until they'd made a try. So for the better part of a year and a half, it was just the five of us.

We did duty at the squeeze like usual, would go for weeks and never see an alabastard. Grady laid it to what he called the Flex Corps effect. He declared that our swarm was chastened and would stay low for a while to come. Dad and I knew better. We'd seen Cracker Daddy. There wasn't a thing chastened about him.

"He's thinking. Scheming. You can see it," Dad told Grady.

"He can talk." I was usually the one to remind them both of that.

"Or say something that sounds like 'No'." That's what Grady always told us back.

I kept hoping that beast would show up in the cavern whenever Grady was around. Just present himself so Grady could see what an unsettling specimen he was. But Grady's knees were failing him, and our alabastards weren't mounting much of a challenge. So Grady stayed topside mostly and kept our paperwork up to date.

He and Dad replaced the roof on our house. Built a new chicken coop from scratch and dug a good two feet of cow flop out of our barn with a front end loader. Brody chased guineas around the yard as kind of avocation, which left me and Leigh Ann and Beauty as our presence at the squeeze.

As it turned out, our alabastards weren't lulling us exactly. Instead, they were busy with surveying junkets, on far-flung patrols of their own in the great black underneath. They left only babies and nurses behind. We finally saw one of the creatures after a couple of months of seeing nothing at all. She was clinging to the cavern roof and tidying up her milk gland with her long cleft tongue. It's a slit on the forearm that looks like a belly button gone astray. Hers was leaking what passes with them for succor. It's thin and the color of curry.

She watched us while she licked and preened. Me and Leigh Ann and Beauty watched her back.

"She's kind of pretty," Leigh Ann said. "If you squint and all."

I was going to call my sister foolish, but that alabastard did have a look about her. Clearly a female. Some of them looked like turtles that had left their shells behind, but this one had authentic girlishness about her. It was in the slope of her face. The tilt of her eyes. She even had kind of a decent nose instead of the old-style drainage holes with a flap of skin laying on them.

"Is that a necklace?" Leigh Ann asked me. The beast was wearing a strip of black fabric.

"A piece of uniform," I said to Leigh Ann. "Flex Corps trophy. They lost two guys."

"They're more than we're banking on, aren't they?" Leigh Ann asked me in time.

I made a show of giving the question some thought before I told her, "Yeah."

We finally got our replacement provisional in August, just after all the work was done. Some civilian drove her up in his truck and put her out in the turnaround. He reached over and opened the passenger door and let her fall to the ground. I was eating a quick sandwich over the sink in the kitchen and watched it all through the window.

She was a dirty blonde, a rangy woman. Gaunt but with kind of a noble profile. She also appeared to be thoroughly drunk. It looked like Kevin all over again.

Brody got to her first. She struck him as an improvement on guineas, so he ran over to pepper the woman with questions.

She answered them all with, "Huh?"

She'd sit up for a bit and then lay flat down. Sit up. Sprawl. Say, "Huh?"

Me and Leigh Ann went out and joined Brody. Beauty had beaten us to her and was giving the woman a sniff. There was a canvas suitcase on the dirt beside her and what looked like an ancient ripper. It appeared to be made of bone and forged steel, rubbed shiny by decades of hands.

She sat up to soak us in. Sprawled again. "You got people?"

"Are you drunk?" I asked her

She laughed.

"Our uncle'll file paper on you," I said.

"Lots of paper," Leigh Ann added.

The woman laughed again.

"Maybe she ought to sit in the barn for a while." That was Leigh Ann's suggestion and immediately seemed sensible to me.

"You don't say anything," Leigh Ann told Brody.

He shrugged in that way that meant 'maybe I won't' and went charging towards a pair of guineas under a boxwood across the yard.

"Come on." I picked up the woman's suitcase. Leigh Ann reached for her ripper, but she wasn't drunk enough to let that happen and yanked it away.

"Can you get up?" I asked her.

That earned me a "Huh?" and some clumsy scrabbling. In hardly more than a half minute, she was standing more or less upright.

She looked like a proper, privileged woman who'd decided to go on a bender, a bout of drinking that had gone on some years longer than she'd hoped. You could tell that she was good looking under the neglect, probably knew how to wear fine clothes and talk to people. But the applejack, as it turned out, kept getting in the way.

I pointed in the direction of the barn. Me and Leigh Ann set out. Beauty stayed behind to herd the woman. We set her up in the far stall. Dad and Grady had left the barn spotless. The floor was all covered with chips from the mill, fragrant pine leavened with oak.

Just before she let herself sink to the floor and pass clean out, she tapped her sternum and told us both, "Clarice."

She stayed out of sight – might even have stayed asleep – for a solid day and a couple of hours beyond it. Me and Leigh Ann took turns checking on her, but she'd just be where we'd left her until I went out at near suppertime the following day. I heard splashing in the old zinc trough back behind the barn and showed up to find her down to her underwear and sluicing herself off.

She was a sinewy specimen and sure had a lot of scars. Clarice had clearly been in her share of swam ups. She'd been clawed and laid open in four or five spots.

"You ever with the Flex Corps?" I asked her before she'd noticed I was there.

She didn't start and shrink like most people would but wheeled around and had me by the throat before I could hope to move.

"There's no profit in sneaking up on people." Sober she had one of those low, smoky voices that surely let her get away with a lot.

"Yes, ma'am."

"Yes, ma'am?" She was a decent mimic too. "Where is this? Kentucky?"

"Virginia," I told her. "Albemarle County." I pointed east. "Charlottesville's over there."

"I guess I slept through the Alleghenies."

"You got here in a bad way," I said.

That didn't appear to be news to her or cause for an apology.

"You've got grown ups, right?"

I nodded. "My dad and my uncle."

That's when I saw it. On the right side of her neck down by her collarbone. A scar that wasn't a scar so much as a signifier. A Q laid sideways in a pointy hat. Her wound was shiny and long healed.

"Where'd you get that?" I pointed.

"Why?"

"The guy before you got one here. I doubt he'll go in a cave again."

"It's never stopped me."

"Where?" I asked her.

"Missouri," she said. "Onyx Mountain. We got caught in a slide."

There were stories in The Great Book about Low Lords who'd been trapped behind slides when rock had fallen and stopped a passage up. But for a few rare exceptions, they'd ended up martyrs. There was a page before the apocrypha, an ornate list, dedicated just to them.

"Why aren't you dead?"

She paused there in her underwear to give me a good once over. "You don't fool around."

"No ma'am."

"There were four of us. Maybe twenty of them. Two of us dug. Two of us defended. We opened a crack I could fit through. It wasn't big enough for the rest."

"So you left them?"

She didn't even bother with caveats and qualifications – how they worked with a fury from the other side but reopened the passage too late. She just shoved an arm in a shirtsleeve and told me, "Yeah."

She collected her bag and ripper from the stall where she'd been sleeping.

"What do I tell them?" I asked.

"How about I just walked up?"

"Our last guy drank, so they won't tolerate it."

"I'm done." She seemed to mean it.

I brought her through the back door, straight into the kitchen. Leigh Ann was making biscuits, and Grady had a casserole going.

Even before I could introduce her, Clarice inhaled deeply. Burned cheese and cream of mushroom soup. Bisquick. Potato spuds.

"Why is it no Low Lords can cook?" she asked.

It was Dad who told her, "Amen."

Grady has a nose for dissolute people, and he got whiff enough of Clarice to disapprove of her on the spot. He let Dad quiz her on her particulars while he leaned against the counter. Grady looked to be deciding which form he'd need to file.

She'd married young, the first time. "As good as arranged," she said. "Cave of the Mounds. Wisconsin. A patrol went bad. He got hauled off."

"Sorry," Dad told her.

Me and Leigh Ann together noticed Dad was looking at Clarice like he hadn't looked at a woman since Mom had packed her satchel and left. We left off with him long enough to glance at each other. Leigh Ann even smiled.

"We had a lot of bad luck," Clarice said. "My brother lost a leg."

"Cave wound?" Dad asked.

She shook her head. "Tractor." She turned towards the stove. "Something's burning."

Leigh Ann darted over and took out her pan of singed biscuits.

"My dad had a stroke," Clarice went on. "Mom lost a foot to diabetes. Regular people wear out above ground. We've got it twice as bad down under."

"How long have you been provisional?" Grady wanted to know.

"Seven years."

I've always been bad with ages, was especially poor back then. It's hard to tell with our sort since caving seems to put hard wear on people, but I think Clarice was maybe thirty-five when she came to us. She looked older in the eyes, like all of us do, so it was a seasoned three and a half decades, and she'd been on the move for an uncommon while.

"I'll need your C-log," Grady said. "I'll be putting in a query."

Clarice nodded and told him back, "I would."

"Show them." I pointed. "They'll want to see it."

She pulled down her collar low enough to reveal the laid over Q on her neck.

It was Dad who told Clarice, "They marked the guy before you."

"I've seen six or eight, traveling around," she said.

Dad asked her, "Know what it means?"

She shrugged. "What does it mean on a cow?"

"Somebody owns it."

Clarice nodded. "Probably like that."

That seemed close to me but not quite right. I'd thought on it since Kevin had come away with the brand on his neck. I'd decided it meant "We could have laid you open, but we just gave you this instead." It was their way of saying they weren't rank beasts. They'd sort of ticked a box themselves. They'd decided to let you live for now, and they'd cash you in when they wanted.

Clarice was with me, more or less. She'd thought about it too.

"There's more going on down there," she said, "than anybody wants to admit."

Grady snorted. He was the type to know what he believed, to have scriptural basis for it he that he could locate in The Great Book. Changing your mind was for people who thought far less of Carlsbad than he did.

"Same old same old," Grady said, the way he always said it.

Clarice had him pegged a quarter hour in. "Keep pushing your paper," she told him.

Dad stepped in to save us from Grady's full-throated defense of the Legion. Grady had enough Jefferson at his fingertips to bury you in the stuff.

"Why don't we eat," Dad said. "Grady's made one of his casseroles."

"I smell it," Clarice allowed. She could have been talking about compost or asphalt.

"Set the table, honey," Dad told Leigh Ann.

Brody wandered over and grabbed onto Clarice's pant leg. By that time, he hadn't run across anything maternal in a while. Clarice might have been as close to a man as women usually get, but Brody could tell what was underneath, and he held to her until it came out.

Brody had gotten a little pudgy — too much cream of mushroom soup — but Clarice still managed to snatch him off the floor and hold him in her arms.

"Hey, little man."

Brody gave her a full accounting of the guineas he'd lately chased and herded.

"Saw a snake," he said.

"Where?"

Brody pointed, primarily at the ceiling. "Chickens pecked him to pieces."

"They'll do that."

Brody laid his head against Clarice.

"Where's his mom?" she asked just generally.

To keep Dad from having to say it, I told Clarice, "Taking a break."

All indications were that Clarice didn't care for Grady's cooking. She forked some casserole in her mouth and dropped it on her plate again.

"How big are yours?"

We all knew what she meant. I told her, "Mostly people sized, but the one in charge is a bigger."

"In charge?"

"He's guessing," Grady said. "You've seen him . . what? Twice?"

I nodded.

"They've got room to be tall around here," Grady said. "It's nothing more than that."

Clarice chose not to say anything back. Me and Leigh Ann did that sometimes. I'd caught Dad doing it lately as well.

Grady was fighting the future. He'd planted his feet and meant to stay just where he was. Instead, she pointed at my ripper that was resting on the breakfront.

"Whose is that?"

"Mack's," Dad told her.

"You any good with it?" she asked.

"I'm all right."

She stepped over and picked it up. She plucked at the draw string, checked the stops and the gearing, drew a bead and told me, "Like hell."

That was the beginning of my remedial ripper instruction with Clarice. She took me out in the pasture the following morning and had me fire some bolts for her so she could have fit cause to inform me, "You stink."

I knew I was a work in progress, but I was having to be self-taught. I watched as she nocked an arrow into her ripper slot and then pointed towards the fence line.

"That post right there," she said. "See the dark spot?"

I did. I nodded.

She took aim, exhaled, and put her arrow in it from what was nearly fifty yards.

"You'll never have that kind of shot down there. Grady says I don't need to aim."

She handed me her ripper. "You going to listen to him or me?"

Her ripper was balanced and solid. I aimed where she'd shot.

"Put the target right on top of the site," she said.

I did. I exhaled. Her trigger was greased. Her works were filed. The action was as smooth as it could get. I missed the dark spot but not by much.

"You're a little jerky," she told me. "We can fix that." She picked up Mom's ripper and gave it sour once over. "Probably fix this too. You got a shop or something?"

8

We had a workbench in a shed off the barn. That's where I came to know Clarice. Not the one that spat casserole onto her plate and said hard things to people. The other Clarice. The sad and disappointed one who shoved folks away when she would rather have held them close instead.

"Ever think about working for Carlsbad?" I asked her. I told her all about Jo Jo, down to the robot fighter and the cleavage and the swarm up he'd survived.

"I don't buy what they're selling," she told me. "They don't go in the caves anymore."

There was plenty of truth to that. I'd seen pictures in the quarterly of the Council at work in Tally House and the Legion brass gathered at Long Acre. They were guys, for the most part, ancient guys with spiky hair growing out their ears. There were two women in the whole assembly and they had faces like old shoes. Go in caves? They probably needed help getting off the toilet.

"They're changing down there," I told her that first day we started work in the shed. She was taking Mom's ripper apart with no delicacy like it was a Thanksgiving carcass and she needed the pieces for stock.

"Uh huh." She examined my ripper bowstring and tossed it aside. "Hell of a fool you've been to go anywhere low with this."

"I'd rather have a groper."

"Not after I'm through with you." She took the last joined pieces of Mom's ripper apart and told me, "This thing's crap."

She was quite the craftswoman, especially given our lousy collection of tools. We didn't even have a proper bench vice, so she made a stop and a kind of clamp. Mostly I watched and handed her stuff, which gave me the leisure to notice that she was nicked and dinged all over.

"How old are you?" she asked me.

"Fifteen."

"What happened with your mother?"

"She left. Dad says this life made her sad."

"Which life?"

"The caves mostly," I said, "but probably the rest of it too." I described the sight of my mother wandering against the horizon down in Tennessee. "Dad did what he could."

"Men can't fix much. They're just slow to believe it."

I thought it was a knock and got shirty. "She wouldn't let him help her. I was there. He tried."

Clarice left off with the ripper stock she'd been sanding. "Easy," she told me. "I'm not even talking about your father. I had my own man who wasn't any count."

I learned they'd been together in Kansas.

"Limestone caves out there," she told me. "Nasty little things. CFs about this big." She held her thumb and finger apart. "I met him in Nevada. We were all right for a while."

"What happened to him?"

"That slide I was in?"

I remembered. I nodded.

"He's the one that brought it down."

"Why? How?"

"Got in a panic. Decided to save his own sorry hide any way he could." She eyed my ripper stock and decided she was satisfied. "Knocked the rocks loose with his groper handle."

"You saw him?"

"I did."

"On purpose?"

She nodded.

"That's cold."

"People do funny things down there. He climbed out. He packed up. Didn't hang around to see if I might have lived."

"Have you run into him since?"

"Once or twice. He works for Carlsbad now."

"Figures."

Clarice gathered all my ripper hardware and shoved it in a bucket.

I sharpened my bolt tips with a file and a stone while Clarice rebuilt my ripper. Leigh Ann came in as we were working and got some advice on groper honing. Clarice was like some kind of estrogen magnet for us. We'd had to too much of men, way too much of Uncle Grady. Brody even left his guineas for Clarice. She parked him on the workbench and told Brody all sorts of fanciful stories about stuff she'd seen, places she'd been to.

After an hour or so of steady and talk and labor, Clarice snatched one of my sharpened arrows, nocked it in my ripper, took dead aim and buried the thing a good inch into a rafter.

She grunted to let me know she wasn't entirely satisfied. "A little more tension," she said of the ripper. Of the bolt tip, she told me, "Nice."

I think I blushed. I know I tingled. She might have been a grown up, a hard use woman, but she was a female unrelated to me who'd approved of me a little.

She complimented Leigh Ann's groper blade too. Then Clarice said to Leigh Ann, "A little more shortening in those biscuits."

"Uncle Grady wants to make it last."

That was true. He was powerfully cheap.

"He'll never know if we don't tell him."

Leigh Ann grinned. She colored some too.

We knew immediately we had an ally in Clarice, a friend and model of sorts. We'd never had anything of the kind in Kevin. Brody kept holding onto bits of Clarice's clothes. She'd take his hand away if she needed to wander, but he'd always put it back.

"Do you like our dad?" Leigh Ann asked her.

I was interested in hearing the answer myself. Clarice took her time and gave the matter some thought.

"Him and your Uncle Grady might be brothers," Leigh Ann said, "but anybody can see they're not a thing alike."

"So?" Leigh Ann's always been dogged that way.

"I hardly know the man. He seems all right." Then Clarice handed me my rebuilt ripper. "Show me what you've got below."

Dad had been down at the squeeze on his own. That was where we'd gotten to after the Flex Corps had driven our alabastards deep. We told Clarice all about the work they'd done, the week they'd spent on the farm.

"Bunch of thugs," she said. "They make everything worse."

"Ours CFs were out of control," I told her.

"They'll come back harder and meaner. You'll see." There wasn't an ounce of doubt in her voice.

Once we'd reached the crease that served as the mouth of our Virginia cavern, we hailed Dad on the walkie, and he came crawling out. It took him a good half minute to stand properly upright.

He waggled his thumb, our all-clear sign. "How are they treating you?" he asked Clarice.

A nod was the best he could get out of her. He put his hands on his lumbar and groaned.

"Ought to stretch first," Clarice advised him. "You guys almost never do."

She showed us how right there in the dirt. She could put her legs places we could barely contemplate.

"You going in?" Dad asked her in the sort of anxious way that suggested he was ready to escort and squire if she'd see clear to permit it.

"We'll take her," I said.

"Any of them around?" Clarice asked Dad.

He shook his head. "I haven't seen even a juvenile in days."

"Dog too?" Clarice asked me once we'd gathered at the mouth of the cave.

"Oh yeah."

Beauty slipped in through the crease and waited for us down at the alcove by the gear box. Clarice let us know she wasn't happy with the state of our cedar locker. The thing was kind of any eyesore and had seen years of rough use. It was largely held together with angle irons and straps.

Her mood didn't improve once I'd opened it. Our helmets and pads and gloves were all just tossed in every which way. There were rusty batteries off in one corner and stray trash in an old knotted pant leg that we'd been a hauling around for years.

She reached for Mom's old helmet without us even pointing her towards it. The battery was shot, so she changed it out, but it fit her without adjustment.

I picked up the hotbox and a plug of fuel the way I usually did, but Clarice shook her head and told me, "Don't bother. Those things don't do any good."

"Is there something better out there?" Leigh Ann asked her.

She enjoyed flipping through the catalog and scouring the ads in the back of the quarterly. If there was some fancy, cutting-edge hotbox update available, Leigh Ann was keen to know what it was.

"Yeah," Clarice told her. "Nerve."

To me, nerve meant blundering into places where you ought not to be. The last time I'd seen nerve on offer, Kevin ended up with a scar on his neck.

Leigh Ann and Beauty led down to the squeeze, which in Virginia was a decent stretch of ledge, about the size of a motel balcony. There was an ottoman on it which I'd largely stopped seeing until Clarice found it with her headlamp. Dad had brought it down for Grady, who still showed up down under sometimes.

Clarice choked back a spot of commentary. Me and Leigh Ann were about to sit down when Clarice told both of us, "Uh uh." She led us off the ledge and into the dark.

Beauty barked. She wasn't used to people with the pluck to just strike out. It excited and unsettled her. She scrambled after us into the chamber below the ledge.

Clarice was scarred up enough to give any follower second thoughts about her tactics, but she was good with a ripper, and she was very much alive, so maybe following her meant nicked and dinged was all we'd ever get.

"Four routes," I told her and pointed.

Clarice found each passage with her head lamp and studied them in turn.

"Dead end." She pointed at the one on the left that went about twenty yards through and closed.

"How can you tell?" Leigh Ann asked.

"Guano. Gravel. Nothing been in out of there but bats."

She pointed at the crease beside it, eleven o'clock. "Goes through but tight and low mileage." Of the third one over, to our far right, she said, "There's water in there somewhere."

She'd settled on the passage at two o'clock. We'd sure seen alabastards leaking from it. It was low and uninviting.

"That one," she said. "They're back there."

Me and Leigh Ann hardly expected we'd actually crawl through the thing. Everything we'd been raised to believe about cavern patrols told us to stay put. So we balked when Clarice said, "Let's go," and struck out.

She dropped to her knees and crawled into the passage, disappeared up to her ankles. We stayed where we were, even Beauty until Clarice had come back out.

"What?" she asked.

Me and Leigh Ann threw in together to explain how we'd been raised, to acquaint Clarice with the cave truths we'd been schooled in and brought up on.

"Crap," she told us. "Let's go." She crawled back in through the slot, and we followed.

"Dog last," was the only piece of instruction she troubled herself to share.

I'd been in a couple of the other channels – the one one the left that quit and the one on the far right that went for a bit and then got soupy. I'd not so much as peeked in the one that we were crawling through. It started tight but opened up soon enough so we could stand bent over. Then the cave roof lifted, and we found ourselves in a spacious cavern chamber. Alone there, fortunately, except for scattered piles of Flex Corps junk.

"Pigs," Clarice said as she kicked at a heap of MRE cans and wrappers.

They'd left a couple of tactical gropers and a half spent box of ripper arrows. There were headlamp batteries all over the place and a couple of busted lanterns. No signs of alabastards but for a drawing high up the far wall.

Leigh Ann found it with her head lamp. It was twenty feet above us, so high that only an alabastard could have put it there.

There was no mistaking what it was, even from down on the cavern floor. A tree. It looked an awful lot like the locust in the pasture. And off beside it, the sun low in the sky.

"What do they want more than anything?" Clarice asked us as we stood there looking up.

Leigh Ann spoke before I could manage to, but I was thinking the same thing. "Out."

9

We carried the Flex Corps gropers and the arrows out, didn't venture any further. We never saw an alabastard. Never heard a thing. Beauty failed to growl even once.

"Where are they?" I asked once we were back topside.

As we headed across the pasture and towards the house, Clarice told us, "I've got a theory."

It was hardly crazy, as theories go, but it ran entirely counter to Carlsbad. The elders had long subscribed to the notion that all low life was confined. Free to wander in a network of channels that quit somewhere and ended. So no matter how adapted the creature and how deep it could go in the earth, it couldn't start in Iowa and end up in Arkansas. The elders gave that out as a truth of the deep dark. One of the verities, they called it. It showed up in The Great Book appendix, and that was enough for them.

Clarice's faith ran in a different direction. "They travel," is what she told us. "Go far enough down, you'll hit the highway. I saw it once," she said.

That stopped us halfway across the pasture, in amongst the sheep.

"Where?" I asked her.

"Oklahoma. My first provisional gig. A clan run by a hotheaded fool."

We waited, me and Leigh Ann did, and let Clarice start where she wanted. She spied the half-dead locust across the way, the one high on the cavern wall. "There's your tree," she said. "Their tree too, I guess."

The guy in Oklahoma —his name was Del — had lost his favorite cousin. "Freak thing," Clarice told us. "Got nicked right here." She laid a finger to her inseam. "A CF laid a vein open just by chance. It wasn't much of a wound at all. The boy bled out in the dark. Del wasn't there, and when he heard, he was hot to take revenge."

A solution cave. Clarice described it to us. It was well back in the scrub of southeastern Oklahoma in the Sans Bois Mountains.

"Looked like a snake pit," she said, "from on top, but once you got in, it went deep."

In a rage, Del threw together what Clarice described as a posse.

"A lot of high feeling. No care much or sense, and all of them bent on blood."

She told us they covered all the usual passages and channels.

"I'd never thought that cave went much of anywhere until we got inside that day."

They plunged into spots they'd never gone before, passed through seams and crawls they wouldn't have attempted level headed.

"We got so far in," Clarice said to us, "I doubted we could get out."

We'd all heard tales about lost Low Lords, foolhardy men primarily who'd chased alabastards down too far to crawl back.

They'd get swarmed or lost. Their lamps would die. Somebody would usually find them but only after a great while, once they'd dried out and mummified and their clothes had gone to tatters.

Carlsbad had an assortment of cave-cured Low Lords in their museum. Their skin drawn tight. Their teeth exposed. Their coveralls in shreds. Those dead guys served as an admonition, a reminder that half of the job was getting out.

"They were crazed," Clarice said. "The way men get sometimes. There was nothing to do but flow along with them."

"How deep?" I asked her.

She shook her head. "Miles," was all she said.

"And you didn't get swarmed?" Leigh Ann asked.

"Nope. Never saw a one. We kept pushing deeper and finally came out in a transit. You could have run a train through it. A regular tunnel that disappeared on either end. There was air moving both ways. We went two miles in each direction. Didn't hit cave wall either way. The thing went on out of sight."

Out of sight in a cavern doesn't count for much. Out of sight is as far as your beam goes, but Clarice said they lit fire knots and explored enough to make her think that channel just kept going.

"It sank as it went," she told us. "Way deeper than you're supposed to go under Oklahoma."

"How'd y'all get out?" I asked her.

"Luck. It took about a day and a half."

"Say that tunnel goes twenty or thirty miles. What does that prove exactly?"

"You're Grady's nephew, aren't you?" she asked me.

Leigh Ann got a kick out of that.

Clarice didn't bother to mount a defense or offer an enlargement beyond telling me, "They travel. I'm sure of it."

"Might want to keep it to yourself," Leigh Ann suggested.

"No worries," Clarice said. "As a rule, I don't much bother talking to men."

"I'm a man," I told her.

Clarice and Leigh Ann laughed all the way to the house.

Grady offered to make a casserole for supper, but Clarice wouldn't let him.

"Save your mushroom soup for end times," she told him, and she sent me out to kill a guinea that she dredged and fried in our electric skillet. It cooked while she mashed real potatoes and stewed greens she'd sent Leigh Ann to gather in the meadow beyond the shed.

Leigh Ann made biscuits with enough shortening in them to make them hold together, and we sat down to a meal that had spice and flavor to it other than salt.

Grady told Clarice, "Hmm," with a thighbone in his mouth. It was about as close to a compliment as Grady ever got.

"Y'all stick at the squeeze?" Dad asked us.

Clarice shook her head. "I had them show me around a little."

Grady grunted his disapproval.

"Any action?" That from Dad.

"Not much." Clarice shot a look at Grady. "Killed an ottoman."

It went like that for the entire meal and so was better than our usual supper. Most nights Grady would instruct us, regurgitate his stories while we shoved casserole around our plates. This was entirely something else. The food was good. The conversation had some spark and humor to it, and Grady was stuck with all the rest of us trying to fight his way into the chat.

"I hear you used to give them sheep," Clarice said at one point.

Grated grunted.

"The guys before us set it up."

"There's no bargain worth making with a CF, and you're getting them used to coming out."

"So?" That from Grady.

"Mission creep," Clarice told him. "They're aiming for up here."

Grady snorted.

"Wouldn't you?"

Grady was disadvantaged by his faith that they were feral and meant only for the deep dark. Cave crackers. Alabastards. Hole hermits or just CFs. They didn't have brains worth speaking of. No long-term strategy. They fought. They fed. They understood main force and groper steel.

"I'm not them," Grady said and shrugged.

"They're sure you," she told him.

Grady threw down his fork. He didn't have much practice at getting talked at. Certainly not contradicted. I feared he might puff up and remind Clarice that she was just a provisional for hire and not some emissary from Carlsbad with doctrine behind her and clout. Instead, he let the clatter of flatware do his talking for him. Grady pushed back from the table and headed for the porch. He was muttering something about the evening air as the screen door slapped behind him.

Me and Leigh Ann and Brody all just looked at our plates for a bit.

Thinking back, that might have been the moment Dad reorganized. Since Mom took off, he'd kept the pain and the heartache of it at the top of his stack. The first thing he woke up knowing. The last thing he thought about before he dozed off. He never said as much, but me and Leigh Ann could see it well enough.

We'd once schemed to send him to a gear show in Bowling Green where we were hoping he'd meet a woman. Grady even helped. He got the truck serviced and allowed that he was in the market for a senior groper — the extra lite model with the hollow aluminum shaft and the diamond dusted blade you never honed.

Dad drove clear to Kentucky on a Friday afternoon but was back home by Saturday midday.

"That senior stuff's all crap," he told Grady as he was climbing out of the truck.

Then Clarice came along and tilted with Grady. She was handsome to start with but seemed to improve on her looks with her starch and pluck. Driving Grady away from the supper table and out onto the porch appeared to do for Dad what a trip to Bowling Green had not accomplished. Mom slipped down a notch or two as Clarice ascended to the top of his stack.

"Sorry," she said in a general way. Clarice was a wretched apologizer. One of those people who makes a brief show of remorse but would do everything the same way again.

"Don't be," Dad told her, which was convenient because she wasn't. "We've let Grady get a little too used to hearing his version of everything."

"Might be easier around here if I just shut up."

That's when Dad reached over and grabbed Clarice's hand. "For our sakes," he said, "I wish you wouldn't." Then he held her fingers long enough to make us all uneasy.

Me and Leigh Ann have decided that was the start of everything. That anyway is how we explained it all to Brody once he was big and focused enough to care how we'd ended up where we were. It seemed like a small thing at the moment it happened – Grady out on the porch and Dad holding Clarice's fingers – but it proved to be significant, even seismic really.

It turned out Grady missed Jo Jo far more than he let on. While Dad was spending those moments just before sleep thinking about our mother, Grady had his mind on Carlsbad and how he needed get there himself. He was built to be a courtier and a Carlsbad functionary. The wonder was that it took him so many years to finally tick the appropriate box. Jo Jo waiting for him finally prompted Grady to action.

I suspect Grady had an instinct Clarice was probably right, or at the very least was sure to win us over. He wanted to go to a place where people were prone to stay mired in the past like him. The Elders wear wigs, for godsakes, and sip from a ceremonial hammered bronze bowl. Carlsbad's not a place for second thoughts and reconsideration. It's not a place for the future or even the actual present. It's devoted to the glorified past.

After that night at the supper table, it was us and it was Grady. We were cordial about it all, but underneath the courtesy and the empty family chatter, Grady kept on thinking what he thought while we moved towards Clarice.

She lead us on deep and ill-advised patrols. All of us – Dad and Leigh Ann and me, Beauty and Brody too. We never got swarmed. We'd go for weeks without spying an alabastard, or we'd catch brief sight of geezoids – they're called ancients in The Great Book. Old wiry specimens well past scrabbling. They lurk and cling instead.

We finally got a lone glimpse of Cracker Daddy. We'd talked him up to Clarice. I feared that we had oversold his menace and probably his stature too until we spied him across a sizable cavern we'd never entered before. That was the thing about following Clarice through a cave. She'd lead you into places you otherwise would have lacked the pluck to go.

We were feeling safe and jaunty. We'd found a geezoid in a crevice. He was back in there deep and panting in a crack where he hardly fit. He was speckled and veiny, scarred and frail. We could smell his breath as we closed.

"Go on," Dad told us kids. That was the way it usually happened when we'd run across a straggler. Dad would send us along and tend to the butchery himself, what they called in

Carlsbad mercy deeds. It was almost like they just sat around thinking up names for stuff.

We moved ahead but not so far that we couldn't see Clarice and Dad and hear her tell him, "Don't."

They had a back and forth we couldn't quite make out. We'd all been schooled in the blunt necessity of leaving no alabastards behind you. The last thing we could afford was to have them fold in on us from the rear. Even the ancients, the frail ones, still had claws and guile.

But whatever Clarice said to Dad, he found it persuasive. Dad left that wheezing alabastard cowering in his crevice, and we pressed on with him behind us. Me and Beauty took the rear. I half expected a force to come sweeping in. Beauty must have too. She'd growl and yip, even though there was no trace of anything back there.

Since I was turned around mostly, I saw Cracker Daddy last. Dad grabbed me to get my attention. I took ahold of Beauty's collar in turn. From across a chamber the size of a high-school gym, he stood and watched us back.

He wasn't bent or crouched, didn't give the appearance of a creature acquainted with scrabbling. He was ghostly white, sculpted. He sniffed the air, so I did too. I only got guano and mineral tang. He got us. He showed his teeth. He made a racket in his neck.

"What did he say?" Clarice asked Dad. She was that far along already. She didn't think the echo had fooled her. She was prepared to believe he'd talked.

"Didn't catch it," Dad said.

Beauty hadn't even growled much. Her fur was down. When I turned her loose, she sat.

"Stay here," Clarice said to us. Then she was on her way across the chamber before anybody could do a thing.

"Don't." That was the best Dad could manage. He followed her but never tried to catch up, trailed a good ten paces back.

Mostly we all just trained our lights upon her. If she talked to Cracker Daddy, we didn't hear her do it. To us, it appeared she was easing in silence over to where he stood.

We'd all been next to alabastards. A groper didn't allow for much distance, and cave quarters were usually a lot more cramped than the chamber we were in. We'd had their white clammy flesh hard upon us. Their foul breath in our faces. We'd known the scrape and prick of their talons. We'd seen up close those black eyes of theirs, like marbles dipped in tar.

Cracker Daddy waited for her. He hardly looked coiled and primed and anxious. He just stood there in repose, a rare thing for an alabastard. They stayed cocked and twitchy ordinarily like jungle cats. They had two settings — pounce now or later — so repose didn't enter in.

Clarice ventured close enough to Cracker Daddy to cause me to clinch all over. I caught myself wondering how we might go on if he just flicked a talon across her throat. We'd die in that cavern, maybe end up at length on display in a glass box at Carlsbad. They weren't showing off any mummified kids as best I knew, and they certainly didn't have a cave dog. So that was something. Immortality at the one place I didn't want it.

Cracker Daddy didn't move. He let Clarice get close. He made a noise. We caught the rumble from it. Then Clarice did a thing I'd not expected. She shifted her collar aside and showed Cracker Daddy her scar.

That earned her more racket, and then that beast raised a massive white hand with one pale finger lifted. The pose was something like Jesus frequently struck in our family Bible where there were colored drawings of Jerusalem, Galilee, the Apostles, and our Lord. Our Bible Christ was almost always pointing at heaven while he talked.

Beauty tilted her head. She was hearing something. I was getting a low murmur at most. Then Cracker Daddy reached out and relieved Clarice of her ripper and her arrows. Dad raised his groper. I thumbed my safety.

I heard Leigh Ann whisper, "Mack."

He broke Clarice's arrows. He crushed her ripper. It would have seemed like a provocative act if it had taken much effort at all. He might as well have been cracking peanuts. The beast turned Clarice's arms to so much litter and dropped the pieces on the cave floor. Then he drifted into the dark.

Clarice picked up her busted armaments. Dad ventured over to help her and then they came walking back.

"He talked?" I asked.

She nodded.

I pictured the guys in the wigs with the bronze bowl dismissing the news out of hand.

"What did he say?"

"Sounded like," Clarice told me, "war."

We were closing on the squeeze by the time Clarice was ready to speak again. We were in the pipe just short of the chamber where the cavern opened below our gate. We were clattering and crawling the way you had to when Clarice — who was in between me and Dad — stopped and rolled onto her side.

"They're gathering," Clarice said. "Like tribes, you know?"

"Where?" Dad asked her.

"We'll hear soon enough."

Clarice was right. We did.

JOURNEY PROUD

1

They were patient and cagey, far more of each than our sort had been trained to expect, which left us slow to come around to good sense and right thinking. We probably would have been better off knowing nothing at all. Faith can be hard to shake and undo, especially faith misplaced and in error. There was a fundamentalist strain that seemed to prevail in the Legion. Grady's ilk would always take The Great Book over their lying eyes.

Looking back, we were lucky a civilian came across them. He knew he'd never seen their sort before and that they didn't belong where they were. His name was Carlos, and he worked on residential boilers, drove a nasty panel truck with a cargo of tools and fittings, grease and boiler soot. Carlos lived in Jersey City and was working a job in Soho, was taking an old unit to pieces so he could put a new one in.

He was passing through the Holland Tunnel at half past five in the morning when he spied four CFs clinging to the tiles overhead. They so captured his attention that he didn't see the one on the roadway, a juvenile he clipped with the bumper of his truck. Carlos elected not to stop. He had his reasons. The creature he hit didn't die. It had claws and teeth and chased him towards Manhattan.

Carlos called the whole thing in to New York One.

The story flashed through the Legion network. None of us doubted they were alabastards, but Carlsbad laid the showing off to an “inadvertent incursion”. The Council directed the New York clan to investigate the matter as best they could. The Legion has long owned property in the industrial waste of the Brooklyn waterfront, in a slot between the bridges where the roads are still cobbled.

The Brooklyn clan has never been known for its rigor. Their sort has long subscribed to the notion that regular New Yorkers could cope with alabastards well enough on their own.

There’d just never been much of an alabastard presence in New York City. The CFs seemed to prefer the Hudson Valley, so the Brooklyn clan patrolled only as a hobby. They made smart money from gray market electronics sold out of a storefront in Chinatown. When the council tasked them about the ‘incursion’, the clan leader promised to have look. In a week or so he came back with some version of “Fuggitaboutit.”

The incident rated only a paragraph in the Legion’s quarterly. It had been decided the Holland Tunnel CFs had fallen out of a crease, the way you might pitch out of your car if your door swung open in a turn.

Clarice snorted when she read the explanation. “You know what I’d do?” she asked us all. We didn’t. She said, “Pack.”

Grady was off in Carlsbad by then. He’d gotten on as the associate curator of the Holdings, Ancient and Storied (they called them). He was sharing a cottage on the compound with Jo Jo and was content at last to be working among wall-to-wall like-minded people. The letters he wrote were larded with Legion jargon. Uncle Grady sounded at peace.

I think we were crowding happy as well. Dad and Clarice had found each other. They'd circled for a while and made mistimed forays. He'd close on her, and she'd back away. She'd close on him, and he'd shy. Clarice had a bad romantic history, and Dad had heartache as well, but after a few near misses they agreed to be wounded together as best they could. They couldn't be bothered with an announcement. We weren't given to family meetings. They left us to watch how they carried on and decide what was what for ourselves.

Clarice kept her bedroom, but some nights we'd hear her slipping into Dad's. They still carped and chafed like grownups will, but they never held onto to it for long. Sometimes when me and Leigh Ann had dish duty, Clarice and Dad would dance on the porch. They called it dancing anyway. They'd stand there wrapped up together and sway.

We observed regular duty and went on our tours like always, but after a while no matter how deep we probed, we never saw a CF. Not even a failing geezoid shoved back in a crevice. Beauty rarely snarled. Our sheep herd thrived. Clarice made herself a fine new ripper but only fired it topside. We'd sit in the deep dark with our lamps off for sometimes a quarter hour and then switch them on hoping a swarm had collected, but it was always only us.

Grady would check in every couple of weeks, and we got the sense from him that Carlsbad had chosen to be triumphant. Alabastards seemed to be scarce and in retreat all over the place. Uncle Grady would quote The Great Book on the rewards of vigilance and name check all the Council members who were convinced the beasts were throttled.

Clarice held a decidedly different view. The rest of us fell in with her. We'd been around her enough by then to know she wasn't wrong about much.

Clarice had a solid sense of the world, both topside and below, and an instinct that she relied upon that rarely seemed to fail her. She was unerring about people and sheep and chickens, so why not alabastards? She could even figure out why Brody was wailing before he seemed to know.

She was the one who finally called us off of duty in our Virginia cave. Clarice had us stay topside and build our arsenal instead. We made backup rippers, a blue million bolts, and hardened gropers with shafts that wouldn't break.

"What are we getting ready for?" was the question we kept putting to Clarice.

"You'll see," was all she ever really told us.

Then finally a story showed up that snared Clarice's attention. A cellar in Bloomingdales, underneath the store on Lexington Avenue, was broken into and plundered from underneath. It had been full of clothes, still wrapped and cartoned. Some intrepid gang had tunneled up and made off with everything.

Then a child got hit and killed by a gypsy cab near the Brooklyn Navy Yard. That "child" proved to be some freak albino thing. It had curious glands and retractable claws and a gizzard attached to its liver. Proper New York doctors couldn't seem to decide on even the creature's sex. The thing had been wearing its new Oshkosh overalls inside out. That was quite enough for Clarice.

"Call your brother. Tell him we want to get rotated and only greater New York will do."

"That'd be Brooklyn," Dad said.

Clarice nodded.

"They're dug in."

That was a truth of the Legion. We all rotated but for that Brooklyn crew. They had interests to consider and business investments to weigh, and it wasn't like they had much use for what Carlsbad had to tell them. That clan had been left alone for decades. They'd as soon go to hell as Cumberland or even historic Virginia where pallets of TVs never fell off trucks.

"They can stay," Clarice said, "but they're going to need some help. It doesn't matter if they don't want it."

Clarice hauled out our massive world atlas and opened it to Manhattan and the boroughs. We all gathered to look at the double spread with her. Even Beauty wandered over from the hearth.

"Tell Carlsbad whatever you have to." She pointed to a spot on the map just west of the Navy Yard basin and smack between the East River and the Brooklyn-Queens Expressway. Vinegar Hill, it said on the map. "They'll be coming out around here."

Grady resisted. It was his native response to everything. So Dad went around him to Jo Jo, and Jo Jo put the paper through. Gotham had long loomed large in Jo Jo's imagination. If he were going to fight robots (or alabastards) and ogle a little cleavage, greater New York was exactly where he'd do it.

Unlike his Daddy, Jo Jo had grace enough about him to wish us well. He commandeered a Legion apartment for us over a restaurant by the harbor, a place down near the old Brooklyn ferry dock that had long since been turned into a park.

Our only official instructions were to check in with Sal. He was head of the Brooklyn clan. We were to do what he decided needed doing.

"We'll see about that," was Clarice's response.

Clarice had a bit more Grady in her than I would have dared mention. Like him, her personal default setting was "No".

The Council didn't trouble itself to replace us in Virginia. Usually, some functionary nominated a clan — one being punished or rewarded depending on where the assignment was — and the Elders signed off on orders and issued a decree. None of that happened this time. We got instructed to weld our cave gate shut, sell our chickens and livestock at the market, get our power shut off and close up the house. Leave the furnishings where they were.

So we just had clothes to carry mostly, our weapons and some kitchen stuff. All that along with the six of us weren't about to fit in our truck, so Dad went and bargained at a car lot out in the valley and came home with a 1989 Ford Country Squire station wagon.

"Smells like Grandpa," Leigh Ann informed us all.

"You barely even knew him."

"Knew him enough to smell him," she told me.

I took a whiff of our Ford. Sweat and tobacco with a hint of Lava hand soap. That was Granddaddy Hoyt all right. I took it as a sign and signal that he was with us somehow.

We spent a day packing the car, or rather we shoved all our stuff into that wagon. We wrapped our weapons in bed sheets to guard against nosy state troopers, and as her last official act in our Virginia home place, Leigh Ann made cookies for us to eat along way. Brody, for his part, sat on the hard pan in the side yard and cried.

I felt a bit like Brody myself. I think we all did at least a little. Part of it was sadness that comes with leaving a spot you've been awhile. But part of it as well was raw excitement and trepidation. We were heading to the grandest of cities and, if Clarice was correct, migrating as well to a monumental fight.

Dad drove the first leg, headed west for the interstate that bisects the Shenandoah Valley. We crossed slivers of West Virginia and Maryland and were in Pennsylvania for what seemed like a week. No place nice, just the outskirts of everywhere with a highway's view of the backs of houses, run down gas stations and family restaurants, more pot holes than a Californian would see in a natural lifetime.

We stopped at a Dutch butcher shop an hour and a half from New York and maybe thirty miles shy of the New Jersey line. A Mennonite lady with some tonnage to her made us sandwiches on soft white bread with pickles, yellow mustard, and Lebanon bologna that gave us all breath I wouldn't wish on a goat.

Dad kept checking his watch and making calculations. He'd decided when we ought to arrive in Brooklyn and was stalling until the time was right for us to roll out again.

He wouldn't tell us when we were certain to leave. He just kept saying, "Not yet."

That was just about when Clarice decided it was her turn to drive the wagon. Dad had left the keys in it, so all she had to do was slip under the wheel.

"Come on!" she shouted.

We all did but Dad. He only joined us once Clarice had blown the horn a half dozen times.

"We're going to hit traffic," he informed Clarice.

"It's New Damn York," she told him. "We're going to hit traffic whenever."

I know now she was right. Gotham is a tangled mess of a place, and even though we didn't arrive in the city until just past 7:30, for all the clotted roadways you'd have thought it was 5:00 p.m. on Christmas Eve.

We would have gotten there a little earlier, but Clarice got pulled for speeding. A New Jersey trooper with an undersized campaign hat and an oversized gut.

He wondered if Clarice was aware that she was going eighty, which gave her the chance to tell him our speedometer was broken. That, in fact, the whole dashboard array was out.

"Probably a fuse or something," she said.

Our tires were in lousy shape as well, and we were driving on 30-day tags. Our tailpipe was making the sort of clatter to that seemed to suggest it was disconnected. We didn't need a law enforcement official looking at us hard. Clarice was making everything worse. I feared she'd reach for her ripper, and Dad was going with, "Now, honey," which was making her iller still.

I had the feeling we were about to get arrested and towed when Leigh Ann chimed in and saved us. She'd never done girlish back in Virginia, but she uncorked a dose of it hard by

Bedminster, New Jersey. She gave us a granny in intensive care somewhere in deepest Queens.

Through her tears, Leigh Ann informed our trooper, "We've got to get there, mister. She's fading."

Once he'd said, "Well," and handed Clarice's license back, I think we all knew we'd be grappling with a different Leigh Ann from there on out.

He slapped the roof of our wagon. "Dial it back a little," he said.

Maybe Clarice did. We couldn't really know since our speedometer didn't work. A fuse or something.

We could have gone through Staten Island and reached Brooklyn from the south. That was the route Dad preferred, and he kept saying how he preferred it until we'd passed the exit near Newark and got in with tunnel traffic.

"Don't you want to see that crease they fell out of?" Clarice asked us all.

Brody did especially and hooted out about it, but it turned out that before any tunnel creases, he desperately needed to pee. It was like that up around the city. We got stuck in traffic. We made pit stops. We got stuck in traffic some more.

"Ought not to drive with your bladder around here." That was the lesson Dad drew.

There wasn't a crease in the Holland Tunnel. There were a couple of access doors and a kind of monorail that ran along the north wall with a cart big enough for one person.

"Nothing spilled out of anywhere," Clarice told us all.

We figured they'd passed through the access door, probably intending to come out somewhere else.

We got to Brooklyn after quite a lot of creeping along Canal Street. We rattled across the Manhattan Bridge and found our way down to the water. There weren't enough street signs standing for us to navigate on the fly. We kept having to stop and reconnoiter. We asked directions a couple of times but from a guy who spoke only Cantonese and a woman who spoke only Spanish.

We found the ferry landing park before anything else, and me and Leigh Ann and Brody took Beauty for a walk. We hooked a leash onto her collar and then allowed her to drag it behind her. She sniffed the ratty grass, the sidewalks, the lamp post footings with a distinct doggy disdain.

Over by the water against the railing, Beauty looked at us as if to say, "You want me to poop in this place?"

Our apartment was over a place called Murry's, a restaurant that advertised itself as "Kosher Italian and Swell!. We were on a side street a half a block from the water. We couldn't know, given that it was dark already, how gloomy and sunless the place would be. We all stood in what would pass for our parlor and listened to pots clanging and kitchen help arguing downstairs. We'd only brought our weapons in and dropped them on the floor.

Dad was the one who finally said, "Well." Somebody was going to have to.

There was enough furniture to make do. We found a broom behind a bathroom door and some rags and cleansers in the kitchen. The general plan was to scour the place before we hauled any of our stuff upstairs.

Clarice kept an occasional eye on our wagon, parked a little ways down the block. When what struck her as disreputable youth lingered to peer in through the tailgate window, Clarice shouted to get their attention and then fired a bolt just over their heads.

Our apartment was sprawling and oddly laid out. A few oversized rooms. A few undersized rooms. Two bathrooms with doors that hit the toilets. A kitchen a trawler might have. The back windows all looked out on a wall that was maybe four feet across an air shaft. Through a window in the front I could see the top of one of the Gothic towers of the Brooklyn Bridge.

Down in the bottom of a built-in cabinet in the parlor, Leigh Ann found a moldy copy of The Great Book. The front cover was off and somebody had written phone numbers on the blank facing page. One for Gil. One for Maggie. One for Fung Chow's with an elaboration —"Ma Yi Shang Shur=Ants climbing trees".

Me and Dad and Clarice and Leigh Ann made trips to the Country Squire and back. That car held about as much as a step van, and we'd loaded it like the gypsies we were. It took so long that Brody went to sleep wrapped up in one of Dad's jackets on the floor.

There near the end, when we were down to shoes that had been pitched in and stuff that had fallen out of boxes, I caught Clarice alone and asked her the thing that had been nagging me all along.

"So what if they come out now? They'll swarm us good. We're nowhere near ready. Might never be."

We were standing at the tailgate of the Country Squire from where we had a view of the front of Murry's Kosher Italian. It was a place with airs. A guy in a jacket with epaulets was standing by a hydrant on his cigarette break.

"We'd be in trouble," Clarice told me, "No sheep up here to give them. They'd probably take a maitre d."

I watched the guy sigh and flick his butt.

We left the keys and title on the front seat of the wagon. By the time the sun came up, the car was gone.

2

The only Legion orders we had were to check in with the Brooklyn clan, but they were so scattered and entrepreneurial as to flummox us at first. We went to where they were supposed to be living, but they'd subdivided and sublet. There were immigrants mostly in pieces of rooms and occupying bits of hallways. That Brooklyn crew had taken a Legion tenement and turned it into a profit center.

Dad went through the place saying, "Sal?" He got everything but English back.

It turned out Clarice spoke a smattering Tagalog or something, enough to find out from a tiny brown lady with pencil through her bun who exactly she paid rent to and how exactly she paid it. She even walked us to the bodega where she carried her cash twice a month.

The guy behind the counter wasn't technically Legion-affiliated, but Sal's clan had been loose enough with talk about their duties and longstanding obligations that the guy just needed one good look at us to know to ask, "You tunnel rats too?"

The bodega guy directed us to the walkway on the Manhattan Bridge and told us how to find Sal's storefront in Chinatown once we'd spilled out on the east end of Canal. The pedestrian walk is attached to the bridge on the south side towards the harbor, so we had a view of the Brooklyn Bridge, Governors Island, and the Statue of Liberty. School bus yellow ferries and the odd freighter on the water. The shipping cranes of Bayonne against the horizon across the way.

Dad had our only phone and handed it around so we could all take pictures. Then Brody got a turn and managed to drop the thing over the rail.

Chinatown proved more than a little disorienting for us. None of the roads ran straight, and the sidewalks were crowded and cluttered. The merchandise from the stores spilled well out into the open air. Most of the locals weren't content to just talk. They far preferred to scream.

Leigh Ann spied the storefront we were after. The sign above the windows was in Chinese and broken English. TV — Steryo —Kitchen.

We all went in. Even Beauty. More screaming. Me and Beauty came back out.

I could see them through the window. Dad and Clarice were talking to the Asian counter girl. She turned out to be Korean and was kind of in on Legion business too. Her name was Eun

Mi, but they all called her Toppy. As she heard Dad and Clarice out, I watched her. Beautiful, delicate features. Shiny black hair. A fierce look in her eyes. I was so little accustomed to being smitten, I had no idea what I was feeling.

A steel door in the sidewalk groaned open alongside where me and Beauty were standing. A loop of steel pushed the plates apart as a freight platform rose and creaked. There were boxes of car radios on it, Bluetooth speakers, a few rice cookers, and guy in a Juventus sweatshirt with sunglasses on his head.

He looked to be about my age but at least a decade more savvy. He gave me and Beauty the hard once over and then said, "Lamphead, right?"

You didn't call Low Lord's lampheads to their faces unless you were a one yourself.

I nodded.

"You on vacation or what?"

"Or what," I told him. "We're looking for Sal."

"Why?"

I knocked on the front store window. Dad and Clarice were still talking to Toppy. Leigh Ann and Brody were studying tiny live turtles in a tank. Right as Clarice swung around my way, I saw them on the wall. They'd mounted their gropers the way you'd show off your collection of ninja swords.

"When did you guys last see an alabastard?"

The guy on the lift said, "A what?"

It turned out his name was Aldo, and he'd never spied a creeper. That's all he'd ever heard them called. He thought his dad had seen one once.

"Back in the day," Aldo told me.

"And that bunch in the tunnel the other week?"

"What bunch?"

Clarice and Dad came out once they'd bought Leigh Ann and Brody a sack of crackers. They were shiny on the outside and lacquered with something that made them taste like crab. Brody shoved three in his mouth and then spat them in the gutter. Since Leigh Ann was a young lady of sixteen, she spat hers in her hand.

At first, Aldo couldn't tell Clarice and Dad anything at all because he was too busy giving Leigh Ann a comprehensive once-over. He looked to me a little too much like he was pawing her with his eyes.

"Hey!" I said.

"Are you Sal's son?" Dad asked.

"One of them."

"Is he around?"

"Who wants to know?"

That proved quite enough for Clarice. She had precious little use for banter. She grabbed Aldo by his sweatshirt and jerked him onto the sidewalk. Clarice might not have had much heft to her, but she was alarmingly strong. Like usual, she'd brought along a bit of gear in her satchel. She snatched out her spike — eight inches of honed steel — and pressed the tip to Aldo's throat.

"Come on, lady. Easy. Dad's at the warehouse."

"Where's that?" Clarice asked him.

He told her, "Secaucus," like that was the only place on earth warehouses were.

"When's he coming back?"

"Hard to say with traffic."

Clarice shot Dad a consulting glance.

Aldo said of the spike, "You want to put that somewhere else?"

"Here's good." Clarice pressed even harder.

"I could call him," Aldo told her.

It was Leigh Ann who suggested in a soft, breathy voice I'd never heard from her before, "Let's do that."

Aldo nodded as much as he could without laying an artery open. He tapped his chest on the crown of the Juventus logo. "Aldo," he said. It wasn't for us. It was all for Leigh Ann.

She told him her name back. Dad looked stricken. Brody blubbered a bit over his poor choice of cracker. Clarice and I glanced at each other.

I told Aldo, in the way of big brothers the world around, "I'll kill you."

Leigh Ann giggled and grabbed my arm the way she never did. "He won't," she said to Aldo. Then she actually giggled again.

"Sal?" Clarice said.

Aldo nodded. "Got to use the land line."

This time even Beauty went in. We all passed through the store. Eun Mi yelled, "No dog!"

She even looked better inside and up close. It was all I could do to keep from giggling.

"Take a picture, Jethro," Toppy told me.

All of my blood went to my cowlick.

The office in the back was a nest of paperwork and stacked boxes with a man-sized hole in it. A bit of cleared desk. A lamp. A chair. A phone as well, but Aldo had to excavate to find it. He speed dialed his dad who sounded to us like a wasp in a bag.

Sal opened with quite a lot instead of hello. He carried on like a guy who didn't welcome phone calls from his son and was under the impression he'd made himself clear about that.

"Got some lampheads here," Aldo explained.

A low restrained hum from Sal.

"Where from?" Aldo asked.

"Virginia," Dad said. "The Council sent us." That was a bit of stretch. Some council functionary – probably Jo Jo himself – had sifted through and stamped our paperwork.

Aldo passed the information along. A brief buzz from Sal.

"Sent you why?"

Clarice told Aldo. "Trouble brewing."

"I think it's creepers or something," Aldo said to his Dad in a way that made it sound preposterous and amusing.

That raised a racket suspiciously like laughter from Secaucus. Clarice then did what we'd known she'd do all along. She took the phone from Aldo and told Sal, "Get back here now."

Sal buzzed a little.

"Now! Or Carlsbad hears you're a slumlord, and all that income goes away."

We all waited for Sal in a park behind the federal courthouse on the southern edge of Chinatown. On his father's instructions, Aldo bought us all Thai takeout from a place nearby. It was fine spring day, so the park was busy with lawyers and Chinese retirees. Grandmothers mostly with toddlers to tend and the odd, slender leathery Asian man reading a Cantonese paper and smoking acrid Chinese cigarettes.

Leigh Ann sat on the bench beside Aldo, but Dad wedged himself between them. He pumped Aldo for his personal history and his knowledge of the duties of the clan.

Aldo had only started life in the Legion's Brooklyn tenement. "We moved to Riverdale when I was eight."

Riverdale turned out to be a tony, suburban part of the northern Bronx where Aldo's mom and dad had bought a house on a leafy quarter acre.

"Mom died when I was twelve. Cancer."

"Ever seen a CF?" Clarice asked him.

"Is that a creeper?"

"I guess."

"Just the one," he told us. "Dad's got it in a jar." With his hands, he described the size of container you'd buy pickles in.

"You guys ever read the quarterly?" Clarice asked.

Aldo squinted. He shook his head.

"Have you got gear?" I asked. "Aside from the stuff that's hanging on the wall?"

"Those blade things?" Aldo asked me back.

This promised to be like raising an army from farmers.

"How many of you are there?" Dad wanted to know.

Aldo wasn't entirely sure. With no need for a clan, the group had sort of scattered and diluted.

"Have you got brothers?" That from Leigh Ann.

"Why?" Aldo said it like he was jealous.

Leigh Ann openly enjoyed the sensation of seeing a boy act the fool over her. "Just wondering."

"Two," Aldo admitted. "Monte's got a couple of kids. Lives in Jersey City. Terry's in school. We're half-brothers. He's eight."

"So your dad remarried?" Clarice asked.

Aldo nodded.

"Legion or no?"

Aldo shrugged. "She's from Long Island. What's all this anyway? Some kind of drill?"

Sal finally showed up in a bit of a snit, one of those "This had better be good, I came all the way from Secaucus" sorts of things. He was fleshy and unkempt, but you could look at him and see that he'd probably been dashing once. Life had just been harder on him than Sal had bargained for, luck far more elusive than he'd ever expected.

To Sal's way of thinking, he and his clan hadn't betrayed the Legion. They'd simply been given so little to do that they'd drifted off over time.

"So?" Sal finally said once the formalities were over.

Dad and Clarice laid out the problem. The 'challenge', Dad liked to call it.

Clarice had little use for that sort of insulating talk. "We get this right," she said, "or we're all screwed."

Aldo and Sal would have probably needed an awful lot of convincing if they'd not neglected their duties and exploited Legion real estate for so long. We had leverage on them with Carlsbad, and if they knew nothing else they knew that.

"When did you last go under?" Dad asked Sal.

"I ride the subway three or four times a week."

"Deep dark." That from Clarice.

"Well, technically . . ." Sal only got that far before Clarice gave him a smack.

Clarice was an effective abbreviator. There are people who try to be economical and incisive, boil everything down to give you just the nugget, but you never know quite what they mean. That was not the case with Clarice. She could say more with her open hand than anybody I'd ever seen.

"It's been a few years," Sal confessed. "Terry got . . . you know . . ." Sal snapped his fingers.

"Baptized?" I said.

He nodded.

"I remember that," Aldo chimed in. "We got pizza after."

Sal nodded again.

"How many years ago?" Dad asked. It was the Grady in him.

"Six?" Sal was cringing already.

"More like seven," Aldo said, past Dad and to Leigh Ann.

"Get your gropers off the wall," Clarice told Sal and Aldo. "Bring all the gear you've got to the store."

Sal told her in a voice that seemed too small and pitiful to come out of a lump of meat like him, "Some of it's in Secaucus."

"Go get it," she told him. "We'll meet tonight."

Sal nodded. He handed over the keys to their panel truck to Aldo who immediately turned towards Leigh Ann and asked her, "Want to come?"

"No," Dad told him. Told her, I guess, too.

Aldo shrugged. Next time. Like Clarice, he was an abbreviator as well.

"Mulberry," Sal told Aldo. "In the alley." He gave his son a twenty. "It's down to a quarter tank."

Aldo loitered like he felt the need to take proper leave of Leigh Ann. The grown-ups all at once and without planning told him, "Go!"

"Time to be what you are," Clarice told Sal. "Like it or not, you're a lamphead too."

3

I argued in favor of Toppy coming in with us. Aldo caught on and argued for Toppy as well.

"She knows everything already," he said.

Clarice gave Toppy a look. "Any skills?"

Toppy picked up one of the gropers that Aldo had moved from the wall to the front store counter. She uncorked a yelp that stirred me, I have to say, and then destroyed three bags of what proved to be Chinese knockoff Cheez Doodles.

"We could use her," I announced.

Clarice got a whiff of something. She swung around my way. "Not you too."

Sal's other sons didn't come that first night. "Terry's got homework," Sal explained. "Let's see what you've got first. Monte has kids and all."

Sal had clearly recovered some pluck since he'd left the park down by the Thai place. Dad and Clarice let him luxuriate in it for about a half hour as they gave him a general update on alabastard evolution and migration. Sal rubbed his eyes. He yawned more than once. Clarice picked up the jarred specimen Aldo had brought in with the gear.

"Where'd you get this?" she asked Sal.

"Old subway tunnel. Under Atlantic Avenue. You climb down through a manhole to get there."

"How long ago?"

“Twenty years maybe.”

“What’s a pig doing in the subway?” Toppy wanted to know.

“It’s not a pig,” I told her. I showed her the earholes. The incisors. “Cavus Ferinus. They live down there.”

“Sal?” she said.

“He’s right. It’s not a pig.”

“Who are you?” she asked me mostly. I felt dangerous, and I liked it.

“Low Lords,” I told her. I’d never been so proud to be a lamphead. “Them too,” I said of Sal and Aldo. “We keep them,” I pointed at Sal’s jar, “from getting out. They’re bigger than that now.”

Toppy didn’t like the turn her world was taking. She far preferred pork to CFs, but she adjusted. She was game. I think that’s what immigrants do. They get to some place. It’s not what they banked on. They tell themselves, “All right then,” and adapt.

Sal’s gear was in deplorable shape. All the coveralls were rotted. The lamp batteries were leaking. The hotbox was of a design I’d never even seen before. It was made out of what turned out to be church pew wrapped in aluminum foil. Big pieces of oak knocked together in the shape of a pagoda with a rotted length of leather for a strap. It probably weighed thirty pounds.

“I don’t even know what that is,” Sal confessed. “My granddad gave it to my dad.”

Clarice wouldn't touch any of Sal's stuff except with the toe of her boot. "We're going shopping," she informed Sal. "Get some coin together."

Sal choked down his objections.

"Got a surplus store around here?" Dad asked.

We all walked over. The place was on lower Broadway. It was half full of recycled junk, but there was old campaign gear as well. Clarice and Dad did all the sifting and sorting.

They'd hand merchandise to Sal and just say, "Here."

Coveralls. Helmets. Lanterns and boxlights. Oil and a wet stone for the gropers. A couple of evil looking tactical knives. I had to wonder if Sal and Aldo were up to fighting alabastards, would have the nerve to lay one open before the talons reached their throats. Next to a sheath knife, a groper is semi-impersonal. A ripper is one step back from that, but I wasn't even sure that Aldo and Sal could kill with a sniper rifle. Once you've spent a life living and letting live, combat can prove a little tough. Even where it comes to alabastards with their claws and their stink and their teeth.

By the time we left Aldo and Sal and Toppy sharpening groper blades at their store, it was half past ten. Instead of walking, we took the subway, went into it on Canal Street. We'd bought a vest for Beauty at the surplus store. She was now our service dog, which gave her access all over.

So we all rode the subway from Manhattan into Brooklyn. We got on the wrong train, of course, like tourists would. The R instead of the N, so we went south to Whitehall and under the harbor to Brooklyn. Though it was a longer trip, it was all underground — the N goes over the Manhattan Bridge — so we had twenty minutes of stations and tunnels to help give us some perspective on how very much territory alabastards had to roam.

By the time we came up the stairs at Borough Hall and got directions to the waterfront, we were all a little stunned at the magnitude of the job we had before us. Except for Brody who was hungry and Leigh Ann who was deeply smitten. They were less focused on our strategic problems than me and Clarice and Dad. I had Toppy to think of, naturally, but I needed to be a warrior first.

"How are we going find them?" I asked Dad and Clarice. "They could be anywhere under here."

"Don't know yet," Clarice said. "Let's think on it while we eat."

There was a small Chinese place up ahead with lacquered ducks hanging in the window and steam beading up the glass. Dad sent me and Leigh Ann in with some cash. We pointed to stuff on the menu, and the woman at the counter screamed out our order to the wok guy in Chinese.

"What do you think of Aldo?" Leigh Ann asked me while we were waiting for the food.

I knew shrugging wouldn't do and hedging wouldn't be tolerated, so I told Leigh Ann the only thing a decent brother would tell his sister when she asked him to size up the first boy she'd had romantic feelings about.

"Seems gay," I said.

Leigh Ann hit me with a napkin dispenser.

We slept that night. At least I slept, and Brody slept through too. We were sharing a room — me and Brody and Beauty — and already it was smelling like a stockyard. Socks and vapors and dog breath along with Moo Shoo Brody had taken to bed on his shirt. Add to that Brooklyn soot and diesel and the general garbage reek from the street, and you had a bouquet that felt about half wilds of Virginia and half urban squalor. The biggest change for me was I couldn't just open the door and let Beauty out.

So it was me and her in the park between the bridges just past first light. For company, we had a guy in his housecoat walking what looked like a sofa bolster with legs and a woman wearing two sweatshirts who had one of those collapsible carts that city people use for shopping. Hers was packed full of treasures (I guess), though most of it looked like spangly refuse to me.

The guy in the bathrobe couldn't even be bothered to say, "Good Morning," to me back, but the homeless-looking woman proved capable of worthwhile conversation. She might have appeared nutty, but she turned out to be in there, just waiting for a kind word to draw her out.

I must have supplied it when I told her, "Hi," instead of just passing by and looking away.

There was the usual trifling stuff at first. The weather mostly. She was tuned into that, living rough like she did. Then she showed me a clutch purse she'd found in the street. It had a pencil, a hair clip, and a pair of surgical gloves inside it. That might have been cause for an APB and a roadblock back in Cumberland, but in Brooklyn it was just something else for that woman to toss into her cart.

Her name was Sally, and she was from Kansas, though not recently or in any chauvinistic sort of way. Kansas was a place she vaguely recalled from a very long time ago.

"Virginia," I told her and tapped my chest.

"Him too?" She pointed at Beauty.

"Her." I nodded.

Beauty finished her business. I picked it up in a shopping bag and tossed it in trash barrel.

"You're a good boy," Sally told me. "You can sit."

It was a nice enough offer. I had no Brooklyn friends. Sally looked interesting to me, so I sat.

Sally once had a shepherd in Kansas. She held out her fingers and got a lick from Beauty. Her hand was chafed, and she was weather worn, but Sally didn't look particularly dirty. She fished in her cart and came out with a hard rubber dog toy shaped like a bee hive. Sally let Beauty sniff it and then tossed it across the lawn. Beauty usually wasn't much of a fetcher, but once I'd unclipped her leash, she took off and brought that chunk of rubber back.

The guy in the house coat with the sofa bolster told us generally, "Hey!" Among the assorted things he wouldn't stand for was a dog loose in his park.

I was going to apologize and hook Beauty back up, but Sally trained a stream of invective on the guy in a voice that sounded demonic. He shouted back, but she was more resourceful and far more energetic and finally succeeded in driving him out of sight. I would learn that's what people in Brooklyn did sometimes instead of coming to blows.

"Don't like that one," Sally said. "Let that dog of his get fat."

He had. I nodded.

"Don't you," she said by way of threat and instruction.

"No, ma'am. I won't."

Sally smiled. "Ma'am," she said it like she was turning it over in her mouth.

I then took a harder look at Sally's stuff in her cart than Sally could stand for politely.

"Naw," she said and put herself in between me and her cart.

But I'd caught sight of something by then that I wanted a better look at, so I smiled at Sally, said, "Yes, ma'am." She settled back on the bench and turned it over in her mouth again.

It was deep in her cart, down by the near wheel and poking through the lattice. It looked a little tortoise shell the way they do – not black, not brown, but both. It was curved and maybe four inches long, a bit stouter than a sailmaker's needle. I felt certain it was a clapperclaw. I'd seen enough of them attached.

The talons on an alabastard will all gouge you open in a swipe, but the clapperclaw is the longest, the one they dig and probe with. They lose them sometimes like cats do, and another grows in its place.

"Want to make a swap?" I asked Sally.

She looked where I was looking. "Depends."

"That thing right there, down by the wheel." I pointed, and Sally came away with a leather bootlace at first. "Next to it," I said.

"Big claw," she told me as she reached down and drew it out.

"Did you see what it came off of?"

She nodded.

"Where were you?"

"Place I sleep sometimes. Used to anyway." She held up the claw and shook her head. "Don't go down there now."

"Big white thing?"

Sally studied me hard. "Maybe."

"Will you show me where you saw it?"

"What are we swapping?"

I didn't have much. "I'll give you my belt. It's leather. The buckle's brass."

She deliberated.

"For the claw and you show us the spot."

"Us who?"

"My dad. My sister. Like that."

"Plus breakfast. Real breakfast. Not that McBiscuit mess."

I nodded. "Done."

I stripped off my belt. Sally inspected it close before she decided to hand over the clapperclaw.

"I'll go get them."

"Naw," she told me. "I'm coming too."

Sally stood from the bench with a groan and a grunt and left the park with me and Beauty, dragging her squeaky cart.

We ended up at a buffet joint just off Cadman Plaza. It anchored a Soviet style apartment complex built out of poured cement. The hostess — a woman with violet eye shadow and a pile of three-toned hair — had qualms about letting Sally in, especially pulling her cart behind her. We arranged to park it in a corner where Sally could see it from our table and persuaded Sally to strip off her outer sweatshirt. The one underneath was hardly stained.

There was eating to be done before any interview could happen. Sally proved partial to bacon and scrambled eggs in between slabs of jellied toast. She drank about a quart of orange juice and an equal amount of thin urn coffee. My little brother — almost as good a judge of character as Beauty — insisted on sitting next to Sally and holding her sweatshirt hem while she ate.

"Who you?" she finally asked him.

With most people he would have sniveled. With Sally he barked out his name.

"Thought so," was all she said.

So we had to wait until the eating was done and wait as well while Sally decided if she was actually finished with breakfast or just taking a buffet break. They kept bringing out steaming pans from the kitchen, and Sally would go to investigate. She sampled the oatmeal. Had a sausage link. Even tried a bit of lox. But it was the bacon and eggs and and jelly and toast that truly satisfied her, and after four of five platefuls, she finally told us all, "I'm good."

Dad held up the clapperclaw. "How long ago did you find this?" he asked her.

"A year maybe. Hadn't been down there since."

"And you saw what it came off of?" That from Clarice.

Sally looked around the place and leaned in before she spoke. "Like he said." She pointed at me. "Big and white. Looked a little like people but not quite finished."

"How big? Like her?" Clarice pointed at Leigh Ann.

Sally made a noise in her neck as she shook her head. "Eat that pretty girl in two bites. Tall as him." She pointed at me. I was crowding six feet by then. "Teeth," she said and held her thumb and forefinger two inches apart.

"Did it come after you?" Clarice asked.

Sally shook her head. "Just woke up, and there it was."

"How did you get the claw?" I asked her.

"Got stuck in the wall or something."

"You'll show us, right?" Dad smiled and nodded.

"I guess," she said. "Going to be a while in the ladies."

She wasn't kidding. Sally lingered so long in the restroom that we sent Leigh Ann in three times just to make sure she was all right.

At one point in the wait, Leigh Ann asked me, "What do you think Aldo's doing?"

Sally had to empty her cart once she got it on the sidewalk and take inventory to make sure nobody had boosted any of her stuff. She was clearly having second thoughts about taking us where we wanted to go and started making noise like she couldn't quite remember how to get down to the spot where she'd seen that alabastard.

"What'll take?" Dad finally asked her outright.

Sally gave the matter some thought before asking him back, "You got a belt too?"

He did.

4

Since we couldn't wander around in daytime Brooklyn with our gropers in hand, we stopped by our place and picked up our spikes and rippers and all our lights and lamps, anything that looked half useful and would fit in a satchel or pack. Then Sally led us up a road between the bridges and down an alley, straight to a boarded-up building that appeared to be a neglected carriage house.

There was plywood over the big front doorway with a semi-circle of shattered glass at the top. The sheets had just been tacked up. Clarice grabbed one at the edge and pulled, which proved enough to get us in. It looked like an army of hoarders had been there before us. There was junk piled everywhere, the sort of stuff in that vague territory between "I can mend this" and rubbish.

Sally was delighted and made no secret of it. I guess the place had been a lot emptier the last time she'd gone in. Brody, for his part, pointed at a furry creature against the far wall.

"Groundhog," he told us.

"Nope," Dad said and scooped up Brody as a precautionary measure.

Clarice nocked an arrow. She hit that rat square in the midsection. It didn't even have a chance to squeak. Sally hadn't known much use for Clarice until then, had exhibited little interest in her.

“What’s that?” she asked of the ripper. She followed it up with, “Who you?”

Sally showed us the hatch. It was standing open – an industrial gauge steel plate that was lifted and leaning against a pillar. When shut it closed off a hole in the floor where a rusty welded ladder descended into the deep. The stink that came out of the Brooklyn dark smelled of low tide and vermin. Sally just needed one whiff to remind her why she’d taken to the parks and the subway grates instead. She got as far as the loop of steel that served as the topmost ladder handhold before she told us, “Naw,” and went back to her cart.

We could tell by looking at her there wasn’t any persuading to do. Sally had brought us to the hole, and the smell had revived her to all that was lurking below.

I fitted Beauty with her harness. Dad went down first with a boxlight and a headlamp to make it as bright down under as he could. Clarice followed just behind him with her ripper cocked. Then Leigh Ann and Brody with me and Beauty bringing up the rear. She was decent on a ladder for a dog if you corralled her in and helped her cling. I lowered her the last ten feet by her harness with a rope.

Then we all met with cause to wonder if we should have said to Sally, “Whatever you do, don’t close the hatch.” We were hardly all on the chamber floor when the door overhead clanged shut.

Ordinary people would surely have panicked, but we’d been in enough dark places to know we’d either force that hatch back open or find some other way out.

Only Dad bothered to comment, and all he said was, "I bought her breakfast, and my pants are falling down."

The chamber we were in was manmade. Rock on rock, big square things the size of hay bales. They looked like granite to me. There were piles of cast-iron pipes around like the place had been city waterworks storage once. You could exit one of two ways, in opposite directions. Big arched openings, twenty feet up, with keystones dead overhead. More rats, too many to bother with.

"Which way?" Dad asked.

Clarice checked out each opening in turn. She sniffed like a good hound might, searching for moving air, for prey.

"That way's the harbor." She pointed. "Chillier through here." The remaining passage. "I'd say this goes down."

Boy, did it. Not steeply and dramatically but along a slope that wouldn't quit. It was a kind of tunnel. I wouldn't have been surprised to find old subway tracks on the floor, but there were just rats and nests and the odd abandoned vagrant homestead. Old blankets and coats and nasty keepsakes. Not a one looked like it had seen use lately. You didn't get the feeling this crop of vagrants was coming back.

Beyond rats and mice and one wayward pigeon, we didn't see anything alive for a solid mile or two. After a bit the passage stopped looking drilled and just seemed ancient and natural. It closed down a little. A train wouldn't have passed, but you could have still traveled along it in a Country Squire wagon.

We got occasional vibrations. You'd feel them in your ankles. A subway train somewhere overhead.

Then we stopped seeing much of anything in the way of life and leavings. We were too far down for people, even too far down for rats.

"Feel that?" Clarice asked. She'd stopped to do her hound thing again.

Air was certainly stirring. When we'd taken the R train the night before, I'd felt a blast of air on the platform, a sign for the locals to step back from the edge. The train was coming, pushing a draft before it, like a plunger in a syringe. This was a fraction as strong, but it felt like something was coming our way. Enough something to still be out of sight before us and yet big enough to make a breeze.

Clarice held up a hand. We all stopped and caught our breaths. Even Brody was mindful enough of the tension to keep his complaints under control.

Beauty made that noise she makes. The one that starts on the roof of her mouth as kind of prelude to a growl and a grumble. She'd been walking free, so I leashed her up. She leaned forward against the hardware, opened her jaws to taste the air.

"Lamps?" Dad asked.

Clarice nodded.

"Dark," Dad instructed us as he shut off his.

Then we heard real noise that we didn't make. Quick. Familiar. The sound of claws on rock.

I thumbed the safety off my ripper. I heard Clarice free hers as well. There was no cover to take, nowhere to crouch and hide. We had no choice but to stick where we were and wait for whatever came. A legitimate swarm up was sure to do us in. We'd just be vanished yokels, and there'd be no looking for us. Nobody left to tell Sal or Aldo or my sweet, dainty Toppy anything about us at all.

I'd never wanted to run before, but I had to suppress the urge just then. In the past I would have flashed upon the torment of talons on flesh. I went straight to Eun Mi this time around. I wondered if she'd even notice I was gone. I caught myself hating Aldo a little because he'd be free to have a run at Toppy. It's funny what your head can get up to while you're waiting for monsters in the dark.

Beauty growled. I shushed her. The racket was far closer now. Claws on stone, without a doubt. If they were rats, they were the size of guernseys.

"Set," Dad whispered to us.

We all reached to find our switches. More clatter. Some sinusy murmurs. They were alabastards all right. Beauty got the first real whiff. She stamped her front paws the way she does.

"Now," Dad said, and we lit them up.

They weren't on the rocky walls like I'd expected. There were four of them. Male. Adultish but young. You could always tell by the lobes and the joints. They only crouched when our light beams hit them. They hissed. They do that when you startle them. Their nasty split tongues came out.

They weren't hunting. They sure weren't swarming. They appeared to be just wandering around.

They all snarled and put their teeth on display. One of them barked out what sounded like an order. We were accustomed to them communicating the way schools of fish do. One darts or turns and the others catch on and follow instantaneously, so fast that it looks like kinetic harmony. All instinct, no thought to speak of. This was something else entirely, maybe because they were surprised. They appeared to be deciding what to do.

"What's he got on?" Brody asked us.

The one in charge was wearing a hat. A Mets cap. Blue with an orange logo. The sales tag was still hanging from it. He was wearing it sideways but less like a homeboy and more like an albino subterranean life form who'd never worn a hat before.

They uncorked on us with that awful screeching they can manage. It's the noise a bat might make if it were the size of a horse. It's a weapon, no doubt. A man hearing it for the first time, especially in the confines of a cavern, is sure to focus entirely on curling up and holding his head in his hands.

We weren't hearing it for the first time. We grimaced and contracted but stayed just where we were.

Those four alabastards scampered and darted back the way they'd come but not before me and Clarice could loose a couple of arrows at them. I missed high. I was over excited. Clarice caught one of them in the hand. The hat guy. He did what they do sometimes. He shoved his wrist in his mouth and bit down. The wounded hand dropped onto the tunnel floor. He'd just grow another.

He lost his hat as well. Leigh Ann went and fetched it while Clarice was reclaiming her arrow and wiping CF sludge off of it.

She dropped that alabastard's hand in her satchel and told us, "Show and tell."

Then we had to get out. Even bold Clarice decided we had wandered deep enough. The plan was to go back up to where we'd started and see if a couple of us together could maybe lift the hatch.

Dad climbed the ladder by himself but couldn't budge the thing. I joined him, and we both pushed, but it was wedged or latched.

"Nope," Dad shouted to Clarice, and she stepped to the archway we'd yet to pass through and gave the air a sniff.

"Moving a little. Briny," she said.

We followed her into the passage. The farther we went, the more evidence we saw that people had occupied that channel more recently than the other. There were bedrolls and scattered possessions, an actual D'agostino's grocery cart. We could tell we were leaving the subterranean air behind, swapping it for something estuarial with a hint of sewage. In the dips, there was water standing. It looked oily in our lights.

Brody started fussing. He'd only picked at his buffet breakfast, and he was tired of wandering under Brooklyn in the dark. There was no talking to him when he got that way. No matter what you said, he'd just scream, "No!"

You'd think with all the responsibility our lineage dumped onto us that we'd be sober, upstanding sorts from the booster chair on up. Not the case. Leigh Ann had been like Brody. I'd probably been like him too.

Brody was doing that percolating thing he does – sobbing and sucking air – when a voice reached us from the dark ahead.

"Hush up!"

That did the trick on Brody. On the rest of us as well. We pressed ahead.

"Hello," Dad called. He raised some vulgar muttering.

We finally reached a pile of topcoats and bedspreads along with what looked a painter's tarp. It was all wedge backed in a crease in the rock, black shiny rock beaded with moisture. Clarice poked the pile with the toe of her boot.

"Quit it!"

"We're looking for the way out," she said to the heap.

More swearing.

"Got kids here," Dad said.

The tarp and the bedspreads and the jackets all got flung back. A guy who looked batter-dipped in mulch and smelled like he'd been glazed in urine took us all in and then asked what struck me as a reasonable question. "Sweet Lord, why?"

He was exposed now and available for queries, and Clarice was hardly the sort to squander a chance for fresh intel. She pulled the alabastard hand out of her shoulder satchel.

"Ever seen the things this came from?"

He snorted and hardly seemed surprised. "Why you think I'm way up here?" He took notice of Beauty. "No dogs in the subway," he told us and covered back up as he grunted and groaned.

There was nothing much for us to do but go on like we'd been going. Another fifty yards, and we were seeing what looked like daylight ahead. It turned out to be a culvert. There was another guy in there, but he was too drunk or high or something to have a conversation.

"Why aren't they dead?" Dad asked in a musing sort of way. "If they've seen CFs, you can be sure they got seen back."

"Urinary self-defense," Clarice suggested. "Would you eat one of them for dinner?"

We'd come out at the Navy Yard, just north of the Manhattan Bridge and across the East River from Chinatown.

Leigh Ann pointed and told us in a dreamy way, "Aldo's over there."

5

Sal had reconsidered his options by the time we caught up with him along with his second wife, Marcy, his three sons and Eun Mi. We all met in front of their Chinatown store, but we were too many to fit inside, so we went off to some Italian legion hall Sal knew where we could talk. Toppy's cousin, Joon, got left to run the store. He was skinny kid with a head of complicated hair.

The legion hall wasn't much to look at, just a storefront by a bakery with a weathered, graffitied portrait of the virgin Mary over the door. Inside, four old guys were playing cards. Two more were smoking and drinking short coffees. We all squeezed in at a big round table in a corner by the toilet. Monte, the oldest brother, went off to fetch a plate of stale cookies and some cloudy juice in a pitcher that tasted like a blend of bandaids and lime.

Sal had a brief back and forth in Italian with one of the men playing cards. Aldo translated after the fact, more dog trouble as it turned out.

"Dad told him you're blind."

I happened just then to slop some juice while pouring it from the pitcher.

That impressed Aldo as the sort of thing a blind guy might get up to. He winked and said, "Nice."

Leigh Ann was happy next to Aldo. She was sitting so close to him they kept bumping against each other. Brody was content as well. He didn't mind his cookies stale, and he was interested in Terry who was just two years older than him but city-wise and showy tough. Monte was plump and balding and quiet and winced every time his stepmother opened her mouth. I could hardly blame him. Marcy was loud and had what I know now for a full-bore Long Island accent.

She hardly let Sal say anything. Marcy was a thoroughgoing alabastard skeptic, and she seemed to think being a Low Lord was like being in the Lions Club. You went to the meetings. You ate the lemon chicken. You sold the brooms and the lightbulbs when fundraising time came around, but you did it all only as long as it was agreeable and convenient. She kept asking us if we got the scenario (she called it). She wasn't much on giving us a chance to say if we actually had.

Dad and Clarice allowed her to rattle on. I got the feeling they were hoping she'd give out, but Marcy just kept on yapping. She'd start each new topic by telling us, "Ok, look."

Marcy was ~~was~~ awfully scattershot. Everything she knew seemed to be piecemeal and fractured, like she'd gotten it off the TV and out of magazines and hadn't let it sufficiently steep and blend in her head. She'd start in on some point she wanted to make and trot out evidence to support it, but she'd forget what it was and how it applied or why she'd dredged it up anyway.

Her main thrust had to do with real estate, since Sal and Marcy were making a handsome living off of rent. The store was a cash sink, Marcy explained. She called on Toppy to confirm that with a nod. So Marcy and Sal could hardly afford to boot out their tenants in Brooklyn and wouldn't do it no matter what we ended up telling Carlsbad. She recited what she claimed to be housing law in the greater New York area, and she let us know it trumped nearly everything.

"We're staying in Riverdale," Marcy finally said, "even if you want us down here chasing gutter pigs or something?"

That's when Clarice brought out the severed hand and dropped it on the table.

It inspired a fair amount of church Latin from Sal and his boys, but Marcy just said, "Gawd!"

She covered her nose, but the thing didn't stink beyond the usual scent of the deep dark — dank and tangy, fungal and exotic. A little bit like frog.

Terry poked it with a drink straw, but the rest of Sal's clan just gaped at that alabastard hand in wonder. It had plainly come off the sort of creature you couldn't hope to shove in a jar.

"Where'd you get this?" Sal finally asked.

Dad pointed at the floor. "All kinds of caverns and tunnels down there. We went under for a look."

"Ok to touch it?" Aldo asked.

Clarice nodded as Marcy said, "No, sir."

Aldo gave her a you're-not-my-mother look and reached over to pick it up. Once Aldo had squeezed the meat of the palm, those wicked alabastard talons extended. That prompted more Latin from Sal and his boys.

"You swore an oath," Clarice reminded Sal.

Marcy nodded. "Sickness and health. For better or worse."

"Before that."

"Sal?"

"I did," Sal allowed. "Got to do this, sweetie," he said to Marcy. "Me and boys. We're all sworn up and signed in. They'll take everything away."

Marcy was flabbergasted, a state she wasn't accustomed to and didn't seem to care for at all. She was plainly the sort of creature who got her way immediately or raised such a stink about it that she was certain to get her way in time.

"He never told you?" Clarice asked.

Marcy laid her hand flat on her sternum. She had more rings and jangly bracelets than I'd ever seen a woman wear. "He did not."

"Sweetie." Sal got a look at Marcy's palm. He turned towards Dad and and me and said, "Didn't think it'd ever matter."

Nobody said much of anything until Aldo asked, "Who killed him?"

"Nobody," Clarice told him. "I hit him in the hand."

The wound was still a little seepy. They run mossy green/gray under the skin. There was a hole through and through where Clarice's ripper arrow had hit.

"Then how'd you get that?" Monte asked us.

"He bit it off," Clarice told him.

"They'll do that," I said.

"He'll grow another," Leigh Ann chimed in.

That got a smile from Aldo. "You know stuff, don't you?"

Leigh Ann colored from her blonde bangs down like I'd never seen before. "Maybe," she said. "A little."

Brody told all of us, "Eeewww."

"Ok, look." Marcy left it at that. She seemed to have spoken as a kind of spasm.

"Can you kill them?" Terry asked. "Or are they like immortal or something?"

"No!" Brody told him. He wagged his finger our way. "They've all killed a bunch."

"What about you?" Terry wanted to know of Brody.

"Cut one once."

It was true. We all nodded, though he'd kind of done it by accident – over his shoulder while getting away.

"How many are there?" Sal asked.

Dad checked with Clarice, but they didn't have a number.

"Let's call it a lot," Clarice said.

"Ok, look."

"Can't we bring in that Flick thing or something?" Sal asked.

"Flex Corps?"

Sal nodded Dad's way.

"Maybe but not straightoff," Clarice told him. "They're kind of a last resort."

"So we fight them ourselves?" Aldo was trying to sound brave, but that big clammy hand and those talons had taken some of the starch out of him.

"Control them," Clarice said. "That's the job. If we can't do that, then we fight."

"Ok. Look. These boys aren't built for that."

"We'll drill them. Train them up," Clarice told Marcy.

"Have you been doing this your whole life?" Marcy asked. "You kind of look it to me."

"Oh?"

"They're hillbillies, Sal." Marcy dared to lay a hand on Clarice's forearm. "No disrespect."

"Loads taken. We swore an oath. We have a job. Them too." She pointed at Sal and his three sons.

"What about me?" Marcy wanted to know.

"You married in. You're a civilian. You can throw in with them or not."

"And me?" Until then Eun Mi had sat in silence watching the whole business unfold.

"You shouldn't even know what we're talking about," Clarice told her.

That's when Toppy uncorked on Clarice a long Jeffersonian passage that I recognized from *The Great Book*. It was the bit about the invisible ties and allegiances of the Order — the part where devotion trumps blood and duty is the loadstar. It also had enough wherefores in it to sound like Marcy's version of real estate law.

We all looked at Toppy. I had the best view since I was sitting right beside her and was grateful for the excuse to look.

"I get bored," she said and then turn towards Sal. "I found it in your office. I've read the whole thing. Twice."

That was a stunning bit of news for us. Aside from Uncle Grady, I don't think anybody in our family had ever read *The Great Book* once.

"Well then, maybe," Clarice said to Toppy. "Why don't you tell them about the CFs and why there's not much chance we'll ever put one in a jar again."

"They adapt," Toppy said. She quoted from the appendix and apocrypha both and undertook an exhaustive rundown of Cavus Ferinus traits and features. Dangers they posed. Tactics they favored. Precisely how they procreated and what they preferred to eat.

"Ok, look. Flesh?"

"They're indiscriminate carnivores," Toppy said.

"If they can't eat a rat or a goat or you," Clarice volunteered to Marcy, "they'll make do with each other."

"Cannibals!?" Terry shouted it loud enough to disturb the card players. Three of them glared. One of them folded. "Cool."

Monte had an idea. "We lock them down there. Let them eat each other."

"Too many ways out," Dad countered.

"Ok, look."

Toppy threw in with a quote from *The Great Book* – a notorious passage from the apocrypha – devoted to the final swam up when topside's swamped and deep dark conquers. Much bone grinding and enslavement. Torment and interminable grief. It was enough to make Brody whiny. Talk of end times always got under his skin.

"Nuke them," Aldo suggested.

That sort of thing routinely came up. Even in Carlsbad where the Elders had long quarreled about the virtues and the faults of exterminating CFs by way of incineration or poison. That would certainly mean failure for us and might even taint the earth. We couldn't be sure.

"It's about hegemony," Dad told Aldo. "Domination and control. We have it. They want it. A pretty old story, just with bigger teeth.

We all walked back to the Chinatown store. Leigh Ann let Aldo hold her hand while Monte complained in advance about the commute he'd have to make each day.

Toppy's cousin, Joon, was standing in front of the store smoking a cigarette and getting some city sun on his coif. Spit curl. Duck tail. A vat of mousse. It was a hell of a thing.

"Does he know?" I asked Toppy.

She shook her head.

"I'll help you," I told her. "With the groper and stuff. There's a right way to do it."

She nodded. "I have a boyfriend," she told me. "Korean."

I tried to smile as I said, "Uh huh," but I'm fairly sure it looked like a wince.

"He's moving to California."

"I like him better already."

Toppy smiled.

Dad and Clarice took notice. Not just of me and Toppy but of Leigh Ann and Aldo.

"We're here . . . what? Three days?" Dad asked her. "And it's already like a commune."

Terry poked Clarice to get her attention. "We get guns, don't we?"

She shook her head. "The bullets all bounce back."

6

We took them in through the culvert we'd come out of. Dad and Clarice had decided the carriage house squalor and the welded steel ladder would have been daunting for Sal and his clan at first.

Even for us, the vagrants and the human filth were new and unwelcome additions. We were used to guano and cave crickets and natural cavern grit. We'd gotten plenty dirty in Cumberland and Virginia, but the Brooklyn chambers and tunnels held a different sort of nastiness.

There was nobody in the culvert this time. Just trash and a trickle of rusty water. Marcy had insisted on coming along on account of her investment (she called it) in Sal. She'd bought 'caving togs' up in Riverdale and was reluctant to get them dirty. She complained that her astronaut jump suit was "choking her canoe."

"Do I want to know what that means?" I asked Toppy.

She told me, "Negatory."

Aside from the trash and the stink, the chief challenge for our newbies was the same as always — the weight and intimidation of the inky dark. All our headlamps together and the light boxes we'd brought couldn't begin to fully illuminate the place. The tunnels we'd be working through were mostly rocky and irregular with the odd section of granite facade and passage arch. There'd be darkness behind us, above us, flanking us to either side, and out ahead past where our beams could reach. You can be tempted to believe that pocket of light is your oxygen and salvation and all that darkness around you will crush and destroy you, given half a chance.

It's like you're in a diving bell but have forgotten water can drown you. Then you suddenly remember, and all you want is up and out.

We knew it was coming. We'd talked about it around the table in our apartment. We were resigned that we couldn't make it ~~make it~~ not happen, so we worked instead on a plan to keep Sal's clan precisely where they were. They'd want to bolt for sunlight, and you can't reason with that sort of panic.

"I could put an arrow in Marcy." I think Clarice meant it. "Nowhere lethal. Maybe through her tongue."

Instead we settled on my war cry. None of Sal's crew had yet heard it. It was a shriek as much as anything, and any sane human was sure to run from it.

So I dawdled and fell back, let Dad take Beauty. I made Toppy come with me. She wasn't part of Sal's clan, to my way of thinking. Toppy was my apprentice, so she belonged by my side.

I'd been instructed to wait until the inevitable cavern agitation took hold. I thought that might be difficult to gauge, but Marcy supplied a running commentary. She'd forgotten entirely about her choked canoe, was no longer worried what her boots might pick up. She was focused instead on every sort of creature that was shifting and scuttling and lurking in the dark.

"What's that?" She asked a few dozen times.

Then she put herself snug behind Sal and held onto his coveralls collar, which made him uneasy too. A rat or something made a racket up ahead in the dark. That's when the dithering and the reconsidering took hold of Sal and his brood.

I heard Leigh Ann tell Aldo, "It's okay."

"Let's go back," Terry said.

"Yeah." That sounded like Monte but an octave too high.

Once they turned and their lights played my way, I hit them with my war cry. The acoustics down there were splendid. You can usually raise an echo in a cave, but from where I was standing the entire tunnel worked like a kind of band shell. So my war cry got amplified, broadcast almost.

Marcy shrieked, "Gawd!" and bolted pretty much all over the place. I could see the play of her light beam. It was lancing and bobbing and bouncing. She got separated immediately, like you do when you panic and run.

The rest of them took Marcy as an excuse to scatter as well. Even Aldo who had to disentangle himself from Leigh Ann to do it. Beauty started barking, which likely didn't help. It was the brand of joyous yapping she often got up to among sheep.

There were headlamp beams all over. The thing we hadn't fully counted on was the breadth and depth of the place. Unlike most caverns, the deep dark under Brooklyn had massive scope and reach. There was almost no end of spots for a spooked newbie caver to hide. When you're trying to get away from a banshee in the dark, you'll shove yourself in places you'd never go in your proper mind.

"Hey!" Dad yelled, but he was late at it.

Somebody fell down and groaned.

Me and Toppy went up to join the rest of my clan. "Too much?"

"High strung, aren't they?" Clarice said. She took a hard look at Eun Mi. "You're doing okay, right?"

Toppy's lamp bobbed. "I'm fine."

Leigh Ann aimed her light beam right at my eyes — a grave breach of Low Lord etiquette — and told me, "If he gets hurt or killed or something, I'm coming after you."

She meant it. I could tell, and the girl had wicked groper moves.

"Aldo," Leigh Ann called out with more tender concern than I'd known her to lavish on anything since Patty, her doll with freckles and penny loafers.

We all held our breath and listened. We heard what sounded like "Ok, look."

They'd covered a lot of territory for first-time cavers from Riverdale and sounded to have gone a lot deeper than we'd meant to take them on a probe to train them up.

We couldn't let them know that.

"We'll walk them back up easy," Dad said.

"Let's find them first," Clarice suggested.

It wasn't so simple as you might think. They'd switched off their lights and were letting the dark conceal them. You can press against a cave wall, kill your lamp, and convince yourself you're hidden and alone and safe. That's when they slip up on you since they can see you all along. They smell you. They hear you. They know where you are. That lamp is all for you.

"Sal. Marcy," Dad called out. We stopped and waited. Nothing.

"Aldo!"

Leigh Ann muttered another threat my way.

"Switch on your lamps," Dad shouted.

Still nothing.

"Form up" Clarice said. "You nocked?" she asked me.

My ripper was still in my satchel. I pulled it out. I cocked and loaded. Gropers went to the ready. We wedged with Beauty on point and Brody and Toppy shielded in back.

"Sal!" Nothing.

"Aldo!"

We heard a Marcy noise from the darkness ahead. It sounded like she was hissing at Sal for getting her where she was.

We went up a notch to double quick.

The way it usually works with civilians underground is you panic and you bolt. The fear drives you, but you'll finally get winded and reigned in enough to stop and think about what you're up to. Then maybe you try to crawl back where you came from or decide to wait for help.

And that's all in the ordinary deep dark, with no alabastards thrown in as a menace. Here Sal and his people were spooked and scattered with that big white hand to think of. Claws. Blue-green seepage. Their imaginations were surely building the rest of the creature on the spot.

"They won't be far," Clarice said. "Did you see Marcy trying to run?"

She was a prancer all right and moved like a lady worrying about her nails. Clarice was obliged to object to that for the sake of womankind. Leigh Ann would have thrown in with Clarice but for Marcy being Aldo's stepmom. Anything that touched on Aldo was now half sacred to Leigh Ann.

"Aldo!" It was more of a rising plea this time than anything else.

We dropped out of level and started descending. It was the sort of thing you could feel more than see. The temperature dropped gradually. Your balance got slightly off. We were in the tunnel we'd visited previously but farther down than we'd dared to go.

As we went, we scoured around for any kind of crack or crevice that might have given Sal and his clan an option.

"How about there?" Brody saw it. A slot in the rock, maybe two feet across.

I stuck my head in. The crease went well back, didn't appear to get much wider but also didn't look to collapse. I heard something back in there. Gritty scraping.

I drew back out into the tunnel. "Maybe," I said. "I'll look. Ya'll go on down, but stay in the main where I can find you."

"Ten minutes," Clarice told me, "or we come in behind you."

That was the typical way, just enough time to be in a swarm up or dead.

"Take this," Dad said. He gave me his *talwar*, a double-edged curved sword that had been passed down through the family. Dad kept lapping steel onto it just to have an edge to hone.

I handed my ripper and arrows over to Toppy. "No room for it," I said. "See you in a few." With that I plunged on in.

There was racket down that crease, though it was hard to tell from what. The fissure was tall enough to allow me to stand. I eased along sideways at a pretty good clip. I'd stop and hold my breath and listen every ten yards or so. Noise, low and steady. Shifting, grating. Too steady for Sal and them.

It could have been a jackhammer somewhere off and away. It could have been the subway overhead causing the loose stones to rattle and shake. I might have been tempted to think that noise was ordinary and benign. Should have been tempted but somehow wasn't. I still don't know just why. Possibly scent. Maybe raw instinct. I knew I couldn't stop.

So I pressed on. That crevice opened and pinched. It got six or eight feet across here and there, closed down to little more than eighteen inches in a couple of places. I kept telling myself it was time to head back, but I'd ease on ten more feet. Then ten more and ten more, and I noticed a change in the darkness ahead. It wasn't absolute like it had been. I switched off my headlamp, and I could still see.

My crevice was clotted up ahead with rocks from the cavern ceiling. Fist-sized mostly, and here and there light seeped through. I could hear noise from the far side of the slide. Not voices but movement, shifting and twitching, snorting too, like you hear sometimes in a barn.

I eased up to the rubble and found a crack I could peer through once I'd taken my helmet off. I knew immediately I was looking at a swarm of alabastards but unlike any swarm I'd ever seen.

The place they were in was vast. I was high up the wall in my crevice. It was an old train tunnel by the looks of it, long abandoned and out of use. The light seeping through a crack in the vaulted ceiling was artificial, incandescent. I heard the rumble of a subway overhead. The squeal of the brakes. The conductor's announcement.

"Bergen Street. Next stop Grand Army Plaza. Let 'em off."

Smoky wisps of soot and grit rained down as the train pulled out of the station. The light flickered and then steadied. They were in an abandoned tunnel underneath the new one. I shifted for a better view, slipped a rock out to open a hole.

That ancient tunnel was as full as it could get with alabastards. Far more than I'd ever hoped to see in one place at one time. They were packed together, standing upright. Some of them were clearly having to struggle to do it, but there was no room to crouch and scuttle, no space at all to fall.

They were moving in a circle, down the length of the tunnel and then back up again, which meant they all passed under the light. That appeared to be the purpose and design. Alabastards were beasts of the deep dark. A full moon was a torment to them. The first thing they always reached for in a swarm up was your head lamp, but there they were suffering the light upon them. They gazed up as they passed beneath it. They were tempering themselves, I had to think.

Some were clothed, not fully but shirts or trousers, skirts or hats. Most were bare and white, their pale skin glistening. They made that sinusy alabastard noise as they shuffled and circulated. The stink from them was thick and musky, like you'd get if you plowed up a bolus of snakes.

I wanted a bigger hole to see them through, and I ended up dropping a rock as I made it. They heard the racket somehow, and the effect was like kicking a beehive. They raised their awful reptile faces and sniffed. Then six or eight of them leapt onto the walls and came my way with alarming velocity.

I eased back from the opening I'd made, retreated to where the crevice bent and hid myself just past an outcropping. An alabastard shoved his entire arm in through the hole where I'd been standing. Talons clicked and clattered on rock. The wall of rubble and wedged boulders shifted and settled, but it held. I peeked past an overhang and saw the CF who saw me as he pressed his face to my porthole. He screeched and bellowed like they do.

I grabbed my helmet and made as headlong a retreat as I could. I was looking backwards most of the way, half expecting to get swarmed on, and so didn't see Clarice coming from the other end until we collided in the crevice and I had all but knocked her down.

"Hey!" She yelled. She had more to say, but I covered her mouth with my hand. That didn't sit well. Clarice jerked and squirmed.

I leaned in close and told her in a whisper, "We've got kind of a problem."

The hole was as I'd left it. Clarice sampled the air. "Piles of them," she told me before she'd even looked.

She had her face to the opening an awfully long time, kept shifting around to gain a better view of the spectacle before her.

"They're getting used to the light or something," I said.

Clarice grunted and kept adjusting.

"I didn't see Cracker Daddy."

"He's there," She told me. Clarice drew back to make room for me. "Back wall. Two o'clock."

I found him. He was the only one not moving. He stayed in the light full time.

One of those sneaky rascals had stayed on the wall. I guess he heard me and Clarice talking because just as I was drawing back, his arm came through the hole. Clarice grabbed me by the collar and jerked me clear before, in one smooth motion, she grabbed Dad's *talwar,* jabbed it through the hole, and skewered the beast.

He jerked back, spouting fluid from his neck, lost his grip on the rock and went down snorting and raging, like they do.

We both watched him land among the circulating horde. They did what their instincts told them. They ripped him to pieces in a frenzy, ate his flesh and crunched his bones.

7

Marcy was still agitated and more than a little indignant. Her jumpsuit was ripped, and she'd gotten cave grit in her eyes.

"Came out of rats probably," she told us, particularly Clarice.

Marcy held with the philosophy that women had a duty to each other, even women like Clarice who hated women like Marcy.

The best Clarice could do was pull a half sympathetic face and tell Marcy, "Yeah, probably came out of rats."

Mostly, we had to figure out how to get from Carlsbad the caliber of help we needed. There's was no form with a box to tick beside "Looks like the Apocalypse."

Naturally, Dad took some convincing at first. He preferred to believe me and Clarice were exaggerating. There were lots of CFs maybe, but not more than we could handle.

"Give it up," Clarice finally told him. "More than we could count. More than we can manage."

"I guess we could call in an assessor," Dad conceded.

"A what?" Leigh Ann asked just before I could. We'd never heard of such a creature.

"An emissary from the Council," Dad explained. "A five-star warrior with a main line to all the right ears to bend."

"Do it," Clarice told him.

Dad nodded. He thought for a second before asking generally, "How?" That was an Uncle Grady job.

Lucky for us, we were standing in Sal's Chinatown store at the time. Eun Mi's apartment was upstairs, and she'd let Marcy in to tend to her cave grit while Sal and his sons were over at the Blue Grotto getting ziti and meatballs to go.

They were in that newbie post-cavern phase of needing to be outside. When our crew found them, Sal and his clan were cowering and disoriented. They were together mostly, but Sal and boys kept trying to ease away from Marcy. Even panicked and trembling, she could dredge up plenty of blame to go around.

Sal and Monte, in particular, got tired of hearing from her, so they kept pushing off to fresh quarters of the deep dark in hopes Marcy would stay put.

"They were going in a circle," Dad told me, "way down the tunnel with their headlamps off."

"Not Aldo," Leigh Ann said with no little pride. "Right, Dad."

Dad nodded. "He was just sitting and shaking."

"Dad!"

"Mostly just sitting."

They were raw civilians who went underground only to ride the subway. There was no shame in sitting and shaking in the dark. I tried to say as much Leigh Ann, but she'd decided we were all down on Aldo. If there was a clan she felt allegiance to that moment it wasn't ours.

"Got to be a form, right?" Clarice asked Dad. She was still on the assessor.

"One thirty-nine stroke twelve," Toppy said and went fishing in a cupboard against the wall.

Every five years, Low Lords get a packet of forms and pamphlets from Carlsbad. They liked to update and revise, clarify the thorny bits, sometimes change the fonts. Toppy brought out Sal's latest packet. She was serving as Sal's Grady. Toppy fished out the stack of forms. Sifted through them. Made her selection. She offered a single sheet to Clarice and Dad.

"Assessor request," Toppy said.

"Fill it out," Dad told her. "It'll need to come from Sal."

Toppy knew exactly which boxes to tick and was adept at forging Sal's scrawl. She pulled one of the official pre-addressed envelopes from Sal's document packet. Council correspondence all went to a post office box in Atoka, New Mexico.

We decided to spend one solid day of boot camp in Secaucus. Our crew rode out there in the back of Sal's empty panel truck along with Aldo and Toppy. We could hear Marcy and the rest of them telling Sal which route to take up in the cab.

In the back, we held to the canvas straps to keep from bouncing all over the place while we settled on the order of business for the day. Basic groper technique. Vulnerable spots on the CF physique.

We passed the time tossing out details, but our hearts weren't really in it. Me and Clarice, in particular, were mopey since we'd seen the whole assembly. Teaching Sal and them basic cavern moves was a little like teaching a castaway how to do the side stroke. It wasn't going to matter in an ocean full of sharks.

"Ok look." Marcy had put on brand new cave coveralls for the Secaucus warehouse. They were violet and covered with all sorts of embroidered butterflies and zippers. "An hour maybe of your stuff and then coffee and pastries from Carmella's." She pointed in the general direction of a pallet of Bluetooth speakers. "Struffoli," Marcy told us. "All year round."

I watched Leigh Ann work with Aldo on his stance and groper grip, but it was clearly just an excuse for her to linger alongside him. Touch his hand every now and again. Bump him with her shoulder. That struck me as a fine sort of thing to be up to, given what I'd lately seen. The same went for Brody and Terry as well, who were mostly just messing around.

I'd always been an optimistic sort until that day out in Secaucus when I decided it hardly mattered what we did. I'd seen what had looked like a thousand alabastards congregated in that cavern. They were organized — to the extent that alabastards ever can be — and up to some sort of tactical no good. I found myself gloomier out in New Jersey than I think I'd ever been.

I couldn't help but picture the brand of carnage a thousand alabastards would get up to. They're bad enough hungry and cave-bound, but they were sure to be catastrophic topside and running free in the world. In a real sense, we'd been controlling them by keeping them weak and hungry. Let even two of them dine on an investment banker and they'd suddenly have the vigor to spoil life for a raft of decent people.

We did end up at Carmella's, half bakery and half diner near the Meadowlands Parkway with a view of the Hackensack River. The channel had ducks floating on it and brownish foam and what looked like a chunk of trailer siding. I had brisket and spaetzle, both new to me, capped off with a pile of struffoli, which turned out to be like doughnut holes slathered in honey with sprinkles.

Sal and his boys had picked up enough pointers to decide they were ready for combat, and they started asking around about all the alabastards we'd done in. It was the sort of thing no proper Low Lord would ever put a number to or even think about in the spirit of triumph. It was always us or them in tight quarters in the dark.

The fights were routinely monstrous and terrifying like you'd been set upon by dragons. I'd never shot one clean with my ripper or groped one in half and put him down. It wasn't like that. They were savage and relentless and would never stop trying to kill you until you'd drained most of their fluid or flat took them entirely apart.

They didn't know fear. They seemed unacquainted with restraint. They were only aware you had meat on your bones and blood in your veins. With them, it was feast or oblivion.

You couldn't say something like that to Sal and his crew. It wouldn't even have made a dent with Marcy. At our table in Carmella's, she was chiefly intent on doing something about Clarice's hair.

"Up maybe," she suggested and reached for Clarice's head, but Clarice dodged away and glared at Marcy.

"You've got the cheeks for it. If you're going do that gaunt thing, you ought to at least show it off a little."

"I wear mine up sometimes," Leigh Ann said, as much for Aldo as Marcy.

Marcy winced Leigh Ann's way like Leigh Ann had broken wind. She reached over and poked Leigh Ann's cheek. "Baby fat," she said.

We passed another couple of hours in Sal's Secaucus warehouse. We'd made an alabastard out of bubble wrap and coached Sal and them as they sliced it up. We could have trained that crew for months and it wouldn't truly have mattered. It's not about where you slash and jab and how you hold your groper. It's about blocking out the idea you're not as savage as they are. That you're a lot less built to brutalize, a lot less ready to die.

We had family dinner back in Brooklyn, up in our apartment. Just eggs and gloom. Everybody had a bath to get the warehouse grime off of us, and then we sat around and were blunt with each other, the way we tend to be sometimes.

It started with Marcy irritation, but the scope widened in a hurry.

"I don't even want to take them down under," Dad eventually confessed to us all. "We're way outnumbered, and Sal's bunch won't help. They'll just get sliced to bits."

Leigh Ann, naturally, was Aldo centric. She couldn't bear to think of him clawed up and laid open in the deep dark.

"If it's as bad as you say, let's give it to the Flex Corps. Can't they gas them or something?"

"Maybe," Clarice allowed. "We've got a guy coming. He'll decide which way to go."

After Brody went to bed, I was still antsy and felt like I needed a walk. Leigh Ann came with me and Beauty, wouldn't be discouraged from it, so I got to hear in detail how delightful Aldo was. We walked up from the harbor on Columbia to the Brooklyn Heights promenade. We'd swung by one afternoon, but this was our first visit after dark.

Our view of the lights of lower Manhattan was flanked by the Statue of Liberty to the South and the stone towers of the Brooklyn Bridge to the north. There were mostly dog walkers on the promenade, a wide brick pedestrian thoroughfare cantilevered above the Brooklyn-Queens expressway. There was a ferry in the harbor, bottlenecks along Manhattan's East Side Drive. A couple tongue-deep on a bench by the railing put Leigh Ann in a kind of an Aldo swoon.

"He wants to take me out dancing. On my birthday, you know. When I turn seventeen."

"That'll never happen."

"Maybe you can talk to Dad."

"I'm kind of with him on this one."

"Mack!"

She crossed her arms and went into a pout. We walked in silence for a few minutes.

"You don't like him, do you?"

"I barely know him. You barely know him."

"We connected," she said.

I didn't want to have this conversation with my sister, and as luck would have it, we both got distracted by a trio of guys up ahead. It was the way they loped that I noticed first. There was something wild-on-the-prairie about it.

"You seeing this?" I asked Leigh Ann.

She nodded.

"Can't be, can it?"

They were all wearing dungarees, flannel shirts, the sort of caps Greek fishermen might wear. Their necks were noticeably white, even in the dim, amber lamplight. They'd clearly failed to find shoes anywhere to fit their cave-hardened feet.

"I don't even have a knife," Clarice whispered my way.

We'd come out for an innocent walk – no gropers, no rippers, no nothing.

We watched them head for a guy with a beagle. He was stout. That must have been the draw. They veered right at him and closed hard. Beauty was snarling and bouncing by then, so I let her go.

We followed her at a dead run. I'd never gone at a CF barehanded, but then I'd never come across one in trousers out on an evening stroll.

The guy with the beagle said, "Hey!" as the first alabastard grabbed him.

His dog lunged at the beast and got joined by Beauty. She knew enough about CFs to home in on their nether parts. The bit one raised the usual sinusy alabastard warble and let go of the fat guy. Him and the other two had their talons extended and were taking swipes at Beauty when me and Leigh Ann came barreling in.

I lowered my shoulder and sent the first beast I reached into the railing. When he bounced back, I put the shoulder to him again and launched him clear over the iron top rail and down onto the highway.

There was more yelling along the promenade by then, and the two CFs left retreated. One of them caught me across the arm with his clapperclaw as he was backing up. They loped off into Brooklyn Heights. There were horns and screeching, the crunch of metal on metal and the sound of plastic fracturing below.

I joined Leigh Ann at the rail. The one I'd shoved was dead in the road underneath us, pale at either end and leaking slimy fluid from the joint where his arm had been. The arm was laying on a drain grate, the digits wiggling and the talons thrusting and retracting like they do. Civilians joined us to look down as well and wonder aloud what they were seeing.

"You're bleeding," one of them told me.

My sleeve was ripped to ribbons. My arm flesh was parted. Dad would need to do some sewing up.

Leigh Ann took Beauty's leash in one hand. Grabbed one of my belt loops with the other. She quickly walked us both back down the Promenade and to our place under the bridge.

8

Clarice did my sewing up this time. She had a lighter touch than Dad. I got a dose of peroxide and a half dozen stitches while Dad tracked down Uncle Grady.

I couldn't hear much of the phone conversation from the kitchen, where we were, but I did hear Dad tell Uncle Grady more than one time, "No, it's worse."

"The assessor's on his way," Dad informed us once he and Grady had signed off. "Leaving tonight."

"From Carlsbad?" Clarice asked him.

He nodded. That meant three days at least. Assessors always took the bus. They didn't even rate train tickets. It was a wonder they didn't make them travel in a Conestoga wagon. The Legion was backwards and proud of it. There was a general philosophy afoot that we couldn't truly honor our calling and the spirit of Thomas Jefferson if we didn't stay a generation or two behind the times.

In their defense, you could reliably get a duffel bag packed full of bladed weapons into the luggage bin of a Greyhound bus.

"What do we do until he gets here?" I asked.

Clarice tied off my last stitch. She nipped the thread with her teeth, uncapped our tub of CF salve, and smeared some over the wound. "Nothing for you," she told me.

"Nothing for us too, right?" That from Leigh Ann.

Clarice and Dad weren't so sure about that. They'd spent most of their lives at cavern squeezes and on forays and patrols. It wasn't in their natures to sit by and wait for a guy coming on a bus from New Mexico.

"A little recon wouldn't hurt," Clarice said.

"But just us." Leigh Ann had Aldo in mind. "Those other guys aren't ready."

"Maybe Sal and Aldo," Dad proposed. "With the three of us and Beauty, they'll be all right."

"We'll take walkies," Clarice said by way of reassuring Leigh Ann. "Mack and Brody can come down and help us if we get snarled up somehow."

"So what'll we do?" Leigh Ann asked mostly Clarice. It seemed like a reasonable question.

"Make sure they're where we left them, so we can take the assessor right there."

It sounded sensibly strategic, as long as they kept an avalanche of boulders and scree between themselves and those alabastards. A swarm up by a horde like that was sure to leave even a full platoon of Low Lords just a heap of wrist watches and teeth.

I hadn't passed a day with my little brother in a couple of years by then, since back when I'd had to drag him around by the hand and watch him blubber. He'd become a guy with enthusiasms. He reminded me of Jo Jo, maybe chiefly because he had a thing for Magnus the Robot Killer too.

Brody owned a half dozen comics — most of them Magnus and his chesty sidekick — and he carried his choice ones down to the old ferry landing park. We sat on a bench overlooking the harbor.

I'd brought the walkie with me. It squawked. Clarice and Dad and Leigh Ann were down in a tunnel somewhere. They'd resolved to go in through the nasty carriage house. Sal and Aldo were patrolling with them.

Clarice was in charge of the radio. "Check, Mack. Check, Mack," she said.

I keyed the mic. "We're here. Boost your gain."

I guess she was cranked full up already because I got nothing but a few partial words and a flood of static back.

"I'm losing you," I told her.

More static.

"I don't want to go down there anymore," Brody informed me.

"Why not?"

"It's not even a cave."

He had a point there. Our experience of Brooklyn was primarily through abandoned tunnels that appeared to the be the work of dynamite and man. They were part regular stonework and part greasy black bedrock. The tunnels were trash-strewn and dank and foul smelling felt thoroughly human tainted. And now they were overrun with alabastards. There was little about them to like.

Somebody had tossed a copy of that morning's New York Post in the wastebasket beside our bench. I could see the front page through the wire mesh. There was a photo in the top left of a terrier that some reclusive dowager had left her riches to. On the top right, a salacious candid shot of the girlfriend of one the Yankee's starting pitchers. Apparently, she was also a kleptomaniac.

The main photo on the center of page one was of a mangled alabastard. I recognized him straightaway. Dungarees. Plaid flannel. White everywhere else with blue-green seepage. He looked like an L.A. gang member who'd spent the last decade in a mausoleum. He was sprawled in a lane of the BQE. The headline was a question mark with an exclamation mark behind it.

I fished the paper out of the barrel, but it had yogurt or something on it. From what I could see, they were running tests on the corpse and calling the death 'suspicious'. They'd interviewed witnesses to a scuffle on the promenade but hadn't decided for certain if old whitey had been pushed or simply fell.

Just then I got a burst of static on the walkie. I could hear what I thought was Beauty snarling and barking. There were people yelling as well.

I keyed the mic. "I'm here."

Nothing for a good quarter minute. I thought I heard Dad yell, "Ladder!" I stood up and told Brody, "Come on."

We swung by the apartment to snag our weapons and our headlamps. Brody's groper might have been puny and brightly painted, but it was hardly a toy. We went at a trot towards the carriage house up between the bridges along the littered alleyway. Me and Brody slipped in past the tacked up plywood, headed over through the heaps of rubbish and peered down into the deep.

We could hear them down there. They were scuffling with CFs. I was more than a little acquainted with that sound.

I swung onto the ladder and climbed down first with Brody close behind. We could hear steel ringing and alabastards snorting. There was some rank panic in the high-pitched warbling of Sal and Aldo as well.

We headed for the racket and the lancing lights and found our crew out in the main tunnel in fiercely contested retreat. He was watching. I think I saw him first. Cracker Daddy without a doubt. He wasn't hanging back exactly. He was right where a groper could reach him, but he gave the appearance of a creature that simply couldn't be bothered with scrapping. He had minions for that, and they were clawing and snarling. Dad and Clarice and Leigh Ann and Beauty were fighting with pitched savagery back.

The trouble was chiefly with Sal and Aldo. They just wanted to get away and were swatting with their gropers at the Alabastards within reach the way men scared of reptiles might try to kill a snake. So my gang was having to beat back the CFs squarely before them and try to pitch in to do some harm to Sal and Aldo's CFs as well.

That's where me and Brody did some good. We took over for Sal and Aldo and let the pair of beasts before us know they were in for a genuine fight. I pierced mine with a bolt right between the ribs, must have nicked that lump of entrails they use for a gizzard because he started loosing juice and giblets in a healthy stream. That freed me up to flank the CF Brody had before him. I pulled out my spike, and together we left him in a pile of parts.

Aldo had recovered some nerve by then. He must have partly been driven by fear of getting humiliated in front of his girlfriend. He came rushing in waving his blade just as me and Brody were swinging around to give Leigh Ann some help. Aldo hung out on our far left flank and left himself exposed. Cracker Daddy took an instant interest in him.

Two strides and Cracker Daddy had relieved Aldo of his weapon and lifted him into the air by his arm. With a talon, the beast made his mark on Aldo, scratched him bloody on the neck.

Leigh Ann yelled, “No!” and lunged at Cracker Daddy. He flung her boyfriend at her, and the two of them hit the tunnel floor in a heap.

Cracker Daddy then made a noise in his throat, and his warriors withdrew with him into the dark.

“Out, out, out,” Dad told us as he and Clarice hustled us towards the ladder.

Aldo argued to be the last one up, but it was too late for that.

“Go!” Clarice ordered him, and he scrambled up the ladder. He was bleeding freely by then.

I brought up the rear, but there was no danger to it. Cracker Daddy was bringing to alabastards the thing that we most feared. He was reigning them in. He was imposing control. We needed them scattershot and untamed to have any hopes of keeping them down.

Dad shut the steel hatch behind me once I'd reached the carriage house. Leigh Ann was blotting Aldo's blood with her shirtsleeve. A Q laid over in a pointy hat. The boy had a lot of peroxide and cave salve in his future.

Apple brandy was traditional with the Legion. We had a jarful from one of the Carlsbad casks in a cabinet in our apartment. Sal and Aldo came up to have a settling dram at Dad's insistence. You usually gave it to a Low Lord after his first kill, but Dad and Clarice decided Sal and Aldo had come close enough to qualify.

"You might sit on this for a while," Dad suggested. "Let the shock wear off."

"Don't tell the boys. Don't tell your wife," Clarice instructed them. "They're sure to just get rattled."

"We're in awful trouble, aren't we?" Sal said. He shoved his empty glass Dad's way for a refill.

We might have all been thinking, "Hell, yeah," but we were accomplished shruggers.

The following evening, we left Beauty at home and took the subway into Manhattan. All five of us in what passed for decent clothes. We came up in the Port Authority Bus Station, a massive eyesore on the west side of the island just at the Lincoln Tunnel.

They'd taken all the seats out to frustrate the vagrants, so we stood and waited for our assessor's bus. The guy was arriving on a connector from Lexington, Kentucky, and it was remarkably close to on time.

Weary passengers came down off the bus and straggled into the terminal proper. They sure looked like they'd been riding the highways for a while — all wrinkled and spent and squinting in the bright bus station lights.

Then one guy came in who was different from the rest. Muscular. Ebony. Fully alert. He was wearing fatigues. They were dark olive and appeared to be tailored. His trousers were tucked into his oiled black boots. He was holding a loaded duffel with such ease he made it look full of feathers.

“Figures,” Clarice said. She waved at the guy. “That’s him. Dirk.”

He lifted a lone finger and waved back.

“You know him?” Dad asked. It sure looked like she did.

“Yeah,” Clarice told us. “my ex.”

SWARM UP

1

Awkward doesn't begin to cover it. Dirk had to stay with us. It wasn't like he could camp at the Waldorf Astoria and expense it. Carlsbad is old-fashioned about that sort of thing too, which is to say achingly cheap.

Fortunately, Dirk had been schooled in palaver. It's one of the assessor training segments. They get strategy and hand-to-hand, certified in demolition, and then they tack on a week's worth of social skills at the academy as well. So it wasn't like he was naturally adept at human interaction, but he could fake it in that Carlsbad sort of way. A frothy question. A smile. A nod. Another frothy question.

Me and Brody and Leigh Ann all decided to dislike Dirk for Dad's sake even if Dad had actively discouraged us from it. Dad had been raised by Granddaddy Hoyt to be a gracious host when occasion presented, so he gave Dirk the bedroom with the bath attached (which meant I got to sleep on the futon), and he went out of his way to try to make Dirk feel welcome and at home.

Clarice did quite a lot less. Plainly, she and Dirk had some rocky history between them. For every cordial remark, they'd indulge together in three or four snide asides. They didn't like each other in that prickly, provocative way that only people who've loved each other once can manage. Almost everything Dirk did that first evening was a problem for Clarice.

"Yeah, why don't you put it there," Clarice said with a snort once Dirk had entered the apartment and set his duffel on the floor. He picked it back up and carried it around until Dad took it from him.

"Something to drink?" Dad asked. "We'll be eating in a bit."

"A pint of gin, right?" Clarice again.

Dirk told Dad, "Water'll do."

Clarice muttered and stalked around the apartment, though with me and Brody and Leigh Ann in the way there wasn't really anywhere much to go.

Dad brought Dirk a glass of water from the kitchen and then told Clarice, "Come here," and led her down the hall.

They went into their bedroom and shut the door, so we could just hear the noise of them clearing the air but not what they said exactly. We could guess well enough. I'm sure Dirk could as well.

"Tell me about your deep dark," he said to us.

Dirk fetched one of our maple dinette chairs and perched on it backwards, provided a guy the size of Dirk could ever be said to perch. The chair joints groaned, and I half expected the thing to splinter and collapse.

"It smells," Brody said.

"Oh?"

"Garbage, sewer," Leigh Ann enlarged. "There are some people down there too."

"Like bums?" Dirk asked. He said it with contempt.

"Hard luck types," I told him. "This is a tough place to make a go."

"And the CFs."

"Loads of them," Leigh Ann said. "Mack and Clarice saw them up to something."

"Spill," Dirk told me.

"Looked to be getting used to the light."

That earned me a snort. Dirk was skeptical. "Listen to you," he said.

"Why you got so many muscles?" Brody wanted to know.

Dirk treated it like a trifling question, made brief mention of his weight training and the diet he followed, but having muscles in the deep dark was ill-advised and problematic. You could look at Dirk and be sure there were a lot of places he'd never fit.

"Engaged them yet?" Dirk wanted to know.

"Yeah," I told him, and then I kept on going. "Clarice says you caused a slide and left her."

"Drinking back then," Dirk said matter of factly. "They fit for fighting?" he wanted to know.

We were bringing him up to date on our encounters with our CFs when Dad and Clarice rejoined us.

Clarice made a stab at being nicer. She softened her tone anyway as she asked her ex, "Do you have to sit like that?"

We got Chinese food delivered, and Dirk ate everything but the boxes. He gnawed one of his chopsticks in half.

"Been on a bus for three days," Dirk explained once he'd caught us all looking at him.

"There's a shower off your bedroom." It came out of Clarice in the form of a suggestion.

Dirk told her, "All right," and left us to convene in the galley kitchen and whisper about him at length.

We had to discount about half of what Clarice told us about Dirk because it seemed matrimonially poisoned. The stuff we decided to believe, however, didn't strike us as all that encouraging. Dirk had a patron at Carlsbad who'd steered him through the ranks and had helped to elevate Dirk beyond where Dirk most likely deserved to be.

"He had the jitters but got past it. He can brutal with room," was Clarice's assessment, "but he's kind of a meathead. You'll see."

Dad took it all well enough. You just knew if Dirk got in deep dark trouble, Dad was the sort who'd wade in and even sacrifice himself to keep his assessor alive. He wasn't petty, and Mom had worn him down enough to leave him passably unemotional. He loved Clarice, but he'd die for the cause. That's just who he was.

Sal and them were convinced they'd rather take their chances on getting overrun by alabastards topside than venture into the deep dark again. Their battle had left them traumatized, and they were all in agreement that nothing on God's green earth could change their minds, but that was before they met Dirk the assessor.

He was just the right tool for the job, as it turned out. He appealed briefly to Sal's sense of duty, the oath he'd sworn, the august tradition he'd been born into.

When Sal responded with his version of, “Listen to you,” Dirk started bending Sal’s joints in directions they’d never been meant to go.

Then Marcy weighed in with an “Ok, look,” and she got squashed by Dirk as well. He didn’t touch her, but he leaned in and menaced her with the brand of glare that suggested he’d have no qualms about bending lady joints as well.

It was quite a show, all performed on the sales floor at the store in Chinatown. The three customers in the shop seemed unfazed. Two of them discussed a rice cooker at length in what must have been Japanese. The third one, a Hispanic guy with a tattoo on his neck — it was either the face of a baby or one of those hairless cats — tried to negotiate with Eun Mi over the price of a cd player.

“No dicker,” Toppy kept telling him. She did a fine job of sounding like she had no English to speak of.

“All right, twenty-five.” He’d come up from ten.

“No dicker!”

“Thirty, but . . .” He examined the player he wanted. “It’s kind of crap.”

Sal let out a yelp just then. It was a tendon issue.

“What’s his problem?” the customer asked.

“No dicker,” Toppy said.

Sal and the boys came to understand the wisdom of going into the deep dark again. Marcy sniveled a bit about it, but she never came out and objected outright. Toppy volunteered her services, and Dirk agreed to take her on as an auxiliary civilian. The Hispanic guy ended up paying retail for a cd player that looked like junk.

"Don't know about the dog," Dirk told me in the carriage house at the hatch.

He was all geared up and looked like something you'd buy in a box at a toy store. He had black tactical everything, right down to his helmet and headlamp.

"Dog's coming," Clarice assured him before I could decide what to say. "She'll probably end up saving your sorry ass."

"Listen to you."

Dad held Clarice by the belt loop. "Lead down," he said to Leigh Ann. "Then you," he told me, and that's how we went.

Dirk had the latest handheld electronics we'd seen in the quarterly. One of them detected movement, and when Dirk wiggled his fingers at the business end, the thing clicked like a playing card in bike spokes. Another was set to CF body temperature. We showed up blue on the screen. Dirk told us alabasters would be bright red.

We formed up in the standard way. Sal had brought down his boys and Toppy. He'd left Marcy minding the store. Dirk didn't think much of the two pole axes we'd bought at the Home Depot to supplement the only two gropers Sal's clan had.

"We'll fit you boys up proper," he said. He had a hard look at the gropers me and Leigh Ann were carrying. "Got an edge on those?"

"Yes sir," I assured him. I'm not sure he heard me since Clarice was telling me at the same time, "Gut him if you want."

Dirk took point, naturally. It didn't matter to him that he'd never been in our deep dark before. To his way of thinking, point was where he belonged, even if Dad and Clarice had to steer him at first away from the culvert and towards the gentle slope that carried us down.

"Does go on, doesn't it?" Dirk said in time.

It was hard not to be impressed with the reach and scope of the place. There was an awful lot of territory for not even a dozen of us to cover.

"No squeezes, I guess."

"Nope," Clarice told him. "A thousand ways out. They can come up anywhere."

"Challenging."

"The crossword's challenging," Sal chimed in. "This stuff here's impossible."

Dirk's scanner clicked before he could go all "Listen to you" at Sal.

Dirk held up his fist. We stopped behind him. Beauty snarled. Dirk glanced her way.

"One," I said. "Maybe two."

That earned me a skeptical grunt from Dirk.

"Her skirmisher snarl," I told him. "We've been together for a while."

"Let's see." Dirk reached into one of his cargo pockets and pulled out some kind of pistol. He dropped a load into the barrel the size of a tomato paste can and fired down the tunnel what turned out to be a flare.

Two of them. Juveniles. Forty yards ahead. They bolted once they were illuminated. One went straight down the channel while the other ducked into some sort of recess in the lefthand wall.

"Here." Dirk handed Leigh Ann his sensor before he took off after them. He loaded a fresh round in his flare gun and handed that to me.

Beauty was desperate to get turned loose, but I hadn't seen Dirk battle yet. I didn't know how wild and free he'd get with his groper once the fighting started. I was worried he might be the kind of guy who wouldn't be careful of a dog.

We followed him but not at a headlong run. That was chiefly because of Clarice. She made his hold back a little.

"He gets himself into messes," she told us. "Got a way of blundering into stuff."

I guess if I had biceps as big around as my waist, I'd blunder into a thing or two as well.

Dirk picked the hollow on the left. It proved big enough to hold him, and he was gone into a cleft of the rock before we got down to the crevice.

"I'll go," Clarice said.

"We'll go," Dad told her. "Just stay here," he said to the rest of us. It wasn't like we were itching to probe further into the dark.

Toppy came over and stood close beside me. I could tell by the expression on her face it wasn't out of fear. It seemed to be just her way of telling me, "You're kind of my human, aren't you?" I wasn't yet sure it applied up out in the light.

We heard some chatter from in the crevice. I had one handset, and Dad had the other. Every now and then his mic got keyed as he passed through constrictions, and we'd get a bit of Dirk and Clarice sniping at each other.

"You'll never fit through there."

"Listen to you."

Then groaning and clanging and triumphant grunts when Dirk, with effort, did fit.

"What if he can't get out?" Aldo asked.

I looked around to take a wordless family vote. It was unanimous. "We'll leave him."

Clarice was ours. Dirk was of Carlsbad and meant hardly anything to us.

We ignored the first few clicks. Leigh Ann was swinging the sensor around, so we all appeared to decide the readings were surely coming off of us. We were milling around and twitching. We were moving. It had to be us.

The trouble came when Leigh Ann swung the thing around exclusively towards the deep dark before us. The contraption looked a bit like a radar gun. You could aim it like one anyway. We heard a few clicks and then a few more.

"Rats?" Monte asked.

Aldo told him, "Yeah," in a way that suggested Aldo was just hoping.

"Form up," I said.

We all did. That was the lone thing we'd gotten good at. More clicks. Then more and more. If that contraption had been a Geiger counter, we would have all been dead by then.

"Light them up," Brody told me.

Terry threw in as well. He said, "Yeah."

I aimed Dirk's pistol as close to the vaulted tunnel roof as I dared, and fired a flare into the dark.

We all immediately met with reason to kind of wish I hadn't. Alabastards were thick before us. Shoulder to shoulder. Wall to wall.

Leigh Ann tried to blame the dog at first. She hadn't snarled at all, but we could all see the flare smoke sucking back into the tunnel with some velocity.

"We're too far upwind," I said in Beauty's defense.

"What do we do?" Toppy asked me.

Aldo was getting swishy with his pole ax.

"Easy," I told him. "We pick a fight and we're finished."

Cracker Daddy was in among them. One gesture from him, and we'd be overrun.

Dad's mic got keyed. Clarice and Dirk were revisiting a catastrophic dinner party from their matrimonial past. There'd been aspic involved against Clarice's better judgment. It sounded like Dirk had been raised on aspic, so it had been a comfort thing.

"What's aspic?" Brody asked.

"Jell-o but worse," Leigh Ann explained. Then she asked me, "What are we doing?"

I handed Leigh Ann the walkie. "Walk them back a little."

I steeled myself with a deep breath and took a step Cracker Daddy's way. He waited and watched. He wasn't just big. He was serene for an alabastard. The rest of them were twitchy, always primed to scuttle and crab away or lurch and leap. They seemed cocked and dangerous. I'd never been so close to so many. One word from the big chief, and I'd be a pile of stripped bones on the tunnel floor.

I got as close as I dared, but he wasn't quite satisfied. Cracker Daddy motioned with a talon for me to ease in a little more. I tried to steer well clear of the minions in the front rank of the alabastard horde. A couple of them were wearing jackets, Members Only rubbish. One of the females – she was was an evil looking thing – had on an I Love New York! t-shirt.

Even Cracker Daddy had gone in for some adornment. He'd wrapped his greasy white neck with a scarf. Black Watch plaid, as best I could tell.

Cracker Daddy motioned. I obliged him and drew closer. So close that he finally reached over and switched off my light.

There's a kind of phosphorescence to alabastard flesh. Once you hit it with a light it tends to glow. So it was me and a clammy pale green battalion. The way they couldn't hold still left me always hearing claws scratching rock.

"Many." It sounded like Cracker Daddy had been working on his talking. He meant him and his horde. He took them in with a look.

"Yes, sir," I told him. I couldn't help myself. It's what I'd been raised to say.

I think he smiled. He widened his mouth anyway, and it was fairly unnerving. Alabastards have more teeth than people do, and they're shaped for butchery. Cracker Daddy had an impeccable set. No fractures. No sockets. No livestock bloodstains.

"Few," I think he said next. He had to mean me and mine.

He reached over and pressed a talon to my cheek. The tip was needle sharp. He could have laid me open with a twitch.

"Many."

I kept from telling him somehow, "Yeah, I got that already." Instead, I nodded. "Many," I told him back.

Cracker Daddy appeared to believe that we had come to an understanding. I wasn't so sure. They were many all right, but we had reinforcements we hadn't even alerted yet. I listened to the alabastard horde shift and make their sinusy noises.

I jabbed my thumb over my shoulder in the direction of up and out.

Cracker Daddy grunted.

I took that as permission to go. I soaked in the horde one last time. It was like looking out on an ocean of jellyfish. Their luminescence was fading a bit, but they still gave off a soft, seafoam glow.

I switched on my lamp and headed in the direction of the world. I could hear voices and clattering from the crevice that Dirk had led Clarice and Dad into. They were easing their way back out and quarreling about it as they came. It even sounded like Dad was pitching in like he'd had enough of Dirk as well.

I waited for them to reach the tunnel while I sifted through my options and decided what I had to do. Dad popped out first. Clarice followed shortly in conversation (I'll call it) with Dirk.

When Dirk saw me, he pointed at the crevice and said, "Nothing."

I gestured towards the deep dark and told him, "Something," back.

We found the others up at the archway that led to the ladder and the hatch. I went over to Toppy and kissed her full on the mouth.

She let me. She kissed back. She told me presently, "Yikes."

2

"One more time."

I couldn't even be troubled to snort. By then Dirk had one-more-timed me more times than I could count. I dropped a word occasionally, added one or two sometimes, but the gist was always exactly the same. We were monumentally screwed.

We'd retired to the pizza place under the Brooklyn Bridge. If you got the right table, the long one against the east wall, you could see a bit of the harbor. I was watching a tiny blue police boat on the chop.

I couldn't muster much of an appetite. I preferred just sitting with my back to the wall, framed snapshots of Frank Sinatra hanging all around me, while I repeated the catechism for Dirk and held tightly to Toppy's hand.

Beauty was tied to a signpost outside. One of the little brown pizza guys — probably Honduran — had carried her out a bowl of water and some cheesy pizza crust.

Marcy had joined us. I'd been all for keeping the trouble we faced away from Sal and his clan since it sounded so dire and unsolvable. If I were them, I'd have panicked and quit. Run up to Riverdale and hoped for the best. Maybe headed to Naples or something. That got me wondering if this was some worldwide alabastard movement or just a local thing.

"Are there caves all over?" I asked Dirk.

"All over where?"

"The world."

"I'm not sanctioned on that," he told me. "I'm domestic."

Clarice got interested. "What the hell does that mean?"

Dirk knew her well enough not to waste his time holding out and dodging. "It means there are caves all over, and I can't talk about it."

"What are you waiting for?" she asked him. "An emergency?"

Clarice was scary hard on guys. I'd never really noticed before. Sure she snapped at Dad every now and then, and for the first three or four hours of every day she had all the charm of something that had crawled out from under a bridge. But judging by what Dirk was going through, I had to guess Dad was getting a tender version of Clarice. She didn't allow her ex any room at all to slip and dodge. She was intense and focused on the guy, like a pilot fish from hell.

"It's a worldwide network," Dirk said.

"The caves?" Dad ask.

Dirk was beyond not sanctioned for that. He just plain didn't know. "The Legion," he said. "We've got chapters all over."

"So CFs all over too?" I asked him.

He nodded.

"Are they all coming up?" Clarice wanted to know.

"We're getting reports," Dirk said.

"Ok, look." Marcy had been mercifully quiet until then. "Maybe we can flood them out or something."

"We're considering all options," Dirk said.

"Drop the Carlsbadese," Clarice snapped. "What are we going to do, aside from die?"

"Die?" Terry and Brody chimed in together.

"She's kidding," Dad told them.

"Grown up table," Clarice said. With that, she sent Brody and Terry out to take Beauty for a walk.

"Has Carlsbad got a plan?" Dad asked.

"Gas or something," Dirk said.

"Have you tried negotiating?" Sal wanted to know.

"With them?" Dirk was sneering.

"Cracker Daddy has the sense for it," Dad told him. He glanced my way.

I nodded. I told Dirk, "He does."

"Ok, look." That was as far as Marcy got. She was too flummoxed and undone and rattled to have much idea what to say.

Hers was the prevailing feeling in fact. Even Clarice was a little stymied.

"How long have you guys been getting . . . reports?" she asked Dirk.

He shrugged. "A few months. Nothing conclusive"

"Gas or something?" Dad said.

"Incendiaries," Dirk told us. "That and a nerve agent together. That's the plan."

"Whose plan?" Clarice asked.

"They've made overtures to D.C.," Dirk informed us. "Regular army and all that?"

"Civilians know?" Dad couldn't believe it.

Dirk nodded. "Classified," he said.

"How far along?" Clarice asked.

"Like I said. Overtures."

That didn't sound far along at all. Still monumentally screwed, I figured.

"If they could just boil out and get us," Dirk said, "don't you think they'd have done it already."

"All right, smart guy," Clarice started in, "what exactly is holding them back?"

"Carlsbad's got a theory." Dirk paused long enough to pick all of the mushrooms off his slice. "They've been testing it out in the lab."

I'd heard all about the lab from Jo Jo. He'd made it sound like a glorified kennel where captured alabastards were kept in cages and boxes made of clawed up plexiglass.

"You wouldn't believe the smell," Jo Jo had told me. "Like a bucket of worms but with maybe a mackerel or two down in the bottom."

We all had to wait while Dirk filled his pie hole. Clarice, of course, was a lot less patient than the rest of us proved to be.

"Are you sanctioned for pizza?"

Dirk tossed his crust in a way Clarice didn't care for. If Dad hadn't grabbed her, there would surely have been a fight.

"Man, you people," Monte said. Life must have been different in suburban New Jersey.

"You know they used to be married, right?" Leigh Ann asked Sal's crew as she wagged a finger in the general direction of Clarice and Dirk.

That explained quite a lot to the New York clan. Sal spoke for his entire family when he said, "Oh."

Dirk claimed to have a special Carlsbad communicator. It turned out to be a Nokia phone with the Legion switchboard number programmed in. No data. Not even unlimited minutes, and the phone was probably five years out of date. That was Carlsbad all over. Low tech to the end.

"Let me have a consult," Dirk said, as he pulled out his communicator. He decided to have it down at the ferry landing park, and we all walked there with him. Brody and Terry had tied Beauty to one of the benches so they'd be free to climb over the rail and onto the rocks by the harbor without her. Dad looked primed to get all fatherly with them, warn them of the dangers of scrabbling around by the water, but he couldn't seem to locate the energy for it and so told them nothing instead.

Sal sure didn't seem to care if Terry fell into the harbor. His world had been fine until we showed up. A house in leafy Riverdale. A wife fifteen years his junior. Tenants shoving money his way every month and all of it off the books.

Sal parked on the bench where Beauty was tied. He ruffled her fur. He shook his head.

"Didn't see this coming," he said by way of a general announcement.

"Feels like some kind of dream," Marcy told him. She sat beside Sal and took his hand.

I have to say, the immediate threat of death by swarming alabastards was serving to make us all a lot less formal than we might have been. If you had an opinion, you volunteered it. An affection, you declared it. A complaint, you delivered it without bothering to dress it up. It was all refreshing really except for the dying in bloody pieces part.

It was a warm, sunny afternoon in the ferry landing park, and all we all tried to eavesdrop on Dirk, especially once he turned away and cupped his phone to keep us from it.

"Yes sir, a substantial threat," we heard him say. "Likelihood of encroachment."

"Who's he talking to?" Aldo wanted to know.

"Bosses," Leigh Ann told him. "In New Mexico."

"Why are they out there?"

"You never told them about Carlsbad?" Clarice asked Sal.

He shrugged and shook his head.

"So you've been like this since they were babies?"

"Before," Sal confessed. "My pops never made me go under. Didn't see the point. I mean look at all the places they can come out."

That was the problem right there. The thing that must have drawn the master swarm to New York. The area was shot through both with tunnels and holes for coming topside. Subway stations. Construction sites. Basements in high rises. Con Ed access shafts. Water traces and steam tunnels. Almost too many outlets to count.

It was hopeless. More holes than we could plug. Too many alabastards to herd. If Carlsbad didn't have some remedy in mind, we'd either have to stay and perish or bug out like cowards and leave ten million savory civilians behind.

"Megaswarm, yes sir. That's confirmed."

Dirk caught us all leaning in and so retreated across the grass.

"Ok, look," Marcy started in. She pointed at Dirk as she asked of Clarice, "What did your people think of him?"

"My people?"

"You weren't hatched, right?"

It was the mood of the day. Sheer liberation. I laid it off to the threat in the air. Marcy was getting lippy with Clarice.

"My people," Clarice started in, "gave me up."

"Low Lords?" Dad asked her. This was clearly new to him as well.

Clarice nodded. "And Low Lords adopted me. They've got kind of a baby racket going."

"They do?" I'd never heard of this before.

"Everybody needs a clan," Clarice said. "Some people need a little help."

"So the people that adopted you . . ." Marcy wasn't going to quit. "What did they think of him?"

"Not much, and that was probably at least half of the attraction. If they didn't like it, I always liked it more."

"Delivered how?" we all heard Dirk say into his Nokia. "But won't it drift up into the subway?" He noticed us listening in and turned away.

"He's so big," Marcy said. It came out half admiring, half mortified.

"Except for the bit between his ears," Clarice told her as they both studied Dirk from behind. "No free weights for that."

"Tell me about it," Marcy said.

Sal was paying attention enough to know to chime in with, "Hey!"

This was about as close to an authentic social gathering I'd ever known in my life. We'd mostly stuck with the clan and, having Grady around, meant readings from The Great Book. We never just sat outside, kicked back and talked, and there we were doing just that with Sal and them underneath the Brooklyn Bridge in the ferry landing park.

We could hear traffic on the motorway overhead. The roar of it and the car tires rattling the metal seams. There were gulls in the air. Boats on the harbor. Unhappy motorists jammed up on the BQE. We could hear the car horns, the pecked toots and extended salvos.

"Why are they coming out now?" Aldo was the one who asked it, but it was the question on all of our minds. After decades, centuries even, why now?

Dad had an idea. He aired it for us. "Now they've got a king."

That had crossed my mind, though I'd not bothered to refine it. I'd long thought of alabastards as herd animals. Yes, they had talons and menacing teeth, but you could drive them before you if you showed enough nerve and steel. They weren't sheep exactly, but they weren't far off. Closer to livestock than to men. Then Cracker Daddy showed up to lead them, to give them something they could aim for.

"Why don't we just kill him and see what happens?" Monte suggested.

"You want to do it?" Clarice asked him.

"Ok, look," Marcy chimed in. "No."

"What would happen?" Dad asked, chiefly to Clarice I guess.

Her best guess was, “Mayhem probably. He must have lieutenants by now.”

“Yes, sir. I will,” Dirk said into his phone as he came back to us from halfway across the park. “We’ll be there. Right.” With that, Dirk shoved into his Nokia into its special cargo pocket. “Carlsbad’s on it,” he said.

“On it how?” Clarice asked him.

“They’re sending an ordinance team to draw up a plan.” Dirk paused and then added proudly, “They’re coming on the train. Get here day after tomorrow.” In legion terms, that was little short of supersonic.

We all ended up in the lobby of the Brooklyn Marriott, the one near Borough Hall, where Dirk paid cash from a ratty roll in his pocket to get the entire ordinance team one room at the corporate rate for two nights.

A bell hop or concierge — some guy in a short jacket with piping — came over to tell us they weren’t pet-friendly.

I asked Beauty to sit. She was impeccable about it.

“Service dog,” I told him.

“What’s your complaint?”

That was easy enough. “I’m depressed.”

3

We stayed out of the deep dark and passed our wait time riding around the city on the subway. We'd split up into crews so we could cover all the lines. The idea was to familiarize ourselves with the entire system and check the stations to see if CFs were bold enough to hang about. Then we'd report to the ordinance crew once they'd shown up in the city.

I went with Toppy and Brody. We knocked around like we were a family unit, a couple keen on each other with a tadpole tagging along. It wasn't much of a stretch since that's kind of what we were. Me and Toppy got to snuggle up on the IRT and take turns telling Brody to leave us alone.

We didn't see any alabastards for that first few days, though we did see a guy who could play a bamboo pan flute and a guitar both at the same time. We saw more tattoos than you'd probably run across on the average aircraft carrier. Watched a pickpocket get tackled and kicked half to death by irate, enthusiastic civilians. We sat through a screaming fight between a woman and her husband. They got on at Spring Street, yelled for a while, reconciled and were lip locked by Grand Central.

We ate off a cart at Union Square. It was farmer's market day, so we wandered through and took in all the produce. The people in the city proved to be so diverse and varied, that I couldn't be sure I'd be able to pick out a CF on the fly.

Toppy thought she saw one on Broadway. We were heading for the station at 23rd. It turned out to be an ancient lady in a trench coat and rain bonnet — one of those plastic accordion-fold things people rarely wear anymore.

One morning we decided to ride the six, the local, up to 125th Street and then take the express all the way back down into Brooklyn. We planned to exit the train at every station along the way just to check the access to any crack or recess that might look deep-dark bound. That was what we intended, but it didn't quite work out that way.

I don't know where he got on, but I didn't see him until we were almost to 96th street. He was one car ahead and looked pretty much like a regular guy from the back. Posture-wise anyway. He was nothing like a Cumberland CF — stunted and bent and crabbing around instead of coming at anything straight. He was taller and straighter even than any Virginia alabastard I'd seen, except maybe for Cracker Daddy, who must have been serving as a standard for them. A model. An ideal. This one was forcing his shoulders and his chin up the way I'd noticed Cracker Daddy did.

"What?" Toppy asked me. She saw me looking.

"Through there." I pointed. "Red plaid."

His back was to us. His collar was up.

Toppy shrugged. "Some guy."

Then he shifted, and we got him in profile. He was wearing wrap-around sunglasses and had his cap pulled as low as it would go. The skin on his face was pale and drawn tight. In the lights from the subway car, I could see his near cheek was slick and glistening.

"Stay with Brody, ok?"

Toppy nodded.

I worked around to get a peek at that CFs chin. They can't do an awful lot about their angular, reptile heads. If people in the subway ever truly looked at anybody, they would have long since backed away from that alabastard strap hanger by then, but it was a city of all sorts and types from every corner of the planet. People probably just glanced — the way New Yorkers do — and figured that boy had come from some far-flung place where a guy with the head of a big hairless bat was pretty much the norm.

I tried to pass between cars, but our end door was jammed, so I waited for the 96th Street station and got off and back on a car ahead. He had his back against the center door. His head down. Most of his face was shielded by his hat brim. He twitched the way his kind tend to when they're coiled and anxious. I had to imagine he'd not known subway lights would be so clinical and bright.

A guy beside him was drinking a tallboy. His can was in a paper sack. He was Arab or something and seemed intent on striking up a conversation.

He said to the CF alongside him, "Hey man, hey man, hey man."

I wondered if this one could talk a little as well. He opted instead for the usual sinusy grunt. That alabastard racket in a subway car sent a chill right through me. It was a noise for the deep dark only, where I figured it should stay.

The train stopped at 103rd Street. A few people got off. Nobody got on.

"Hey man, hey man."

Still nothing. Beer guy was getting a touch indignant. He appeared to be accustomed to having people answer him back.

I was holding to a pole beside a woman with the pinkest fingernail polish I'd ever seen. I swung my shoulder bag around, lifted the flap, and reached inside. I'd gotten to the point where I could nock an arrow blind.

Beer guy jabbed that CF a couple of times with his elbow. "Hey man."

That earned him a sidelong alabastard look.

"You get burned or something?"

That was the thing about people in the city. I'd noticed it from the first. They either said nothing to you or asked you questions they should have kept to themselves.

That alabastard might not have been chatty, but he appeared to understand well enough. He shook his head.

"Acid, right?" Beer guy took a sip. That CF went back to watching the floor of the car. "Hey man, hey man." The elbow again.

When that alabastard raised his head this time, that's when his eyes caught mine.

They know, some way or another. I can't say how exactly, but he tuned in straightaway to precisely what I was just like I'd tuned into him. I still can't say if he panicked or just decided, "What the hell." All I know is he turned trifling nothing into gory something in an instant.

The beer guy got it. That alabastard (his hat read Def Yo! in purple on black) extended his talons. One sweep down the front of beer guy's torso, and he was laid open. Four furrows. Those claws were so sharp and the action so sure that beer guy had to look down and see the damage before he felt it at all.

That CF took off. He hit the end door, jerked it open and passed through to the next car up. I pulled out my ripper and chased him. That was my job after all.

I passed through to the next car up. That CF had cleared it already, and here I came with a ripper. That put everybody in a state. I got met by a blend of shrinking and yelling. People turned their backs and got small, though a few were loudly unhappy about it.

I closed on that beast four cars ahead, reached the car that alabastard was in just as the train doors opened. He darted out onto the platform, and I followed hard behind him.

"Move!"

People just looked at me like a guy running full out through the station with a crossbow might have been an inconvenience but wasn't all that queer a thing. I chased that CF up and over to the downtown platform. I got a clear view of him halfway down the stairs and put a bolt in his back.

My tips are all dipped in bleach and lacquer. I read about it in one of the quarterlies. It's supposed to work like poison on CFs, corrosive and straightaway. This one didn't really get the chance. That alabastard reached around and gouged the bolt out with his talons. A plug of meat and skin came with it. He dropped the whole business on the platform. It hit the slab with a splat.

He didn't even slow down to do it. Aside from pausing to shoot, I'd kept running as well.

That beast jumped down onto the tracks where the platform ran out, and I was fairly determined to follow him and finish him off. I wasn't really focused on how foolish that might be. Risking my neck for a lone CF when there were thousands massing in the deep dark. Knocking those beasts off one at a time wasn't likely to help awfully much.

So I was reconsidering at full tilt as the platform was quickly running out, but the decision got made for me by a couple of transit cops.

I heard one of them tell me, "Freeze!" as his partner fired his taser darts.

I froze all right. I toppled over. I broke my fall primarily with my nose.

By the time I came to, I'd collected a crowd. Civilians, mostly black, were gathered around me and grinning down. The cops had cuffed a white guy for once, and they were all pretty chuffed about it.

One of the transit cops — the young one who looked like an actuary — was going through my satchel. There was nothing to find in there but ripper bolts. He pulled out a half dozen in his fist and showed them to his partner — a fat guy whose uniform was linty and wrinkled. He was examining my ripper until he noticed I'd woken up.

"What's all this?" he asked me.

We were not, as Low Lords, supposed to elaborate or explain. It wasn't in The Great Book proper, but it was in the appendix twice and even figured into one of the mottos

Carlsbad featured on the quarterly. Security in Silence, Strength in Duty, Safety in Vigilance. It usually ran just under the address sticker, unless it got covered up. I didn't know what it all meant exactly beyond probably, "Hey man, shut up."

Actuary cop wrestled me into a sitting position, put my back against the wall. His partner pointed to the chunk of alabastard skin and flesh with one of my arrows in it.

"Hit something?"

Security in Silence.

He kicked the bottom of one of my shoes. Not violently but sharply enough to let me know he meant business.

"Who were you chasing with this?" He showed me my ripper.

"Might be one of those games," his partner volunteered.

"Who?" fat cop asked me. Then he kicked my shoe again.

Actuary cop walked me up to the street and handed me over to regular topside patrolmen. They weren't interested in anything I might have to tell them. They were taking me to the precinct house and talked about the anatomy of the driver's girlfriend's sister along the way.

I got fingerprinted in a grimy squad room and then shoved in a cell for a while. They didn't offer to let me call anybody. They didn't ask me any questions.

After a couple of hours in a holding cell with six or eight grimy civilians, who seemed less in withdrawal from freedom than cigarettes and alcohol, I got called out by the warder.

He pointed. "You," he said.

He walked me to a grubby room with a steel table, a trash bucket laying on its side. I got handcuffed to a U-bolt fixed to the table top and left to sit for a quarter hour.

Even Uncle Grady, who was a stickler for eventualities and procedures, hadn't ever advised any of us on what to do if we got arrested. In Cumberland and in Virginia, that hadn't seemed much of a threat. I knew I'd sworn an oath as a Low Lord, and I was well acquainted in practice with the subterranean parts of that. I didn't know much, however, about my topside obligations.

So let's say I was unresolved when the guy I would come to know as Les stepped into that room and joined me. He was lean and neat. His tie knot was shoved full up. His shoes were proper oxfords and shiny. He smelled slightly of sandalwood or something like it with no burly tobacco back note. His holster was empty. His badge was gold.

"Now," he said as he pulled out the chair across from me and sat. He wore a wristwatch that looked old enough to have been his father's. A gold wedding band that he kept worrying with his thumb.

He'd brought a stiff green folder in with him. He opened it on the table. There was paperwork on top and what looked like photographs underneath. He'd carried my ripper and my bolts in as well. They were in evidence bags.

"Want to tell me what you were doing?" He waited.

I sat and looked at my hands.

"Ok." He pulled a pen out of his shirt pocket and ticked a box on a form.

"Detective Lester Hayden." He offered his hand. I couldn't imagine I was barred by oath from shaking it, so I did. "People call me Les."

I just sat.

"Got a name?"

I tried to be uncooperative while looking genial and polite.

"You can talk, right?"

I nodded.

"Huh?"

"Yes," I said.

"There we go." He ticked another box. "Let's save the name for later." He cast an eye on my ripper. "Tell me about this stuff."

That wasn't going to happen.

"We get pistols, knives, like that. Don't see too many bows and arrows in the subway."

I squirmed. Bows and arrows? I couldn't help but want to correct him. A ripper was a compact and excellent battle weapon. The tackle and pulleys produced a high-velocity discharge. The cocking was quick and simple. The aim was true. Bows and arrows?

He watched me shift, listened to my restraints rattle. "So?"

Nothing.

"Ok. Me first."

Les slid my way a photograph of the plug of flesh with my arrow in it.

I did him the courtesy of looking. It was, sure enough, a chunk of seepy alabastard flesh.

"Funny thing. Looks like antifreeze."

It did a little. Not blood exactly but more of a green meat bath. They don't have much in the way of veins.

"The guy in the subway's going to make it, but he was sliced up pretty good. Everybody says he did it with his . . . claws."

I just sat and looked at Les.

He tapped the photo of the chunk of alabastard flesh. "DNA's going to come back with a bit of crocodile in it."

That was something I hadn't expected. Low Lords weren't much on forensics. Certainly little beyond the toxins we'd need to destroy the sons of guns. It didn't matter if they were part crocodile, though it proved idly interesting to me.

"How do you think I know that?"

I didn't offer an opinion.

He laid another photograph before me. "Because we found his brother or something."

It was a picture of the CF I'd knocked off the promenade in Brooklyn. Somebody was holding a sheet up in the roadway so the photographer could get a decent snap.

"Him we tested." Detective Hayden fiddled with his watch. Thumbed his ring. "I say him, but I don't know. Lab couldn't be sure." He shrugged. "I guess that's what part crocodile will get you."

He shoved another photograph across the table. An autopsy shot of the dead Brooklyn CF laid open. There were ducts and parts and organs that would have scared most pathologists half to death.

"Guys in the lab, actual doctors, don't know what the hell it is."

I treated Detective Hayden to my best blank gaze.

"Now here you are chasing one on the Lex."

I was under the impression I was due a phone call or a diet Pepsi or something, but I felt like I was making decent work being silent and didn't want to spoil that by chiming in.

"You know what these things are, don't you?"

Nothing from me, not even a twitch.

"Mind if I swab you?" He pulled a cue tip in a tube from his trouser pocket. It had a long enough handle to make me worry where he'd end up sticking it. I was relieved when he told me, "Open your mouth."

That was fine with me. They were sure to discover I was just some regular earthling, an authentic human kid.

He stuck the thing in my mouth and swabbed. Into the tube it went and then out the door. I couldn't reach the file or I would have rifled through it. The Detective Hayden who came back demonstrated far less patience with me.

"How old are you?"

I didn't care to say.

"Have you got family here?"

That seemed worth nodding about.

"Why don't you call them. Preferably one that talks."

He pulled his iPhone out of his pocket and offered it to me. I only knew one number. I punched it in on the keypad and then handed the phone back to him. I was onto his tricks. Let him do the talking.

Toppy answered. I could hear her.

"This is Detective Les Hayden. I'm calling from the 25th Precinct, Manhattan. Who am I speaking with please."

Toppy told him.

"We have a young man in custody. He dialed your number."

That put it right in Toppy's lap, and she saw to it from there.

Sal brought Dad and Clarice uptown in his panel truck. They must have decided Dirk would be a liability. I still hadn't said anything to anybody. No one had offered a diet Pepsi. They'd moved me to a bigger room where the three adults could join me. Detective Hayden brought his partner in with him. A guy named Tony who admired his fingernails for a while.

"Tell me you talk," was the first thing Les said.

"Yeah," Dad told him, "we do."

"Refreshing." Les opened his file. "Got some questions for you."

It was a delicate interview and required a fair number of sidebars and thorny exchanges between Dad and Clarice. Sal some too.

"Hell, bring them in on it," was Sal's standing opinion, but then Sal had all but forgotten (if he ever knew) what being a Low Lord meant.

Dad had placed a call to Uncle Grady who'd piled on the brand of poor advice that you can only give in earnest if you're working out of Carlsbad. They cleared their caverns of CFs years ago to save them the aggravation of running a bureaucracy and fending off swarm ups both at once. So they were routinely dictating policy and consulting on problems that had come to be largely theoretical for them.

Yes, there was trouble across the land (under the land anyway) but not anywhere they could see it regular and up close. I think Uncle Grady told Dad to talk around the details. That was going to be a challenge, given the carcasses the cops had collected.

"This is your son?" Les asked, mostly to Clarice.

She pointed at Dad. "His."

"Residents? Tourists? What?"

"Got a place in Brooklyn," Dad told Les. "Been here a little while."

"The boy probably wants a soda or something," Les told his partner. Tony knew what that meant. He left the room and stayed gone a while. He never actually brought back a soda.

Les gathered his paperwork, his forensic photos. He stacked them neatly and shoved them into the stiff, green folder. Left it to lay on the tabletop. He intertwined his fingers, leaned forward and rested on his elbows.

"I know you know what's going on," he said to Dad. "I need to know about it too."

Sal leaned towards Dad and Clarice and said, "Tell him," in a hissed whisper.

Les waited. No revelation ensued.

"This is not going to end well," Les said. "Not for any of you." He took us all in with a panoramic glance. "Some cop'll see a kid with a crossbow and feel free to put him down."

"I appreciate the advice," Dad said.

"What advice? I'm telling you your kid's going to end up dead chasing some crocodile man through my city." Les thumbed his ring. Adjusted his watch. "Does that sound like advice to you?"

"They can't tell you," Sal piped in. "They're sworn and all."

"So are you," Clarice snapped at Sal.

"Sworn?" Les said. "You guys in a club or something?"

Sal very nearly nodded until the point of Clarice's elbow collided with his ribs. He just grunted instead.

"I could charge him," Les said of me. "Ought to charge him."

"Wish you wouldn't," Dad managed.

"Then give me something."

Dad and Clarice consulted with glances.

Dad told Clarice, "Go on."

He knew like I did that she'd be stingy. Clarice weighed her options before she spoke.

"Not a club exactly," she said to Les. "More of a calling. An order."

"Like the priesthood?"

"A little."

"Have you got bosses?"

Clarice nodded.

"Is this federal?"

That was the out she was looking for. She nodded again.

"Who can confirm?"

Clarice let Dad have that one. He brought out his bulging, sweat-rotted wallet and fished around in it until he'd found what I saw to be one of Jo Jo's cards. It was impressive, as business cards go, even Dad's bent and abused one. It had the embossed Carlsbad logo — a triangle in a circle with the stylized head of a bat.

He handed the card to Detective Hayden who gave it an exhaustive once over before he pulled out his phone and dialed.

"Four seven nine eight," Dad told him.

Once prompted, Les repeated the numbers into his phone. That connected him with Jo Jo. We could hear the tinny version of Jo Jo through Les's earpiece.

"Detective Les Hayden, NYPD. We picked up one of your . . . operatives . . . on a weapons charge."

A chirp from Jo Jo.

"Does he have a name?" Les asked Dad, pointing at me.

"Mack," I said.

"It speaks." Les said, "Mack," to Jo Jo, and my cousin did what he'd been trained to do. They may not be much in the way of warriors at Carlsbad, but they're accomplished scammers and prevaricators. Civilian troubles all get pointed their way, and they're reliably slick with a response.

Jo Jo went on at some length. It must have been all the usual deep cover, deniability stuff. Les didn't look impressed exactly, but he let himself be persuaded. Not to his core but enough to decide he'd put me back out in the world.

Once he'd hung up from Jo Jo, Detective Hayden unlocked my cuffs. I imagine he'd left them on chiefly to rattle Dad and Clarice and Sal. He reached in his front shirt pocket and pulled out a stack of business cards. Not bent. Not sweated up. Pristine. He handed one to each of us.

"One of you'll get picked up again. Maybe all of you together. Call me." He shook his phone at us. "I know earwash when I hear it."

We all mumbled and nodded.

"I guess you'll need this." Les shoved my bagged ripper across the table.

He walked us out. We passed his partner, Tony, sitting at his desk considering his nails. He gave us a good riddance look as Les squired us towards the precinct house doors.

Out on 119th Street, Les said, "I can probably help, you know?"

Tight smiles from Dad and Clarice. That's all.

Les was still standing on the sidewalk watching us as we turned the corner onto Lexington Avenue.

4

We met the ordinance team at Penn Station that very evening. Dirk made us all dress to do it. Not dress dress but business casual. The sort of stuff no cave crawler would wear. I don't know why we bothered since they needed us mostly just to haul equipment.

The ordinance team was passing as two couples on a lark. They'd clearly been closeted too long at Carlsbad since they came off the train looking chiefly like Mennonites on the prowl.

Dirk knew both the guys and one of the girls.

"We had a thing," he told Clarice.

He seemed to be fishing for a jealous response, but Clarice just shrugged and said, "Whatever."

Marcy was wearing some kind of running suit with rhinestone hummingbirds on it, some of them perched on rhinestone flowers. She clashed powerfully with the ordinance team who'd gone in for frontier plain.

They all had undercover names. Doug and Bob. Fay and Mary. It hardly mattered what we called them since they'd only talk to Dirk. Carlsbad was funny that way. A club within a club. We were the functionaries. The help. We were nothing without their direction, which they only provided grudgingly while they kept pretending they'd rather do stuff themselves.

The more I saw Dirk around them, the more I wondered if he wouldn't turn out to be just one of them as well. A guy with a ripper in one hand and a groper in the other who was so far removed from battle that he hardly knew what to do.

We subwayed to Brooklyn with all the team's gear. You'd have thought they were immigrating. It was packed into musty steamer trunks and battered suitcases. Those four didn't blink at the fact that Dirk had rented them one hotel room. They even seemed to think the Marriott was posher than their usual digs. We all piled in with the gear, and the one called Bob or Doug told Dirk how they planned to proceed so he could pass it onto us.

Dirk even started explaining a little before Clarice said, "We heard."

Then she went all Clarice on the four of them. "Hey, Doug/ Bob — you and yours got something to say, you say it to everybody."

Doug/Bob looked to Dirk for clarification or something. Dirk was well enough versed in Clarice to know to tell him, "That's what I'd do."

So they talked to us after that but like we were sanatorium patients. The guys let the ladies explain their equipment to us as they went around to check it, unlatching the suitcases and opening the trunks.

That stuff wouldn't have been out of place at the Normandy invasion. Some of the consoles even had tubes in them. There were rubber bellows. Copper reducers. Fay/Mary tended to tell us what each item did by reading the faceplate tags.

So when they opened, for instance, the valise containing a brown metal box with three gauges and two dials marked Vitalink Thermobarometer, the strawberry blonde told us, "This is a thermobarometer."

The other one, the brunette, added, "Vitalink's in Indiana."

Clarice made her predetonation noise.

Marcy said, "Ok, look."

They had a lot of stuff but none of it seemed ordinance related exactly. They were the ordinance team after all.

"What are you hoping to find out," Dad asked. "This trip anyway?"

"It's technical," Doug/Bob told him.

"Try us." That from Aldo. He had his Dad's savvy and, lucky for us, only his mother's green eyes.

"You're talking about an infestation, right?" It was Bob/Doug doing the asking.

We could agree to that, even down to Dirk. We all nodded at Bob/Doug.

"So we need reach and intensity. Full saturation. High toxicity but limited duration."

"The most you've killed at once? " Clarice asked.

"Need to know," Fay/Mary said dead quick, almost by reflex. I couldn't help but get the idea that was the ordinance team's default.

"We do need to know," Sal told them. "Topside around here is like sitting on a colander turned upside down. A lot of ways out. An awful lot of holes."

"If we gas the deep dark," Dad said, "It's coming out all over."

"That's why we're here," Doug/Bob allowed. "Big job. Weird terrain. Got to do some tests."

The ordinance team made plain that they wouldn't have wanted us with them if they'd not needed sherpas to carry their precious gear into the deep dark. Sal supplied two hand trucks and the sort of rolling cart with over inflated tires that people use to haul their crap to the beach.

Fay/Mary was in charge of the packing, which meant every thirty seconds or so she'd snap at one of us, "No!"

They started taking readings topside, well before we'd even reached the culvert. Air gasses. Humidity. Ambient temperature. They were particularly keen on the local yield (they called it) of auto exhaust.

"Diesel sweetened," Doug/Bob announced significantly. His teammates made appreciative noises.

We had to roust a homeless lady and her belongings from the culvert. There wasn't much choice. We could hardly hope to get the gear down the carriage house ladder, but to move that lady we all had to handle her goods — old shopping bags full of nasty, tattered clothes, rubbishy treasures, take-out containers of cast-off food.

She caterwauled and threatened us. Dirk gave her dollar bills until she stopped. The ordinance team just stood and watched and looked a bit queer at it. They were all wearing proper respirators by then.

"Do we need those?" Clarice asked.

Doug/Bob shrugged and told her through his filter canisters, "Probably not."

They did have super duper head lamps. Some sort of halogen we couldn't find off the shelf and weren't about to pay Carlsbad prices out of the catalog to get. They were bright and the beams were broad.

"How many hours you get out of one?" I asked just generally of the team.

One of the ladies appeared to give the question some thought before she told me, "Move."

Between our clan and Sal's, we'd all about reached Clarice's pitch of animosity by the time we'd descended through the main tunnel, with its high vaulted ceiling and long gentle arc, and had gained the breezy transit that qualified as legitimate deep dark. No rats. No bums. No draft-blown human litter. Nothing but us and alabastards and inky black where our lamps couldn't reach.

They all had sensors out and equipment switched on. We'd brought a car battery down with us on the cart, and it was harnessed and rigged to run everything they needed. They were looking for movement. Testing the air. Reading the temperature of the tunnel down to fractions of degrees.

"Let's go dark," Doug/Bob said. The ordinance team all put on goggles.

Going dark for us truly meant going dark. Dirk didn't have goggles, but he had his gun that measured body temperature and registered wayward movement. The rest of us just had our gropers and our imaginations along with the most reliable sensor of all in the form of a half-breed collie somebody had tossed out of a car.

One of the Fay/Marys was wearing elaborate earphones that were plugged into what looked like a directional mic on a telescoping pole. She had a knob on one of her earpieces that she kept cranking up and cranking down.

"Two o'clock," she said. "Probably fifty yards."

The rest of the team oriented their sensors. We could hear them all shifting around. Some of their gauges were dimly illuminated, but all was dark beyond two feet.

"I've got six," Dirk said. "No eight. Coming out of a crease, maybe ten o'clock.

Clarice and I ratcheted back our ripper strings at precisely the same moment. We eased up to put ourselves just ahead of and flanking the entire crew so we wouldn't put a bolt in the flesh of anybody who wasn't white and clammy and savage.

"I'm getting CO2 nil," Doug/Bob announced. "It's like scuba air down here."

"Twenty plus," Dirk said. "Thirty yards dead on."

"Lights?" Dad asked.

"Hold off." That from Fay/Mary.

"I've got the males at fifty-five degrees. The females at fifty-seven."

"See if that holds. That's a full two down." That from the Doug/Bobs talking to themselves.

Even staring into the dark and seeing the usual phantoms and floaters, I left space in my brain to soak in their chatter and think about what they were saying. The air in the deep dark was far less contaminated than they'd expected and the core alabastard temperature was lower than they'd seen before.

"Accelerating," Dirk announced.

"Screw it," Dad said and switch on his light.

The rest of us did too, and there they were, maybe two dozen altogether coming on us at a jog that was graduating to a run. There was no scrabbling to it at all and hardly any sinusy snorting. As they closed, their claws extended. They all showed us their tearing teeth.

"Throat," Clarice said by way of reminder.

She'd been concerned from the start that I was overly showy with my shots. I could bury a bolt in an alabastard's eye from forty yards in good conditions, but the sure kill was the hollow in the neck. Dead center, halfway down.

She let fly and dropped a male. An adult with some seasoning, by the looks of him. Clarice was always strategic enough to get the warriors first. After that, you can hit the gray tufts and hope the juveniles will lose heart and run off.

I picked out my target. Another warrior. He shifted and crabbed a little as I fired, so the bolt went through his cheek instead. He snarled and wailed and kept on coming.

"Close off!" Dirk barked at us as the ordinance team drew well back behind us all.

They were nerds at bottom. You could see it all in that moment. The prowess was show, technical savvy married to sneering condescension. Once the fighting started, the ordinance team was about as useful as Jo Jo in a cave.

I heard the reassuring twange and ring of groper steel as Dad and Leigh Ann and Brody all banged their blades on the stone tunnel floor. That was an old custom Granddaddy Hoyt had insisted we observe.

"Give them a scare," he'd always said, "and get yourselves stirred up."

Aldo imitated Leigh Ann. He banged his blade too, and it sang.

Me and Clarice kept nocking and firing. We put down seven alabastards between us. The one I'd hit in the cheek closed on me hard. I buried a second bolt center shot torso, but he kept coming anyway. I had a flash of understanding as he piled in on me — that's what happens when you miss the soft spot halfway down the neck.

I'd long since lost my fear of alabastards. Sure there was anxiety and no little bit of dread. I knew my scratches would get infected. If I got bit, that was sure to go septic. But I was confident and capable with my ripper and my spike. I had my own clan to back me, and now I had Sal's clan as well. That included Toppy, and she was for me just like I was for her.

So when that wounded Alabastard came charging in — with his seepy bolt holes, his refuse breath, his teeth and claws, his greasy pale flesh — I had my spike at the ready. It was as sharp at the point as steel could get, and I was aiming to lay his middle patch open like a felon in the yard.

He was on me with a shriek, and I was reaching to skewer him when Toppy came in with a yelp and a growl and took his head clean off.

She didn't pause to be thanked but wheeled around and swung her honed blade again. She laid two geezoids open straight across the middle. They squeaked and retired gripping their wounds to keep their giblets from spilling out.

Unfortunately, Toppy caught Dad with her backswing. That was the danger of going to war in the deep dark in anything close to a rage.

"Hey!"

She didn't hear him. It must have been all battle roar to her by then. The steel was ringing. The alabastards were snorting. Beauty had a warrior by the arm and was mostly through to the bone. It's a wild thing to contemplate. One day you're living topside and selling people boom boxes and rice cookers and then suddenly you're down under, well below the subway, fighting off a pale greasy horde.

Seeing alabastards in repose is different from battling with them. They go from being a startling curiosity to trying to put you to ghastly death. So I wasn't about to take the edge off Toppy's ferocity, but I did keep well wide of her. I wasn't keen to lose an arm.

She inspired Sal and his boys. Provoked them anyway. They weren't about to be bested by Toppy. She wasn't even an American.

Marcy who was laying back with some kind of garden tool (she had her Frenched nails to think of , after all) watched Toppy lay open a trio of CFs and told anybody who cared to hear it, "Gawd!"

The ordinance team didn't help out at all. They had spikes to unsheath and did so, but the things looked ceremonial in their hands. I got the feeling if circumstances started looking dire, that ordinance team would wheel and run.

They'd get overtaken, of course. They'd get flayed and filleted and eaten, so I had that to console me while I fought.

Our clan had done plenty of pitched battle in the past, though we hadn't fought much recently. But in Cumberland with our puny CFs and those first couple of years in Virginia, we'd spilled quite a lot of fluid and probably a dinghy's worth of giblets. Things might have quieted down in the last couple of years, but once you've battled in the deep dark, you never forget how to fight.

For Sal and them, they were still new to this stuff. Those boys had been convinced it was harder to be a Rotarian than a Low Lord, so first they had to shake the shock off and then they had to keep alive. Lucky for them, they'd brought Toppy in. She had instinct enough for them all. They proved wise enough to fall in behind her and cleaned up the stragglers her blade spared. Dirk was doing harm to alabastards as well but at a slower, musclebound pace.

CFs never give up exactly, but they're not the type to fight to the last beast. They come hard as long as they're making way. They'll war against stiffening resistance, but they all seem to have a primal sense of when enough is enough. This swarm was taking a beating. They knew it like we did, and they were there in front of us clawing and snorting until sudden they weren't .

Toppy was all for full pursuit. I found an angle in to grab her before she could put her blade somewhere it would do me harm.

"They'll be waiting," I told her.

"We can take them!"

"They want us to chase them," Clarice said.

Toppy was slick with fluid. It was splattered all over her.

"You did good," I told Toppy.

"You all did," Dad said.

Sal and them looked haggard and shocky.

"Except for you lot," Clarice told the ordinance team as she broke with cavern courtesy and played her lamp right in their faces.

"Not our job," Doug/Bob said. "Right, Dirk?"

Dirk's black tactical coveralls were soaked and giblet splattered. He looked a fair bit less happy than he'd looked before to have the ordinance team from Carlsbad for his colleagues and his friends.

"Let's put one on a pike and leave him," Clarice suggested. At first, I thought she meant one of the dead alabastards at our feet, but then she pointed at Doug/Bob, the sneerier one, and said to him, "You'll do."

5

They had to file reports, the ordinance team did, and Dirk was the one who volunteered our apartment. So the Doug/Bobs and Fay/Marys sat at our eating table and ticked boxes and wrote abstracts while ignoring all of us but Dirk. It didn't seem to matter to them that they'd probably be dead without us. They had a full appreciation of the order of things across the Legion at large. We were deep darkers. Cave hounds, they called us. We were supposed to keep them alive. They didn't have to appreciate it. It was the natural way of things.

One of the Fay/Marys did trouble herself to speak to Toppy in time.

"Sweetie," she said, "you're kind of in my light."

Toppy let her keep her entrails, though it looked a close call there for a moment.

We'd all cleaned up by then and had sent Marcy to the laundry. Alabastard fluid will eat right through even the stoutest duck canvas if you don't get your coveralls in hot water and detergent straightaway. Marcy volunteered for laundromat duty. Unlike the ordinance team, she was properly grateful we'd kept all the CFs from getting to her.

Nobody had said much on the way out of the tunnels until Marcy announced, "I nearly plotzed."

Toppy was indignant and agitated. She didn't like that the ordinance team was so calm and bureaucratic when we'd just been underneath Brooklyn battling for our lives.

"What's with them?" she asked me.

I shrugged and told her, "Carlsbad." There was no explaining the ossified nature of the place to a civilian, so I didn't even try. "Let's take Beauty out," I suggested instead.

We walked her to the dog park briefly, but Beauty kept knocking down Schnauzers and beagles and yellow labs and standing over them with her teeth exposed. So we strolled on the Promenade and then down to the ferry landing between the pizza place and the River Café.

Toppy went for a bench in the afternoon sun. Beauty rolled in the grass beside us while me and Toppy looked out over lower Manhattan in silence for a while.

"It was awful," she finally told me. "And it's the best thing I've ever done."

I knew that feeling. I'd had it myself. Terror and delight.

"You're lucky then," I said. "It stays just awful for some people, and they can never get around it."

"Monte," she told me. "Probably Sal too."

I nodded. I'd noticed as well.

Among our crew, we only had a few scratches. Sal's arms were pretty clawed up, and Aldo had suffered a couple of talon punctures. Clarice had applied CF salve to help stave off infection. That was the one thing we bought from the catalog now since Grady wasn't around to make his concoction anymore.

They were sure to feel viper bit for a day or two. But they'd recover. Their wounds would scab over and heal in the regular way. Untreated, the skin would slough and rot. Infection would take hold.

"What do they do?" Toppy asked me. "If they get you and drag you away?"

I was about to go shruggy and noncommittal, but this was warrior Toppy talking. She deserved to know what would happen if her blade and brothers failed her.

"Feed on you," I told her. "Not all at once, but in chunks and bits and pieces. They know how to keep you going for a while."

"How do you know that?"

"I saw a guy once. He got hauled off. It took the better part of three days for his clan to find him."

That was a Cumberland memory for me. I'd pushed it well back in my head. We'd gone to a regional meet up, one of the yearly lame attempts that Carlsbad mounts to make us socialize. This one was in the Ozarks, some hillbilly wasteland between Rogers, Arkansas, and Eureka Springs. Carlsbad had covered the cost of a Methodist fellowship hall and what they called "full catering," which turned out to be white bread sandwiches and price club chips dumped into bowls.

There was music by happenstance. A few of the Low Lords had brought their instruments and played. Uncle Grady, of course, had been keen to attend.

"We'll network!" He'd told us all brightly. He meant he'd network, or at least hunt up people he could use to help him get to the home office. I don't think we would have attended if my mother hadn't wanted to go. She was morose by then, worn down by Cumberland isolation and tedious cave duty.

"Forget the little buggers for a weekend," she told Dad of our alabastards. "Let's go to this shindig."

They danced some, Dad and Mom did. Mom drank more brandy than she should have. It was home brewed stuff an Oklahoma brother had brought in from his truck in a pickling jar. I ate cream cheese and olive sandwiches and kept an eye on Leigh Ann. She was just big enough to get in all gauges of trouble at the time

I finally saw him in a corner. It was hard to get a decent view. People stayed crowded around him chatting him up, keeping him fed and irrigated. But the kids in the place finally flocked in for a story, so I grabbed Leigh Ann by the arm, and me and her went over too.

He was a Hadley from Texas, sand cave country, and he was doing the regional circuit at the behest of Carlsbad PR. The man was a living warning and admonition. He was talking proof of what The Great Book told us about our adversaries.

That Hadley from Texas was missing one arm entirely and another in part — it quit at the elbow. He didn't have either foot. Apparently, the feet are a delicacy. One of his legs stopped at the ankle and the other at the knee. A chunk of his spare tire was missing as well. It was like they'd scooped out his left side and left a divot where blubber had been. He had an ear and a half and had gotten his cheeks rebuilt so he could chew solid food and talk. I'm told the meat between the eye sockets and jaw line is very much like caviar for discriminating alabastards.

It had always been bad enough until then to know cave crackers would eat us. It was worse somehow to learn they wouldn't do it all at once.

That Texas Hadley was dressed so he could readily show us his scars. He was an after school special for Low Lords. He knew his job and did it to mortifying effect. We were all kids around him, so at first we were thrilled by his ghastly revelations until we started getting scared and didn't care for them anymore.

I remember being little short of mesmerized by the way his jaw moved when he talked. It roamed a bit like the whole works were held together with string and rubber bands. He'd lose control of it every now and again. It would flop up, and his teeth would go clack.

He walked us through his entire ordeal. There was some negligence involved. In the telling, it was all on his part. He'd been sloppy and inattentive.

"They come out of a crease," he told us. "Two of them. Grabbed me and that was that."

He'd had a cousin in front and a brother behind.

"We got spread out like they tell you not to."

We all nodded, us kids. We were most of us at the age where we were hearing everything we shouldn't do. The list was long. The details tiresome.

That Texas Hadley was in the deep dark for seventy-two hours. No lamp. No sun seep. Hardly any air stirring.

“I remember the smell,” he told us. “Like a bear den or something. All of them packed in close. On top of each other. On top of me too.”

We squirmed. We were meant to. He pointed down with his nose.

“That foot went first. I don’t know how they took it off, but it was mighty quick. Didn’t even hurt. Deep dark, you know. Couldn’t see a thing. Seeing would have made it worse.

“They cook you?” one the boys asked. Him and three brothers were up from Pine Bluff.

“Naw, son. Ever seen a possum or a raccoon cook?”

The kid shook his head.

“These things ain’t no different.” Then he went on to say, “They smeared something on me to keep the blood from pouring out.”

I had to think nobody had seen a raccoon or a possum do that either.

He worked his way through every amputation and all the melon balling (he called it) that he’d endured in the course of three days with alabastards in the dark. It was gruesome stuff and was meant to be. We all resolved to be more vigilant. Then he reached the part where his clan came to save him.

“Never quit looking,” he told us. “Never gave up.”

“Big ol’ fight, I’ll bet,” one of the boys declared.

“Them cracker cowards run off,” that Texas Hadley said. “My folks got to me just in time.”

Ever Watchful was the catchphrase they were pushing back then. Carlsbad had even supplied that Texas Hadley with buttons, about the size of a half dollar. There was a drawing of groper blade on them, that Hadley's initials, and EVER WATCHFUL! across the top.

I didn't tell Toppy everything but did mention a couple of that Hadley's amputations.

"And he lived?"

"Kind of." I allowed.

"It's exciting, you know." Toppy said it almost apologetically. "Us or them. I like it. It's simple. Hardly anything else is."

"You sure you weren't born a Low Lord?"

That's when Beauty growled. She's got a range of noises and is easily irritated. You might even call her grumpy for a dog. I saw the Pomeranian first. It was dragging a leash behind it.

It was looking back where it had come from like it was being chased by something. I thought maybe the leash was spooking it. All I could see was a man over by the waterfront rail. A big guy. His back was to us. Hat. Jacket. Dungarees. Big white slab feet instead of shoes.

"Get up," I told Toppy.

We only had one blade between us, and it was three inches worth of pocket knife. I'd left my spike soaking in WD-40 at home. My ripper and bolts were in my satchel on the parlor window seat. Toppy's blade was wherever she'd left it. It was just us as we were — at least with Beauty, thank goodness — pitted against King Wog. Big Chief. Cracker Daddy.

He was right out in the bright sunlight. He was gazing across the water. When he swung our way, I could see he had on big sunglasses like grandmothers wear.

Toppy drew breath.

He motioned for us join him with one of his big, pale hands. His claws were retracted. His hat was floppy. His jacket was oversized. At a glance, he'd have a passed for a pigment-challenged pituitary case.

"What do you think?" I was the one doing the asking. I found Cracker Daddy intriguing, but I didn't want my foolish interest in him to leave me with no feet.

"A little closer," Toppy said.

Beauty had the right idea. She just kept on growling. I tied her leash to the arm of our bench, and me and Toppy headed slowly towards the water. He'd turned back around to look out on the city. Here was the king of the alabastards leaving himself exposed to us. We were warriors. He had to know that by now. And we were fresh from battle. I couldn't decide if it was a sign of haughty confidence or maybe a show of trust.

I put myself between Toppy and Cracker Daddy as we closed on the rail. Toppy was working to look over and around me. She was keen to soak him in.

It was awfully peculiar to be standing in a park in the open air, under a bright sun in a teeming city in the company of an alabastard. I couldn't help but flash on Granddaddy Hoyt and wonder what he might think.

Cracker Daddy watched a puny blue and white police boat head up the East River. "Out," he said.

I couldn't argue with him. There he was. In the park. In the sun.

I heard some racket off to my right. Telltale alabastard snorts. There were three more on the far edge of the park. They were off behind a stand of shrubbery, busy near the fencing. A couple of them had on shirts. One was wearing just cargo shorts.

Beauty snarled and barked. She strained against her leash. The bench I'd tied her to wasn't fixed and properly bolted down. Once Beauty found out she could move it, she dragged it behind her across the park.

Those three alabastards on the far side of the bushes were hauling something down a drain hole. They'd pulled the grate aside. I followed Beauty towards them. Toppy followed me.

Cracker Daddy stayed against the rail from where he growled the way they do.

It sounded threatening enough, but when I swung around to meet him just in case he was charging our way, I saw that he was shaky. He looked to be holding the rail for support. What skin of his I could see wasn't just greasy – the way it is underground – but wet with what I took for alabastard perspiration. He had some color to him as well, an unnatural blue-green flush from fluid rising. All in all, he didn't look awfully well.

His minions by the fence line appeared to be in poor shape too. They were like a trio of drunks trying to change a tire. They did everything slowly and out of order. I finally got close enough to see they were attempting to make off with a hipster. He had a gash on his head where they'd pounded him and the sort of beard a man should need to live in a treehouse to grow. He was wearing a gray twill uniform shirt with the name Hank embroidered on one of the pockets and plaid pants that might have been pajama bottoms.

He was kind of coming around as they tried to shove him in the drain hole. He kept saying over and over again, "Hey, no."

We might not have had traditional weapons, but I fished a bottle out of a trash barrel, and Toppy armed herself with a fractured hunk of granite cobblestone. We had a snarling dog dragging an entire park bench and a yapping Pomeranian. That proved enough to get the attention of that trio of alabastards. They were sweating as well, looked weak and staggered.

I knocked one over with my shoulder before he could extend his talons. Toppy caught one flush with her cobblestone. He staggered back and seeped some fluid. He looked morose about it.

The third one didn't bother to battle us at all. He turned loose of that hipster's ankles, jumped in the drain hole and disappeared.

We grabbed the guy and dragged him free. His Pomeranian shifted around to bark at me and Toppy. Those other two alabastards disappeared down the drain hole as well. I glanced towards where Cracker Daddy had been. He'd bugged out and vanished too.

"Hey, man."

"You ok?" I asked the guy.

He kind of nodded, grabbed one of his elbows and said, "Ouch."

"This your dog?"

He nodded. "That was like weird, you know."

He sat up. The dog came scampering over to lick him. Beauty warbled and stamped her front feet until I'd untied her from her bench.

We helped the guy stand up. He found his Freightliner cap on the ground and popped it back onto his head.

"Like really weird," he told us. Then he got a text and eyed his phone. He took his dog and left.

6

"Inconclusive," Doug/Bob was announcing as we got back to the apartment. He read off some figures and percentages. "We'll crunch all this back home." He meant Carlsbad. They were finished. Inconclusive is all they had.

"We had sort of a thing at the park," I told Dad and Clarice mostly.

Aldo and Leigh Ann were holding hands on the sofa and whispering to each other. Terry and Brody were watching a cartoon on the lousy TV that had come with the place. Sal and Monte and Marcy were back at their store or somewhere. Dirk appeared to have attached himself to one of the Fay/Marys. The strawberry blonde with the lipstick.

"A thing?" Clarice asked.

"Three drones and Cracker Daddy," I told her.

"They were sweating and panting," Toppy added. "Weak, you know. Trying to make off with a guy."

The ordinance team perked up and left off with their equipment. They were all listening in.

"Sewer drain," I said. "But it was like they were drunk. You know, stumbling around."

"It's the air, isn't it?" Toppy aimed that at the ordinance team.

It wasn't their custom to respond to a creature with even less rank than a provisional, but the Doug/Bob with the bald spot broke with practice and said, "Yeah." He checked some sort of ticker from one of his boxes. "Foul stuff." He gestured towards the air around us. "Soot," he said. "Particulates. Exhaust."

"So they can come up but they can't stay?" Dad asked.

"That's what it looked like," I told him. "At least for now."

That's when the buzzer sounded. We didn't even know what it was. Nobody had buzzed us before. The downstairs bell, yes, but this was somebody just outside in the hallway. A knock followed.

Dad threw back the bolt and opened the door.

Detective Les Hayden chirped, "House call."

His partner, Tony, followed him in. He had a new haircut and smelled of Barbasol and marinara. Tony was hardly across the threshold before he checked his fingernails.

"What's all this?" Les asked.

We waited for somebody to kick off the lying so we'd know just how to throw in.

Doug/Bob started us off with the wrong question entirely. "Who are you?"

Les stepped over to the dinette and showed Doug/Bob his detective shield, provided Doug/Bob could see it through his forehead. Les pressed it there hard enough to leave an NYPD impression.

"How can we help you, gentlemen?" Dad asked.

"Who are they?" Les wanted to know.

Carlsbad offered a course in conversational evasion. They must have used a textbook from the eighties or maybe just from northern California. Fay/Mary volunteered that they were on a spiritual quest.

"A journey," she told Les.

"To where?"

"Oneness."

"And that's in Brooklyn?"

"It can be anywhere." Fay/Mary pressed her thumbs and ring fingers together and made a decent overtone.

Les turned to Tony. "Go call us in, will you?"

Tony nodded and stepped into the hallway. He behaved like a guy who was used to being sent away to sit and wait.

"I've got a problem," Les said to all of us, "and I'd like to hash it out."

We mumbled. We nodded. The Fay/Mary with initiative told Les in her best soothing commune voice that he had the talking stick.

Les fished a folded piece of paper out of his inside blazer pocket. He unfolded the paper and offered it to me. "Know what that is?"

I looked. Two charts. Some numbers. "Nope."

"Your DNA."

I looked again. Still charts and numbers.

"Know what it says?"

I shook my head.

"It says you're your own thing, brother."

Clarice took the paper from me and had a look for herself. She couldn't decipher it either and so handed it off to Dad.

"What do you mean?" Clarice asked Les.

"Not quite like the rest of us."

“How?” Dad asked.

“Anomalous. That’s what they told me. Got some chromosomes out of whack.”

“Meaning what?” That from Dirk.

Les stepped over to the dinette to see what Dirk and the ordinance team were up to. “Not sure,” he said in response to Dirk’s question. “They’re still chewing on it.”

Les looked over some of the forms Doug/Bob and Fay/ Mary were ticking and filling.

“What’s all this?” Les plucked up a sheet for a glance. “Thermobarometric balance?” he said.

“What do you want exactly?” Dad asked him.

Les laughed and shook his head. He dropped the form back on the dinette and strolled over to the big bay window where we had a view of an industrial block and a grimy, truck-lined street.

“I want to know what the hell’s going on. You’re chasing crocodile guys with crossbows.”

“Rippers.” Me and Clarice corrected him together and at once.

Les gave us a look and kept on going. “Tell me you’re from the future or Alpha Centauri or something.

Dad and Clarice went blank on Les in that old-school Carlsbad way. Dirk and the ordinance team looked marginally better at it.

Les drew a weary breath and kept on going. “The guy holding the lease on your apartment died in 1958, but he’s still paying the rent somehow. Awfully conscientious of him. And I checked on your buddy, Salvatore De Luca. He’s got a building, not four blocks from here. Your dead guy owns that too."

Dad said nothing at all to Les, so the rest of us said nothing as well. All of us anyway except for Dirk. He couldn't help himself.

"What's your point, chief?"

"Who's this guy?" Les asked me mostly.

"Her ex."

He glanced at Clarice. She shrugged. Everybody has a past.

Les stepped back over to the dinette. He considered the ordinance team and Dirk. "Home office, right?"

That was close enough to the mark to earn the full attention of the Carlsbad gang. They all stopped shuffling papers and dithering around and took occasion to consider Les.

"Croc trouble?" he asked. "Maybe more than usual?"

We'd reached that point you get to sometimes in this sort of conversation when you can't be sure who's got what details and why.

Les sounded clued in, but he was a New York City police detective, which meant he'd know how to play us. We were rubes by tradition and calling. We were well versed in just one thing nobody else was supposed to know.

"I don't follow," Dirk told Les. You could believe that coming from Dirk.

"Here it is," Les said and then paused. He had a cop's fine sense of drama. "You take me to the crocodile guys, and I'll leave you to do what it is you do."

As propositions go, that one put us in a bit of a fix. We'd have to admit to an officer of the law that there was such a thing as alabastards. That went against scripture and code and Council decree. It qualified as a grievous offense, and Detective Les Hayden was asking for it in front of Dirk and the ordinance team. They were sure to have the proper form in their files to sanction the whole pack of us.

But then Carlsbad was making active overtures to D.C.. That was bigger and worse than anything we could do.

Fortunately, I guess, Sal came charging in while me and Clarice and Dad and Leigh Ann were gawking at each other and trying to figure out what to say.

Sal was hardly in the door when he yelled, "One of them's right downstairs! Get your gear!" Then he saw Detective Les and told everybody, "Oh," but it was a bit too late by then.

We grabbed rippers and gropers and spikes, and our clan plus Les went down the stairwell.

Sal led the way. Les followed close. There were two alabastards in the street, in fact.

They were busy getting talked at by a guy in Swahili or something. A wiry jet black man in Genesee t-shirt – "Always ask for Jenny" – and one alabastard had ahold of him by the arm. The other alabastard's claws were descending just as Clarice fired a bolt.

It planted deep in that CFs torso. It was the cleanest shot she could get. The beast wailed like they do. I'd never heard one bleat like that outside of a cavern. It made for an arresting racket. Everybody within earshot stopped what they were up to and turned to look.

"Go, go, go!" Dad shouted, and we all charged up the block.

I let fly and caught the other alabastard in the backside. They'd let their civilian go by then and were just trying to get away.

They were scrabbling and running, lurching and crabbing. They rounded the corner. We were twenty yards behind them. By the time we made the cross street, there was no sign of them anywhere.

Les had a radio on his belt. His partner had seen us and the thing was squawking. Les keyed his mic. "Sit tight. Sit tight."

That was all Tony needed to hear.

Beauty nosed up those alabastards and led us into a truck bay and onto a warehouse floor. The place looked recently abandoned. There were pallets about, torn down boxes, strips of packing plastic. Les pulled out his side arm.

"Uh uh," Dad told him.

Les was stranger enough in a strange land to pay Dad a little heed. He holstered his gun. Dad offered his talwar. Les took it. Eighteen inches of hardened steel, bronze pommel, hammered silver cross guard, an edge that would cut a parking meter in half.

Les eyed the sword. "Who are you people?"

"Stay to the rear," Clarice advised him.

Les was no fool. He did.

Beauty went down a stairway. We all packed in to follow. Only Toppy had thought to bring a light. It was all she had.

"Hang back," I told her.

She laughed. It sounded like something she'd picked up from Clarice. Toppy squeezed ahead with her lantern. It was Beauty and her and then us.

The far cellar wall was buckled and opened up to the underneath. Beauty passed right through a crack in the foundation. Toppy followed, and we scrambled in behind her.

"Kill that radio," Clarice told Detective Les. He didn't make her say it twice.

I had to hand it to the guy. He knew when it was time to be a good soldier and exactly how to do it. I figured Sal's clan — mostly Monte and Marcy — could learn a thing or two from Les.

Once we'd climbed down into the deep dark, we closed on those CFs from the street. We could see them up ahead. They looked like a winded sprinters, were struggling to fill their lungs. Me and Clarice and Dad and Leigh Ann took full notice of their condition. We'd been in caves our whole lives and had never known CFs to tire.

The air tasted tangy in my mouth. It tingled in my nose. Like it was distilled or ionized or something. It hurt me a little to breathe it. I was having the CF experience in reverse.

Clarice thought she had a shot and let fly. Her tip sparked against rock right beside one of the creature's heads. They accelerated as best they were able. We charged on behind them.

"Can we take one alive?" Les wanted to know.

"Why?" Dad asked.

"Study him, you know. Figure them out."

"We've got people on that," Clarice told Les. She said it like they were worthwhile people and not Carlsbad techs and clinicians all living in the past.

"Then why chase them?"

Clarice paused to pick up her wayward arrow. "It's what we do."

I wondered for a moment if that wasn't just a Carlsbad brand of thinking.

I sensed them up ahead before I saw them. It's the movement you feel. The stirring air. The knowledge the wild is encroaching. I'd been underneath enough to know there was a nest of them up ahead.

"Swarm," Dad said. He felt it too.

We only had Toppy's lone beam. We all slowed to a walk. Clarice and I had arrows nocked. Leigh Ann banged her blade on stone.

Dad raised a hand, and we all stopped. Les had a question but saved it once Clarice had leaned towards him and put her finger to her lips. You could hear them. I could hear them anyway. Like bugs in a plank. Beauty snarled.

"They can come to us," Clarice said. She reached over and switched off Toppy's lamp.

"What are you doing?" Les asked. Otherwise, he stayed cool and true to form.

He didn't ease back like I probably would have. He didn't instinctively pull out his gun. He stood and waited. We waited too.

Once it sounded like we were in the plank, Clarice switched Toppy's lamp back on. They were wall-to-wall before us.

Those lizard faces. That shiny pale skin. Teeth and talons. Coal-black eyes. There must have been a hundred of them. They stretched back into the gloom.

Les drew a short, sharp breath. They didn't seem to want a fight. Me and Clarice kept our rippers on them as the rest of our crew retreated behind us. They didn't give chase. I picked out the injured, winded pair that we'd pursued off the street and down into the dark. They'd been surrounded and insulated, were getting protected by their kind.

Not even a single skirmisher forayed to menace and push us. Those alabastards remained in tight formation. The order was out to let us go. We passed back up along the tunnel, climbed through the crack in the busted foundation wall. We crossed the littered warehouse and down the truck bay steps into the street.

Les appeared to have given up on asking questions. Instead, he just looked at us hard. He gave our entire group a deliberate and comprehensive once-over. We were the people who'd just upended his world and kicked his life apart. We probably looked harmless enough, certainly rag-tag by paramilitary standards, and the weapons we carried were nearly medieval. I would have been lost for words myself.

In time Les switched on his radio. We all heard Tony calling to him. Les answered, and Tony showed up from around the corner on foot.

Tony had quite a lot to say. Tony was irritated. Tony was hungry. Tony had a thing about Brooklyn. It wasn't where he wanted to be.

When Tony paused to check his cuticles, Les laid a hand on Tony's shoulder.

"Do something for me," Les told his partner. "Shut up."

7

The ordinance team was packed and gone by the time we returned to the apartment. They'd left all their trunks and valises and equipment with Dirk.

"We've got to ship all this," he said when we came in. He was leaving too. We meant us.

"What's the verdict?" Clarice asked.

"Wait for the report."

"Give us the highlights," Dad told him.

Dirk made a show of looking at Toppy and Detective Les in a significant and incriminating sort of way. "You're going to get dinged for civilians. Might as well count on that."

You could always depend on Carlsbad to focus on precisely the wrong thing.

"Yeah, and?" Dad gestured towards Dirk with the business end of his groper. I liked his thinking and his method. I still had a bolt nocked and only had to level my ripper and swing it around Dirk's way. Leigh Ann joined in. Clarice as well.

"Need him arrested or something?" Les asked.

"Depends," Dad said. We all waited for Dirk.

"Ok. Here's how it is," he told us.

Dirk started out with everything they already knew in Carlsbad, even before they'd put him on a bus and sent him out our way.

"Water's rising. That's item one," he said.

"What water?" Sal asked.

"All of it. Everywhere. Driving them up."

"Then they're sure to come out." That from Toppy.

"They've still got room," Dirk said. "Just not as much."

Tony had come in behind Les. He'd been taking it all in and looked to be having a fairly novel experience for Tony, distracted as he was from his fingernails and the thoughts of his next meal.

"They who?" Tony asked.

Dirk and Dad and Clarice all consulted with glances.

"This stays here," Dirk told Les and Tony. Once they'd nodded, he said to Dad and Clarice, "Go on. Tell them."

Dad and Clarice tag teamed it. They brought me and Leigh Ann and Brody in for the odd enlargement and confirmation, but they hardly needed our help to trace the history of the Legion from Constitutional Congress days all the way up to ours.

"*Thomas* Jefferson?" was the only question Les asked.

"Yeah," Clarice said. "Busy guy. He invented the swivel chair too."

They did a quarter hour on Carlsbad with more scope and tone than Dirk could approve of. He kept telling them, "All right. That's enough," but they just ignored him. Clarice in particular ragged on the general stratification of the Legion. The Council. The Elders. The whole lot.

"You saw the ordinance team," Dad told Les and Tony. Some of their equipment was still sitting around unpacked. "Look at this crap." They did.

Les and Tony got an accounting of our years in Cumberland, Tennessee and Albermarle County, Virginia, mostly as tours that were emblematic of the sort of policing we were charged to do. They heard about all the adaptations we'd seen our CFs make.

"Maybe they'll get civil too," Dad said, but he added — like he had to — that with all of their physical alterations and subterranean adjustments, he'd never known alabastards to grow less dangerous and less fierce.

"They'll eat livestock if you make them," Clarice told Les and Tony, "but they'd always rather eat you."

Dad had Leigh Ann provide a groper history and brief lesson in blade work. I went through the evolution of the ripper from oversized encumbrance to the lethal item it was now.

"He says Carlsbad's talking to the army." Dad eyed Dirk as he spoke.

Dirk nodded and said one more time, "This all stays here."

Everybody wanted a plan and wanted it right away. Even those of us who didn't come out and say that's what we wanted. Those of us who weren't sure, after years with Uncle Grady, that plans were all they were usually cracked up to be.

Sal and Aldo sure wanted one.

When Marcy showed up, she wanted one too. Then she studied Les and Tony and asked Dirk mostly, "Who called the cops?"

Dirk had it straight from the ordinance team that we were six weeks away from a solution.

"What kind of solution?" Les asked him.

"Need to know," Dirk said.

Clarice punched him in a way that appeared to be left over from their marriage. She caught Dirk in a vulnerable spot. Just left of his belt buckle. It turned out he'd long had a muscle tear just there, and Clarice could always find it in a pinch.

Dirk groaned and doubled over.

"What did they tell you?" Clarice asked him.

"Gas," Dirk said.

"What gas?" Les wanted to know.

"String of letters and numbers. Heavy toxin. They tell me it'll stay where they put it, and they plan to put it low."

"The army's all right with that?" Les wanted to know.

Dirk couldn't say. He shrugged.

"Sal, honey," Marcy said. "I want to go home, and I mean Riverdale."

"For a night or two?" Sal was asking Dad and Clarice. They could tell well enough we were all in for a Marcy fit unless they gave the go ahead.

"Sure," Dad told him. "I doubt it can hurt."

Dirk checked his oversized tactical watch. "I've got a bus to catch."

"Bus?" Les asked. "Honest to God?"

Clarice and Dad told him, "Carlsbad," both at once.

Aldo stayed on in town to be near Leigh Ann. We let him sleep on our sofa, and Dad threatened to gut him if he wandered in the night. Monte stuck in Jersey City while Sal and Marcy and Terry went up to their house in leafy Riverdale. I got leave to help Toppy in the Chinatown store.

"I'll train her and stuff," I proposed to Dad and Clarice.

Dad let Clarice sneer and tell me, "Right."

Unfortunately for us, it turned out the alabastards had a plan of their own. Something beyond snatching the stray dog-walking hipster or grabbing the odd Kenyan off the street. It was a smart plan too. You had to give them that. I couldn't help but believe the credit belonged entirely to Cracker Daddy.

We had two quiet days. We passed one of them packing the ordinance team's gear and arranging to have it shipped to Carlsbad on the cheap. We trundled off everything but an old Bearcat police scanner that we found shoved in a valise. That was a thing we could put to practical use. Our hope was we could distinguish between human-on-human New York mayhem and the sort of stuff CFs would get up to in the subways and around.

That was a taller order than we'd expected, given the strange stuff that routinely goes on in the city. There was a report of a gorilla in Central Park, some kind of blood-sucking ghoul in Chelsea, and a winged dragon perched on a ledge of the Pan Am building in midtown. No alabastard involvement at all, as it turned out. Fortified wine, absolutely. An uncorrected astigmatism and pharmaceuticals as well.

The attack, when it came, was ambitious enough that we couldn't help but notice.

A bus full of prisoners left the criminal courthouse on Centre Street in lower Manhattan with two guards, one driver, and twenty-three convicts all heading for Rikers Island. They got as far as the Brooklyn side of the Williamsburg Bridge where a raiding party came over the railing into stopped traffic on the elevated highway. All the witnesses sitting on the BQE said essentially the same thing. A gang of maybe dozen guys kicked in the bus door and climbed on board.

Les came to meet us when the first details started trickling in. He sent Tony over to have a look. Tony had friends in corrections, and he took this occasion to prove he was something more than just a fellow with a manicure and a poor work ethic. He kept Les informed on the two way, and Les passed everything on to us. We were in Sal's storefront with Toppy. Me and Clarice and Dad anyway. They'd left Leigh Ann and Aldo watching Brody at home.

"By themselves?" Toppy kept wanting to know. That made me a bit uneasy since she knew Aldo far better than we did.

"Is that a problem?" Dad asked her.

"Want a grandbaby?"

"I trust my daughter." Dad said it like he was trying it out in his head.

"Hmm." I knew that tone from Toppy.

"Should I go home?" I asked.

Clarice said, "No sir." Then she informed us all, "Me and Leigh Ann had a talk."

That made me worried for Aldo. Leigh Ann was an artist with a blade. I was just relaxing a little when Les arrived and told us, "I think they grabbed a bus full of cons."

For a while, it was chiefly intuition on his part. The guards and the driver had gotten scuffed up pretty good. They were cut and beaten but left behind alive. The witnesses agreed about a gang of thugs. No mention of teeth or talons, no hint of crocodile DNA. But Les had a nose, and it was twitching.

"How are they working it?" Les asked.

"Half convinced it's *Trinitario.*"

Les explained to us, "Big Latin gang around here. They'd get up to something like this."

"So maybe they did," Dad said.

"Let's hope." Les raised the walkie and keyed the mic. "How'd they get on the highway?"

"Came over the barrier. Climbed up somehow."

"And the getaway?" Les asked.

"That's the weird thing," Tony told him. "The cons were all chained together and got lowered down like a string of pearls."

That was quite an image to contemplate.

"He's got kind of a way with words," Clarice told Detective Les.

Les nodded. "Tony writes poems. They stink."

"Let me see who I can find," Tony came in through the static.

"Come back in ten," Les told him, and with that he turned the two-way down. "So?" he said.

"Maybe." Clarice was the only one of us who was prepared to go that far.

New York was a funny place. People got up to peculiar mischief. If you read the *Post* regularly, like I tended to, you'd think New Yorkers capable of almost anything.

"What are we not seeing?" Dad asked Les. "We're from out of town. Remember?"

"Right." Les paused, I guess, to consider everything he'd heard from Tony. "Here's the odd bit. Nobody got shot."

Those *Trinitario* boys were fond of their guns, the way Les explained it to us, and wouldn't have thought twice about shooting (especially) a corrections bus driver and a couple of guards.

"Then it must be them." Clarice was the one who said it out loud, but we were all thinking the same thing.

"Kind of brilliant." Dad said. "Convicts."

Les nodded. "There's plenty the city won't do to get them back."

"Sal's truck's in the alley," Toppy said.

We all knew us-or-nothing when we saw it.

Les drove with Dad and Clarice in the cab. Me and Toppy rattled around in the back. Dad took the Manhattan Bridge to Brooklyn where we picked up Leigh Ann and Aldo, Brody and Beauty.

We loaded up all the weapons we had while Clarice and Les quarreled about where we ought to go and what we ought to do. Les wanted to swing by the scene of the crime. That was the way he usually worked cases. Clarice felt sure we didn't need to since she'd seen the alabastard hive already.

"It's under here." She pointed at the nearest sewer grate. "You know they'll take them home."

Tony came in on the two-way to tie the business up in a bow.

"Found a guy," he said. "Says he saw them go in a hole."

"This isn't your fight," Dad told Les. "You don't have to go."

"My city," Les said. He keyed the radio mic. "I'll be dark for forty-five."

"Where exactly are you going?" Tony asked through static.

Les just told him, "Down."

8

We decided on the culvert instead of the carriage house and the hatch. That was all we had for strategy until we were too far in to turn back. I understood at that moment that, without Uncle Grady, we were doomed to be the sort of crew that always intended to plot and plan but only ever improvised.

It's one thing to be spontaneous about where you have your picnic or what movie you decide to buy tickets for once you've reached the cineplex, but it's something else altogether to blunder into the deep dark with just your weapons, raw pluck, and some hope.

Detective Les had brought his shotgun from his trunk. We'd tried to talk him out of it, but he wasn't ripe to be persuaded.

"I hear you," he told us as he shoved shells into the breach. "Call me new fangled," he said and left it at that.

We made him agree to carry a groper too — actually one of our hardware store pole axes that Toppy had used a time or two. She was armed with Sal's blade, a fine old specimen with leather bindings and a carved bone handle. It was alabastard femur darkened by palm grease and years.

We kept Beauty on her leash, which she didn't much care for, but we couldn't be sure what sort of mood we'd find our CFs in. If they were stealing convicts off of buses, they'd rounded a corner and crossed a line. That was a very long way from grabbing sheep staked out in a pasture. We could no longer be sure just what they were up to and what they might see clear to do.

As we passed into the deeper dark — below the cellars, below the subways — I felt the moving air from the transit before us. It smelled antique, a little sweet and rank and minerally, like parchment dipped in blood.

We were moving at a decent clip, mostly on the downslope, so we'd covered a lot of territory before we bothered to stop for a blow.

"We're just grabbing cons right?" Les asked.

"Let's hope so," Dad said. "Could turn into something else."

"I don't mind telling you," Les confessed, "I don't much like the dark."

The tunnel we were in dead ended into a massive cross channel, deep under the city and the harbor. It was all black bedrock. The walls rose to an arch overhead, and the tunnel floor was so grit and guano free that it had a luster to it. There was air moving, east to west.

Talon on stone. We all heard it and stopped.

"The Port Authority sure didn't build this." Les played his lantern beam overhead. The highest point of the ceiling was probably twenty feet above us.

"Where you figure it goes?" Aldo asked.

"All over," Dad said.

"Alabastard interstate," I volunteered.

We heard a human yelp in pain. That shut us up and focused us. Whimpering followed. Some pitiful muttering. A tunnel like that can fool you, the way it bounces and amplifies sound. That racket could have coming from just ahead or halfway to Pennsylvania.

"Save your lights," Clarice told us. We switched ours off, all of us but Les. "Kill it," she hissed at him.

I finally reached in and extinguished the thing. That left Clarice's solitary beam to help guide us down the tunnel. She slapped a filter on the lens. Blood red. Close by was dim and gloomy. Everything else was inky black.

"Why don't we get some help?" Les was prattling now. Nerves. You see that in the deep dark even without alabastards. "Get SWAT down here."

"Our job," Dad told him.

We got the raised fist from Clarice. We could see that if nothing else. It was our sign for run silent. I put a finger to my lips for Les. He was working his way back to steely cop mode. He nodded, made no sound.

Toppy grabbed a fistful of my coveralls. That was her form of comfort, and it consoled me a little as well.

We stopped. We listened. Distinct voices. Complaints. Brief bits of talk. The odd clank of chain. Bursts of swearing.

We crowded in for a consult. Even Beauty stuck her head in the scrum.

"Foray?" Dad asked.

Clarice nodded. She pointed at me. At herself.

It always made sense to slip up with rippers. No danger of steel clanging off rock, and we could rain bolts on the beasts and hold them back if a headlong retreat became – what was called in the cavern battle manual – "advised". Of course, this was the same manual that insisted you could make potable tea out of cave crickets and rock mold.

We had to go full dark. That's never less than a twingy ordeal for even the most seasoned Low Lord. Cave black is like being in your casket. It's complete. Engulfing. Deceptive. Everything you think you see is never there until it is. You make up a landscape and manufacture a threat. The real stuff grabs you while you're dodging the phantoms. I usually close my eyes when we go dark. That way I know I'm seeing nothing at all.

Me and Clarice had our rippers and a dozen arrows each – enough bolts to get us back to our crew in lamplight at a run. We let the draft guide us. We were moving west into it and following the odd clank of shackle chain, the occasional forlorn human noise.

I held to Clarice they way Toppy had held to me. That was the protocol for creeping in the dark. We were trying to stay in the dead center of the channel as we went, but your gyroscopes get off in the pitch black, and you convince yourself you're moving true when instead you've bent to a tangent. Suddenly you're nosed up to the cavern wall.

We did that twice. Once with Clarice in the lead. The other time was my fault. Then we stopped and squatted. We let our pulses slow and our breath get unlabored and steady.

Only then could we hear the stirrings ahead, feel the contours of the breeze. The temptation is always to switch on your lamp, if only for a second, but then you'll have floaters for a quarter hour and be more confused than you were to start.

We meditated. Clarice had taught me how. We slowed everything down. We made everything still. We eased back out to the center of the channel and proceeded into the draft on a dead straight course until we reached a confusion of air that felt like a schism in the rock, some kind of intersecting channel. We stopped again. We waited and settled. The lone *tink* of a chain link gave them away.

We had small, disposable lights we carried. They were the size of your little finger, ran on watch batteries and hardly worked at all. They were dim at full brightness straight out of the packing and got weaker immediately. That's why we used them in the deep dark. They were nominal illumination at best. You could switch one on and only barely find out where you where. It was as close to darkness as you could get and still see at least a little.

Clarice used hers to find the crevice. It was a fissure where a massive block of granite had fractured eons ago. They were back in there somewhere. We could hear them now. Alabastards were bad at holding still. Claws on rock. Sinusy snorts. It sounded like the convicts had largely gone docile. I could only imagine what those guys were thinking, snatched off a bus on the Brooklyn-Queens Expressway and dragged underground by a bunch of clammy beasts.

This was nightmare stuff and must have made Rikers Island seem like Bible camp.

We entered the crease. I took point. We had to turn sideways to clear the first five feet, but it opened up after that. I could stretch out my arms and guide myself by running my hands along the walls on either side. The shaft bent once south and then straightened again. No serious kinks after that. That fissure was acting like a megaphone for any sound the swarm made ahead.

They never post sentries. Alabastards are predictable and cocky that way. If you come onto a clutch of the creatures, they never have prior warning. They depend on being fierce and ruthless. That must have been the crocodile in them.

So we didn't expect to bump into a scout, and in truth the alabastard we tangled with wasn't on watch exactly. She was napping on a ledge. I ran right into her. Quite literally. I rammed her dangling clawed foot with my face.

I knew enough to grab her ankle, jerk her hard and stun her by banging her violently against the opposite wall.

"What?" Clarice whispered. We were working blind, even two feet from each other.

"Help me," was the best I could manage, and Clarice came piling in on me and my alabastard. The beast was just waking up to the fix she was in. We couldn't let her snort and shriek. It was clearly her or us.

She did that thing they do sometimes when the combat gets dire and lethal. She made a pitiful noise through that lump that passes with alabastards some for a nose. It goes right to your sense of decency and spirit of fair play.

That can't be by accident. She made her noise. I backed off a little.

Clarice heard it too, and she was hissing at me, "No!" when that harpy of a thing swiped me with her razor claws. She was aiming for my neck and the artery there. I dodged just in time to leave her clawing at my chest.

Clarice bore in with a bolt in hand and found the spot she was after. The gap above the breastplate that usually lets the life right out. Clarice plunged in the tip and got bit for her troubles, but she drove the shaft in up to the plumage. That touched off a solid half minute of spastic alabastard writhing. They whip around like they've been electrified right before they die. There was nothing for us to do but draw back while she flopped and whined.

It sounded to me like a monumental racket. I was sorely afraid she'd give us away and we'd get swarmed any second. But lucky for us (and unlucky for him) one of the convicts had gotten up to something that had cheesed off a bunch of his keepers.

We could hear alabastard gurgling and human wailing coming from up ahead. It sounded like somebody was learning first hand what claws and tearing teeth could do. Our alabastard snorted one last time and went quiet.

I would have wondered of Clarice if we shouldn't head back and round up the rest of the crew, but the narrow passage we were in made numbers almost meaningless. We could only go through single file and so were bound to spill out in the opening ahead like gum balls from a machine.

There wasn't any help for it. Even Les' SWAT team wouldn't have mattered.

I eased ahead with my ripper cocked. A lot of good our bolts would do us if the swarm ahead was even half the size it sounded. We could hear them shifting around on the rock. The cons had gone quiet. I pictured a row of gutted prisoners like bass on a stringer.

I felt air — rank air — as our channel funneled open, and finally we could even see a little. The CFs who'd been out on the raid were glowing still from exposure to the sun. They were pale green phosphorescent like cheap night lights scattered in among the swarm.

Lucky for us, the CFs before us were hardly the entire hive. There were maybe forty of them. That's all the chamber would hold once the shackled civilians were added in. Those guys were thoroughly scuffed up and half of them looked to be in shock. One was cut across his torso and bleeding pretty freely. We had to hope they could still run headlong for their lives.

The nearest con was hardly three feet in. Given half a step, I could grab him. In the dim, green glow me and Clarice consulted as best we could. She picked out a female, a regal creature as alabastards go. She was off across the way hard beside Cracker Daddy. He'd clearly been in on the raid as well. He must have gone out shirtless because he was glowing seafoam green from his middle on up.

He was breathing hard. All the glowing ones were. Their hive brothers and sisters looked to have piled in on them by way of comfort.

Clarice pointed at me. At Cracker Daddy. She tapped the hollow in her neck. Her target would be the female beside him which she gestured about as well. Then she wiggled two fingers to let me know the basic plan was to run like hell.

That's kind of all it ever came down to in a cave with alabastards. You were always trying to hold them off long enough to find some way to scramble out. It hardly seemed like a worthwhile calling when you broke it down like that. They wanted up and out. We wanted them down and in. You didn't need *The Great Book* to understand that or a teeming bureaucracy in Carlsbad.

I nodded. We aimed. Clarice's ripper was just off my left shoulder. She had that female's kill spot in her sites. I drew a bead on Cracker Daddy's.

Clarice counted down, her head right next to mine. "Three. Two . . ."

She fired first. I was milliseconds after. Clarice's alabastard went full-bore operatic with Clarice's bolt buried up to its feathered nub in her neck. My bolt planted in Cracker Daddy's shoulder. It wasn't a misfire exactly. I just realized at the very last moment I didn't want him dead.

Clarice nocked and fired again. She hit another hollow flush while I grabbed the closest con and told the pack of them, "Let's go!"

They must have been used to getting ordered around — that and they were hungry for sunlight — because they all rose as one with a metallic clang and slipped past us into the crease.

The furor among the alabastards was savage and unchecked. We could barely hold them off with bolts flying at them thick in the air.

"I'm out," I told Clarice.

She fired her last bolt, and the only thing between us and alabastard retribution was a pile of fallen CFs clotting up the passage. That bought us a quarter minute at most. We slipped and scrambled at full velocity. I caught up with the string of cons. The dark had slowed them down. They had no idea which way was out.

"Go! Go! Go!" Clarice and I both shouted at them and pushed them from behind until finally we all spilled into the transit where we both switched on our lamps.

"This way," I said and grabbed the lead guy. He was big and brown with a mustache and muscles. He was wide-eyed and grimy, authentically terrified.

"Run," Clarice told them and made herself emphatic by given the last con a firm kick in the ass.

He shifted around to snarl and swear. That's when he saw them pouring out.

Lit and unlit alabastards, phosphorescent and ghostly pale. They came tumbling out of the crevice making their grunty warrior noises. We couldn't do much but run. We just had Clarice's spike between us. They were gaining. We were tiring. They were almost on us when we heard the first shotgun blast.

Les was no fool with a weapon. He'd aimed high and bounced the shot off the cavern roof. It cleared us for the most part and found the CFs like so many hornets. They made their aggravated, put-upon noises. After that, they usually just get angrier, and ours had started out enraged. We'd shot them up with ripper bolts and made off with a week's worth of food. Fury propelled them. Les fired again. I felt the sting of some pellets this time.

Our crew charged past us as we reached them. Leigh Ann and Aldo. Dad and Toppy. Brody and Beauty. Les as well. They went in blades up and met our swarm. The goal was just to stun and stop them, knock them back a little. Buy enough time for me and Clarice to run our guys up out of the deep dark and towards the light.

That's just what we did. The shackles rang and rattled. The cons coughed and wheezed, but they kept running. Even the gashed and bleeding one. His buddies helped him along, little short of carried him. They'd all had enough of the underneath to last them for a while.

When you're coming out of the deep dark, you don't trust the light at first. Our guys were like that. Up ahead, there was sunshine seeping in through the culvert. They couldn't believe what they were seeing, had given up on topside already.

They headed up towards daylight and safety. We turned back towards the dark. Our crew had left our satchels in the middle of the tunnel where we were sure to see them. We scooped them up and kept running, loading as we went.

We heard them. They were fighting a classic rear action and backing towards us as they battled. Steel was ringing. Beauty was snarling. The alabastards were raising a godawful savage fuss. I could hear Toppy in the mix. She had a wild battle cry.

We reached them in time to give the CFs a fresh push with a flurry of bolts from our rippers. Our crew retreated fighting, facing those alabastards that kept pushing and scrabbling forward. I caught sight of Cracker Daddy. He was directing his forces from the rear. Growling and grunting. He looked right at me. Shiny green fluid was draining from the bolt hole in his shoulder. He hardly appeared weak and wounded. I put him more in the way of incensed.

We backed out of the transit and up along the tunnel, firing and fighting as we went. Les and Brody were side by side. Lucky for Les since Brody was a demon with a groper and low enough to make real trouble. Brody sliced CFs in places they couldn't reach to shield.

The closer we got to the culvert and sunlight, the thinner the ranks of CFs grew until a lone suicidal geezoid – he was gray-tufted and warty with a scarred nub where an arm had been – kept scrabbling at us and making swipes with his lone set of yellowed talons.

I took Toppy's groper from her. "I'll knock him back," I said. "Go on."

They did, all of them. Up towards the daylight and into the mouth of the culvert. Mad grandpa kept coming at me, and I kept whacking on him with the flat of my blade. I couldn't see the point of dicing him up. That would just be piling on.

"Go on," I told him. I was feeling cocky by then, confident enough to let myself forget what I knew about alabastards. You showed them mercy at your peril and you never ever turned your back.

Grandpa kept coming. I kept swatting. I wasn't so troubled and occupied that I couldn't enjoy the moment. If this was our Bull Run, at least we'd taken the first battle. They'd snatched convicts in broad daylight. We'd ventured down and snatched them back. Word was sure to get out about alabastards now. There'd be cons on every cable channel, all over the *Post* and the *Daily News*. Carlsbad was about to come, blinking and balky, into the twenty-first century.

Life was going to change for us Low Lords. Change for Carlsbad and the Legion at large. Our veiled days were over. We needed new blood. New tactics. New weapons. New thinking. If we started fresh, we'd have chance.

I felt no dread. For me, it was all just sweet anticipation. I might have been swatting my geezoid, but in my head I was topside and clear. Back with my crew. Back with my fine dog. Back especially with Toppy.

I gave that geezoid one final blow with the flat of my blade and then pivoted and headed for the culvert. I guess I'd decided everything was different already and the old rules didn't apply. I faced the light the way you shouldn't. That's when he caught me by the tendon. Not the frantic geezoid I'd been swatting. It was Cracker Daddy.

He grunted. He relieved me of my groper with one swat. Broke my ripper strap and sailed the thing against rock wall.

I yelled loudly enough to be heard outside, in the open air at the mouth of the culvert. I could see shadows racing towards me.

I heard Toppy cry out, “Mack!”

Cracker Daddy was fast and sure. He threw me over his good shoulder and raced with me down the tunnel towards the transit. The one arm geezoid I’d been swatting kept up with us, scrabbling sideways. If I didn’t know better, I would say he was grinning as we went.

I heard Toppy’s voice. Distant. Faint. We reached the transit and veered into the draft. The only light was from the wan, phosphorescent glow of Cracker Daddy’s glistening flesh

He smelled of musk and fluid, of fungus and vermin.

Cracker Daddy told me, “Mine.”

Nil Plus

1

We went deep. Far deeper than I'd ever been. It stung to breathe. Darkness was upon us like inky satin. I rode slung across Cracker Daddy's shoulder for probably a half hour. Then he stopped and the horde closed around us. I remembered the guy from Texas. The footless one with the teeth that clacked. "Melon balled," was what he'd called it.

I did the kind of struggling I guess you have to do once Cracker Daddy sat me down, but there were fangs and talons everywhere. Damp alabastard hide all over. I barely had room to shift my shoulders. There was nowhere at all to run. Even if they'd parted and turned me loose, where would I have gone? That bait geezoid had taken my headlamp. I still had the pocket flint we all carried. It was stuffed in a tube with some cedar shavings, but they'd only give me enough light to show me where I'd die.

As it was, I couldn't raise my arms. Alabastards were packed tight around me, and if I didn't move the way they wanted, I got a wealth of talon pricks. So on we went. Down, I could tell that much. Deep dark like I'd never known it. Claw on stone and sinusy breathing was all I could hear for a very great while.

I thought about Toppy. Quite a lot about Toppy. The last human thing I'd heard was her calling, shrieking for me, her voice going distant and tiny until I could no longer hear her at all. I hated the idea of being just a brass plaque on a slab at Carlsbad. I remembered sitting for the photo they were sure to use. Their circuit photographer had come through Virginia. They always tell you it's for the directory, but that's just an old-time courtesy. It was a portrait for the Lost Lords wall. I'd seen a picture of the thing in the quarterly after an ambush in Delaware. Four of ours got dragged to the deep dark after weeks of barren forays. They were holding gropers in their photos just the way I'd had to do. Same look on their faces I'd had on mine. I guess they'd been told, "Say guano" too.

The Lost Lords wall was covered mostly with provisionals. Damaged, itinerant sorts like Keith, and now I'd be with them as well. I'd been fool enough to show a bit of mercy to a geezoid, and there I was down in the far underneath doomed to be a meal.

I probably would have felt sorrier for myself if I'd not been so stinking tired. The swarm of alabastards minding me only stopped about once an hour. That's what it felt like anyway, and the longer we went, the more pricked all over I got.

I finally said, "Hold on," and quit running. I was ready to have it over with and hoped they'd start with my feet so I could sit.

They grumbled — the ones right around me. It was a lizardy sort of racket. Then they raised me and kept on going, and I rode on top of the swarm. Up there I could smell the untainted air. It was sweeter than normal cave quaff but still sharp in my lungs. I had to guess we were in the transit going to Missouri for all I knew.

I wondered what I'd do to rescue me and worked through plans and tactics. Nothing I could come up with seemed like nearly enough.

We went somewhere particular. By that I mean we left the transit and took a side channel that was closer and tighter. The air was damper and warmer the farther we travelled.

I heard more alabastards up ahead. They were chuffing and screeching the way they sometimes do. Then my bunch did the same thing back before they all went in for some kind of *Huzzah!* The sort of noise you might make if your were half crocodile and expecting a barbecue.

I was lean, maybe one hundred and seventy-five pounds in my boots. I decided to take pleasure in how little of me there'd be to go around. It wasn't much pleasure, and I only took it briefly. Anything to keep from wailing and begging and letting them know how I truly felt.

When the two forces joined, I got poked and prodded. Then they set me down on a sizeable ledge with what turned out to be about a dozen alabastard babies. I'd run across one or two before, always dead and left behind.

They weren't at all like human babies. They didn't need coddling or protecting. They were more like new born rattlesnakes – had all the tools but no control. They hadn't yet learned how not to be ferocious all the time, so it was like I'd been inserted into a sack of angry tomcats. I suffered worse with those babies than I had in my entire cave crawling life.

They climbed all over me and bit where they pleased, clawed everywhere they touched. I decided the big chief wanted me infected as a flavor booster. One of the little demons nipped off a plug of my left ear.

That's when I started flinging babies and guessed I'd get laid open for it. I'm pretty sure I bounced a couple of them off the cavern wall. I yelled as I did it, "Eat my damn feet. I don't even care."

I kept expecting the sensation of having both of them lopped clean off, but instead I heard what struck me as alabastard murmuring. Cracker Daddy, I decided, was the loudest of the bunch. He'd make a noise by himself. Then the rest of them would chuff and burble back. It was a bit like talking, just no words and no sense as far as I could tell.

It worked for them, though. The geezoid with my headlamp got directed, I had to think, to switch it on. Because that's just what he did, so I got a look at my situation. The alabastards instinctively shrank from the light, but they couldn't go much of anywhere.

We were packed into a vaulted cavern that was the size of a cathedral. Hundreds and hundreds of alabastards and only one of me. "Pipe down. You're done" was the message I took from that quarter minute of illumination. There was nowhere for me to go. No escape for me to make. I'd get what they'd decided I was due.

It worked after a fashion. I had nothing more to say, and they finished clearing the ledge of babies and let me have it all to myself.

I'm pretty sure I slept because I'm certain that I dreamed. I was somewhere sun-splashed with my dog and my girl. Not in the city but out in the world where there was open sky and trees. We were eating some of those weird shrimp-flavored chips from Sal's Chinatown store and making the kinds of plans you make with people when you're dreaming. We'd decided to drive to Australia because Toppy knew the best way to go.

"What's that smell?" I asked her.

She didn't seem to hear me and talked at length about camper vans. Then Beauty snatched the chip bag and ran into a leafy thicket. I called her, but she wouldn't come back, so me and Toppy went looking for her, and soon I found myself in the woods alone.

There were toads on the forest floor. Big tropical lizards in the trees. I heard Toppy calling from off somewhere.

"Mack! Mack!"

I tried to answer but couldn't. I sniffed the foul air and reached to scratch a spot where my neck was itchy. That's when I woke up in the deep dark with my fingers in an alabastard's mouth. The tips were resting on his lower sharpies, the ones he tore flesh with. He didn't bite me. He didn't prick me. He didn't slice me with a talon. He just moaned and resettled the way, I guess, any creature does asleep.

Alabastards were piled up all around me, sleeping in tangled heaps. That cavern had warmed considerably and felt about like a terrarium. It sure smelled like one. After a few hours in among them, I'd decided they stank like a combination of laundry basket and mud wog with a pinch of python musk thrown in. It wasn't unpleasant, just intensely earthy.

The creature hard to my right rolled over and laid an arm upon me — not in anger or agitation but just by drowsy happenstance. The talons pricked me through my coveralls. I got a blast of alabastard breath — about what you'd expect from a creature that lived on cousins and raw livestock.

I don't know how long we slept. I'm not sure how long we did anything. Four hours? A day? I had no way of knowing. Granddaddy Hoyt's old pocket Hamilton watch had ended up with Dad, and he kept it in a sack with the bracelets and rings my mom had left behind. Down under, we tended to measure time by how long our headlamps lasted. We could tell by how dingy they went how long we'd been and how long we could go.

In the deep dark with those alabastards all I knew was I got hungry. At first, I'd been too rattled and scared to spare a thought for food, but after that nap I woke up aching for something to shove in my mouth. I searched my pockets and found mostly lint and grit but did discover a chunk of almond. It was left from the mix Clarice made every few weeks. Dried fruit. Mixed nuts. M&Ms.

I blew on that nut and popped it into my mouth. I tried to chew and savor the thing and was making a decent job of it when my alabastards all woke up. The ones close around me stirred and sniffed the air. The racket of them waking woke the ones out from them. Pretty soon the rustling and rising was general along with the sniffing too.

A creature next to me stuck a talon in my mouth and dug out with it what puny bits of almond I had left. I think it sniffed them. That's what it sounded like. Then it made a throaty noise. That got spread and communicated, went out through the horde like a breeze. Then everything started reorganizing. I could hear claws on rock and feel the stirring air, but I couldn't see a thing until Cracker Daddy switched my headlamp on.

He was across the way towards what turned out to be some kind of spring fed pond. Or more likely we were down with the aquifer, and some of it had leaked into a natural basin. He made enough of a motion to make me understand I should join him, and the alabastards parted sufficiently to give me room to pass.

Cracker Daddy pointed at the water. I went down on my knees and scooped out a mouthful. The stuff was cold and sweet. When I stood up, Cracker Daddy offered me a strip of jerky. It hardly looked like the beef or the turkey stuff we carried, but my chunk of almond hadn't satisfied, so I took it from him with a nod.

I sniffed it. That met with general approval. Alabastards were big on sniffing. It smelled like nothing much the way jerky often does. There wasn't a thing else to do but take a bite, so I closed my eyes and clamped down and tore off a bit. I chewed and hoped it wouldn't be snaky. It could have been alabastard, but I prefer to believe it was goat. Sheep maybe. Not cow. Certainly edible. Not salted, but there was distinct spice to it. It was food for sure, and I was grateful to have it to hand.

Cracker Daddy had some sort of poultice on his shoulder where my ripper bolt had gone in.

I pointed towards it and told him, “Sorry.”

The creatures around me all murmured in a low, creepy way some version of “Sorry” back. Cracker Daddy, for his part, laid the tip of a claw on the hollow of his neck. Somehow he seemed to know that I’d not taken dead aim the way I should have.

I nodded and told him, “Right.”

The alabastards said that too.

Some of them were wearing hats and shirts. Usually not both together. They appeared to have quit on the trousers. Given the strapping way they were built down below, I couldn’t blame them much. I saw two in housecoats and one in some kind of denim ladies’ jumper. But the rest were as God or whoever had made them. White and slick and treacherous looking.

I jabbed my thumb nowhere much and said to Cracker Daddy, “I should go.”

Hundreds of them repeated it as best as their split tongues would allow. Cracker Daddy might have smiled. That was a hard thing to tell with a CF. I do know he pointed at the rocky cavern floor and told me, “Here.”

Then they squatted. All of them and pretty much at once. Just went down on their haunches and stayed there. I tried to join them, but a pair of alabastards lifted me back up. Then a third one pricked me with her clapper claw. She was a vile old thing, tufted and groper scarred.

"What's that for?"

They all said it back, and not badly.

Cracker Daddy switched off my headlamp, and him and the beasts around him glowed. I waited. They waited. I got pricked again.

"What's the deal here?"

They said that too.

"You want me to talk? Is that it?"

They were more confident now and louder.

"Alright."

"Alright."

"So this is some kind of practice?"

"So this is some kind of practice?" They were all in on it. Many hundreds — my own weird, murmuring echo that was slightly laggy and out of sync.

"Fine."

"Fine."

I tried to think of what to say, as if it really mattered. They were just working to get their mouths and tongues to make the words.

I got pricked again.

"Quit it."

"Quit it."

There I was miles under New York City looking out on scores of squatting alabastards bathed in their own phosphorescence and all of them repeating every syllable I said. What if they boiled out and killed us all because I'd helped them enunciate?

I was troubled and torn, but the talon pricks had a way of taking care of that. So I did what they wanted.

"I'm going to tell you about Magnus, the Robot Fighter."

They pretty well butchered that one.

"He lived in New York with his girlfriend."

Better, but still a bit split-tongue plagued.

"They had a place up high. Skyscraper."

A mucousy relapse.

"They'd watch the sun come up in bed."

Solid. Almost in harmony.

"Magnus," I said, "the Robot Fighter."

"Magnus, the Robot Fighter."

It went like that for a while. I would have guessed a week, but it turned out to be four days. We stayed put. I lived on sweet cave water and what I hoped was livestock jerky. I can't say I saw an alabastard eat or drink a thing. They squatted. They slept. They milled around. They got dosed with my headlamp beam.

I remembered the sight of them circulating through the band of light beneath the subway station. They clearly had plans that involved them emerging into the sunlight and open air. Or moonlight maybe. I couldn't really say.

Cracker Daddy healed in the time we were there. The poultice he used was spit and something. It smelled worse even than alabastard breath. I could always locate him with my nose. All I know is his bolt hole closed and vanished. There was just the slightest scar.

My headlamp was running out of juice. I could see that much. Cracker Daddy would switch it on for maybe eight or ten minutes, and always different alabastards (I could tell them apart after a while) would take up positions in the beam and let themselves get lit. It appeared to be sharply painful first, but the discomfort dulled with time.

I talked, no pricking required. We moved off Magnus to Bible verses. I didn't know many. My people were kind of agnostic, given our job. I still had scraps in my head of Granddaddy's circumcision spiel, and I took a bit of pleasure in hearing the particulars of hillbilly pruning murmured my way. I ran through an assortment of Uncle Grady's casserole recipes, all of them more or less the same but for the addition or exclusion of canned beans. I recited the words of a song my mother used to sing me about a pony, and I told the story of Leigh Ann and her chicken nuggets and how we'd taken turns holding her hair.

I once pressed Cracker Daddy, with my chorus behind me, to tell me if I'd get eaten. I think I was having a desperate moment and was sick of the suspense.

He laid a talon to the spot on his neck that I'd elected not to shoot. I decided to take that as a "maybe not."

Whenever I eased off my ledge and felt along the wall to do my personal business, some of them always went with me. Not hard on but close enough. I could hear them, feel them. They watched what I got up to and inspected, I do believe, whatever came out. Students to the end.

It all got tedious after a while. I knew we'd be out of lamplight soon, and then darkness would uninterrupted. The thought of that did a thing in my head I hadn't really expected. I'd spent much of my life in caverns and chutes, in muddy crawls and pinches. You would have thought I'd have made my peace with the darkness, but in the deep dark with the alabastards, it felt to me like doom. No light. No people — especially dear people. No dog I loved. A steady diet of goat jerky and water. And me saying whatever stuff I could conjure so they could say it back.

I figured we'd move in time. Go deeper and farther, and my best hope was that they'd take me up and out some night on a raid. Who knew where we'd be by then. A bit of fresh air and the dark of the moon seemed all I had to hope for.

But then I heard it right in the middle of another general lesson. I was down to country music lyrics. I worked through a pack of trashy songs before I remember one that suited.

"I got four walls around me to hold my life."

They said it and did okay.

"To keep me from going astray."

That proved a twister for them.

"And a honky tonk angel to hold me tight."

They'd gotten sharp with their Ks.

"To keep me from slipping away."

They made porridge out of that one, and I was going to try it again when I heard the noise that stopped me short.

Not a growl exactly but a racket in a dog's throat I'd heard scores of times before.

"Beauty," I said.

And hundreds of alabastards said it too.

2

I know now how it all went. Five days, six hours and change. Dad, Clarice, and Toppy especially agitated to go deep and save me, but in showing themselves, the alabastards had stirred up the hysterics. Some of them were regular run-of-the-mill over-excited civilians, but quite a few were New York politicians, and there was a claque in Washington too. Senators mostly. Men exclusively. The kind built to keep people scared.

So the NYPD supplied tactical units in their helmets and black trucks, and the army sent in some super secret force in helicopters, and they all went under Brooklyn. Then they all came right back out.

"Nothing down there but rats" was the general report. "And not an awful lot of them."

They wouldn't listen to Dad and Clarice at first. They had no use at all for Toppy. They put Aldo in cuffs for about half a day once a soldier had talked to Leigh Ann in a tone that he couldn't sit still and take.

Detective Les was the one who finally got through to the army brass and police bosses. "These people," he said of my clan, "know exactly what's going on."

Dad gave our history to an army captain, an assistant police commissioner, a couple of elite SWAT officers, and the whole crew of special forces. There were eight or ten of them. They didn't require persuasion, only orders. But they sat and heard Dad out in polite silence nonetheless. He could quote Jefferson but hardly to the extent of Uncle Grady, and Dad knew our traditions and lore about like most people know the Old Testament. The flood, the ark, the pillar of salt — like that.

It was a waste of time. Clarice had to know it right from the beginning. She was good about efficiency where people were concerned. So she didn't trouble herself to try to back Dad up with chatter. She let Leigh Ann and Brody throw in. Marcy uncorked a few "Ok look"s, but Sal was enough of a Brooklyn boy to know better than to talk to the cops.

Clarice let it all go where it might, and once Dad and them had quit, she fished that alabastard hand out of her satchel and unwrapped it. The one she shot through with the ripper bolt and the owner had gnawed off. Alabastard parts will stay semi-fresh and seepy for a pretty considerable while. That hand was still shiny and fluid damp. The talons extended if you knew where to push. Clarice did. She made sure they saw the claws and then tossed the thing onto the table before them.

"Here you go, boys," Clarice said. She singled out a moose of a cop, a strapping guy in body army. "And the little ones are big as you."

"We're going down," Dad said. "You can come if you want."

My people left. Les went out with them. A half dozen special forces boys caught up with them in the culvert. They'd been tasked and charged and properly ordered. Somebody had even thought enough about it to give them reasonable arms. They were carrying what looked like tactical machetes and had brought along enough night scopes to go around. They tried to object to a dog on the mission. Beauty had some years on her and surely could look old and balky, but she'd just learned to save herself for when there was an alabastard to bite.

"We take orders from you," the head special ops guy said, the one that talked for the bunch anyway. He wasn't looking at Dad or Sal or Aldo, at Les or Leigh Ann or Brody or Toppy. They'd picked out Clarice. Those boys knew a natural warrior when they found one.

"Alright," she said and turned to Leigh Ann. "Tell them what to do with those."

Leigh Ann relieved one of the army of guys of his flat black machete. She tested the heft and edge. "Not bad," she said and then ventilated that soldier's shirtfront for him as she instructed those boys, "You cut them here and here."

It went like that as they worked their way into and down along the transit. They all made do with army food you could just tear open and eat. They stopped and slept when they felt like they had to. They tried to keep up with the passing hours, but those lose meaning after a while. They took turns switching on lamps and night scopes, kept untouched spares for getting out. Mostly they came quiet with Beauty in the lead. She got sprier and younger the deeper they went, the closer they inched to alabastards.

The special forces boys warmed to her and tried to pal with her after a while, but Beauty was all attentive business. She had a friend already. Me.

Days passed. They couldn't say how many. The compasses the army boys were carrying went haywire early on. Their radios kicked out static only, so they left most of them behind in a pile along with anything that fired a bullet. Les was allowed to keep his shotgun since he'd shown already he knew to aim high.

"What did you tell your wife?" Dad asked Les after a while.

"Conference," Les said, "in the Poconos."

"We're probably there by now," from Sal.

The special forces boys were starting to ask about turning back. Low on pouch food and out of water but for what trickled down the cavern walls.

"Go on," Clarice told them as her and my people continued deep and down.

They followed, of course. They weren't about to get shamed by civilians and a cop, and not even a proper meathead cop but a savvy, fit detective who knew his place in the crew and kept to it, didn't let on to have rank to pull.

Those boys were scared probably, but they weren't allowed to show it. They'd make mutinous noises and get left behind, but they'd reconsider and catch up. Then the chafing trailed off and the misgivings dried up as they hardened to their circumstances. So the crew was all together and about as ready as they'd get when Beauty, who was well ahead, finally made her noise.

I didn't for a moment think my mind was playing tricks, that an alabastard had shifted and moved in some way to make a noise like Beauty's. I knew it was her. I'd heard that racket a couple of thousand times. It hit me like a jolt of main current, and somehow I figured out exactly what to do.

My job was to keep the alabastards talking so they'd both be distracted and give themselves away. Toppy would have been proud of me since she was a wiz with the Great Book. I landed on a chunk of Thomas Jefferson that I could recite full and true. It was larded, of course, with heretofores and thoroughly seasoned with nonethelesses and was largely devoted to Low Lord duty and took the form of an oath.

So there the alabastards were swearing fealty to our legion and then blessing a Low Lord's traditional stable of tools — the groper, the talwar, the spike, the ripper. We capped it off with a rousing tribute to fuel oil and the cave lamps. They were even making a decent job of it when Beauty charged in on their flank.

I don't think alabastards are quite built to warble with surprise, but this pack came as close to doing that as any might. They sure knew something was after them, something with teeth and will and fury, and from the noise they made I could tell they were falling back in disarray.

I was trying to tuck beneath my ledge in case they decided to kill the hostage (and make a snack of my feet on the spot), and that's when I heard Toppy's battle cry and the tang of steel on cave stone. The thunk of a ripper bolt tearing into alabastard flesh. Beauty's growl. Brody's screech. Some guy's bout of swearing. My clan, more or less, in full push with some recruits for support.

I kept expecting a headlamp beam, kept looking for enough light to guide me away from the CFs and over to my crew.

But I couldn't find one. It stayed pitchy everywhere but for the occasional dancing green dot. I know now they were the lozenge-sized indicator lights on night goggles they all were wearing. They looked like a swarm of fireflies from where I was.

"Mack!" It was Dad calling out.

"Over here." I moved once I'd shouted. I kept forgetting that I was the only one around who couldn't see and didn't want one of my CF buddies to take initiative and slash me. I kept shifting until I'd found a cleft in the rock face that would hold me, and I slid in sideways as far as I could manage.

It felt a touch cowardly given the battle raging all around me. I caught the occasional spark of steel glancing off of stone, heard the scratch of talons as CFs climbed the rock walls and scrabbled like they do, and I could sure hear beauty snarling and yapping, Toppy snarling and yapping a little herself. Then some sort of explosive went off, and a dull hum was all I heard for a while.

Those special forces guys and their concussion grenades. They started pitching them all over. Clarice and Dad were yelling for them not to, but they'd forgotten about everything but saving their skins and so cut loose with all they had. As I understand it (I couldn't see squat) Les finally made an impression on those soldiers with his shotgun. He brought the barrel to bear on the pack of them and made them understand he'd shoot. They'd get left in the deep dark and eaten for sure, or they could raise their machetes and fight.

All they'd needed was an ecourager, as it turned out. Throw another grenade and I'll kill you proved exactly what they had to hear. They scrapped well after that, waded in flailing and swearing, and them and my clan together began to force that whole horde back. Alabastards started streaming through a channel at the rear of our cavern. It had to be on orders from Cracker Daddy since they had the numbers to swamp us all.

He had something better in mind for his clan. That's what I decided. Something grander and more lasting. They weren't getting adjusted for nothing. To the light. To the language. To the general idea of leaving the deep dark behind. They didn't need to kill us because we didn't matter in Cracker Daddy's great scheme of things.

They did grab one special forces guy and leave him nearly naked. Sure they snatched his machete from him, but they took all his gear as well. His night scope. His remaining concussion grenades. His first aid kit. His radio that he'd refused to leave back up the transit with his gun. Then they spat him back out once he'd gotten the mark — a sideways Q in a hat on his neck.

Finally, Clarice switched on a proper headlamp and I could see at last. My crew was a beautiful sight even if they all looked like they'd been dipped in alabastard fluid. Toppy charged up and punched me hard in the arm for letting myself get snatched. She kissed me too, in front of everybody.

"Where's Beauty?" She should have been by me by then.

Then I heard her. We all did. She was deep in the cavern, maybe down the channel already chasing the alabastards out. I whistled for her. I called. I took a lamp and a groper and ran her way. Toppy was right with me. Sal and Aldo and Leigh Ann too.

I caught a glimpse of her in the channel fighting six big alabastards. A wounded one was biting her back left leg. She was lurching and nipping at the other five when they closed on her and swallowed her up. Then the whole scrum moved down the channel, around a kink and out of sight.

"Come on!" I tried to follow, but Sal and Aldo held me back.

Clarice and Dad were closing on us by then.

"Mack," Clarice said and wrapped one of her wiry arms around me.

They all crowded close to comfort me and, I have to think, hold me in check.

"Beauty!" I yelled. I whistled. I got nothing but echo back.

I can't say how long it took to get out. We never really stopped entirely. The special forces guys were awfully proud of themselves, and they wouldn't any of them shut up. They'd fought monsters under New York City. Cannibals with teeth and claws and stuff.

One of them kept saying, "Osama who?" And the rest of them would cackle and hoot.

I straggled, kept hoping that Beauty would race up to join me out of the dark. They were waiting for us on the lit end of the culvert. It was late in the day, and the sun had just about set over Manhattan. There was army brass and police bosses. The special forces guys had radioed up. Carlsbad was represented as well, and not just by a Flex Corps squad. They'd sent an elder as well. He was wearing a boxy suit and beard down to his sternum, but I looked right past him because he'd come with Uncle Grady and Jo Jo too.

"They got Beauty," I said, and Jo Jo came to me.

He'd slimmed down and neatened up but was Jo Jo to the core.

"I'm sorry, Mack," he told me, and I pressed my face to his shoulder and wept.

The army and the city officials decided it was a triumph. Hostage saved. Dog lost. Alabastard swarm routed. But it only sounded decisive if you'd spent your life in the sun. We knew better. Cracker Daddy and them had retreated, but they'd be back.

Grady and Jo Jo joined us in our apartment where we all cleaned up and ordered Chinese. Uncle Grady told stories about the old days. We had a few tales about Sal and his clan. Clarice gave Grady and Jo Jo (and me as well) a blow by blow of the assault in the deep dark.

Big changes were afoot in Carlsbad, and Grady told us all about them. The army and the Flex Corps would help Sal and his clan keep the city holes plugged. "You and yours," Grady told dad, "are getting reassigned."

"Not me," Leigh Ann said.

We all looked at her and waited for more, but she just took Aldo by the hand and said nothing else. She'd turned seventeen, and she'd do what she wanted within the community. That was the way with Low Lords. She knew it. We knew it too. And I'm sure Dad could tell like I could that Leigh Ann had flat made up her mind.

There was nothing to say back but, “Well.” The “all right” was implied.

That’s when Toppy set the balance right. “I’m going.” She took my hand.

A lieutenant came up to invite us all to join him for a debriefing, but we decided to stay with the moo shoo and dumplings instead. Carlsbad could throw in with the army and make alliances out in the world, but we knew we weren’t for everybody, and we preferred our kind. That’s how the deep dark works on Low Lords. It’s our fate and our cement.

3

It was Kentucky for us. Rich with holes to plug. Detective Les Hayden brought us a Volvo station wagon from the police impound lot.

"They won't miss it," he assured us.

His partner had followed him in their official sedan, so we all got to see Tony inspect his fingernails one last time. Les promised Dad he'd keep a watchful eye on Leigh Ann.

"Just topside, though," he told us and pointed at the ground. "She's on her own down there."

It was a tough leave-taking for all of us. Grady and Jo Jo were there as well, and Brody did quite a lot of wailing. He was keen on his sister now that he'd lost her. He wanted to go. He wanted to stay. He wanted to sit on the pavement and whine.

We didn't have a lot to pack beyond gropers and rippers and spikes. We'd go to a big box in Kentucky and get some fresh clothes, new coveralls for cave crawling. Even Toppy only brought one suitcase, and it was hardly any size.

Marcy had packed us a lunch. "Ok, look," she said and then explained how we should eat it. Soon we'd run out of stuff to tell each other, and our lot piled in the car and left. That Volvo was a far sight cozier than the country squire we'd driven up in, and we were down a dog and so had more room, especially once Brody had climbed into the way back to ride on top of our gropers and pout.

It took Dad several passes to find the ramp to the Manhattan Bridge. Then we crept in clotted traffic along Canal Street to the tunnel. Crept some more out 1&9 to the highway west across New Jersey that went into Pennsylvania at Allentown. Brody fell asleep, and Toppy went quiet. We were farther into the country at large than she had ever been.

We stopped for gas near Harrisburg. Clarice had decided to count our stipend — a bundle of cash that Grady had handed over in a Holiday Inn envelope. Dad had shoved it in the glovebox unchecked. Clarice was more of a natural checker, so we were pulling into a Flying J when she got a tally and snorted.

"Shorted us," she said. "A hundred and a half." She showed Dad a sheet of notepaper Grady had done his figuring on. Additional charges levied. Deductions disallowed. "Sometimes," Clarice informed us, "I think a swarm up's just the thing."

We stopped for a night of rest and a proper meal in Morgantown, West Virginia. Dad nosed up the sort of restaurant that seemed to specialize in gravy. The kind that's thickened with flour and speckled with skillet crunch They put it on everything but the pie. We had Salisbury steak and meatloaf and chicken and scattershot, idle conversation. They all avoided talk of the deep dark and the days that I'd spent down there. It was like I was just home from prison or some ghastly war and all people wanted to do was talk around it.

That was okay with me. I sopped about a pint of gravy with biscuits the size of coasters, and then Toppy told us what exactly she could remember of Korea. She was reminded of some stretch of mountains there by the rugged terrain of Morgantown.

Dad got us two rooms in a motor lodge and handed me one of the keys. He and Clarice didn't say a word, just took Brody with them. It wasn't like me and Toppy had ever dated or anything. We'd had a few meals. Been on a few walks. Fought some close combat under Brooklyn. Looking from the outside, people would say we were from two different worlds, but Toppy was as close to Low Lord as any human could get, especially one born civilian and (for our clan) way the hell somewhere else.

We got in the bed in lots of clothes and watched some rubbish on TV. Toppy let me decide when to switch off the lights. She probably thought I wasn't ready for darkness given where I'd been and how.

We laid close. She waited. I started slow, but it all came out — everything I could remember. The smell, the dread, the constant sound of alabastard claw on rock.

"They're coming up," I told her. "In their time. They're down there getting ready."

Uncle Grady would have chuffed and doubted me. Not Toppy. She asked me, "Wouldn't you?"

We fell asleep in our clothes. Woke up in the small hours and shed them. We were both ready to do something about what we had by then.

Jo Jo had given Dad directions to the compound in Kentucky with a significant turn off missing, so we drove around for a bit. It's a pocked landscape. You could hardly find a pasture without a solution hole in it. Sometimes three or four of them in a thirty-acre stretch. That whole central run of territory is dimpled like a golf ball. You're constantly reminded that you're standing on the crust and there's an awful lot of hollow underneath.

We eventually blundered on our new home. We were looking for a cellphone signal. Dad was aiming to call Carlsbad and figure it all out. We'd stopped at the end of a long gravel track. There was a hand-lettered sign on a gatepost. No words, just a symbol. What looked like a Q laid over and wearing a hat.

As Low Lord digs go, our Kentucky spot was swanky. We had a rambling farmhouse the previous crew had renovated and dressed up. It looked yokel as hell on the outside but was updated under the roof. A kitchen with all the fineries. A proper formal dining room. All kinds of electronics in a den with a wet bar. A library of a sort. The books turned out mostly to be spines glued to planks for effect.

There were plenty of bedrooms and toilets all over. A screened-in back porch with fans overhead.

"Got to be a catch," Clarice decided. "Our CFs must be hellions."

That seemed more than likely, so we avoided our cavern at first. We had sheds to inspect. A lawn to mow. The leavings of a garden to harvest. Jo Jo had assured us there'd be a herd of sheep, but we couldn't find them at first. Our land went for a bit. We had pasture and woodlands, and we took a couple of days to walk the fence line. It was stout and unbroken from end to end.

"Got to be in here somewhere," Dad said and eyed the woods at the head of the pasture.

We all went looking. It was a rocky, snaky trip, but we finally found all forty head crowded on the highest lump of ground. They peed when they saw us. That's what you get from sheep instead of any sort of proper cordial acknowledgment and affection.

"What are they doing way up here?" It took Brody to ask it.

The rest of us had already decided we knew: Because nothing good happens down low.

We drove them back and closed them in the pen behind the barn. We didn't stake one at the cavern mouth since we'd not been in the cavern and, after Brooklyn, I think we'd all decided the livestock didn't matter much. It was like giving the devil a stick of gum. He might stop for a moment to chew it, but he was still sure to bring hell with him and keep on being the devil himself.

Clarice announced that she'd make sweaters. There was some kind of loom in the barn loft and spinners and bobbins and racks and such. She was an awful long way from getting put out of the truck she'd rolled up in drunk.

We'd probably been in Kentucky a week before we trooped in force to the cavern. We had new coveralls from the Tractor Supply, new cave sneakers, the latest halogen headlamps. Same old gropers and rippers. Dad brought his talwar. We'd all buffed our blades and sharpened every edge that we could find.

It wasn't dread exactly that had held us back from our duty in Kentucky. We were still spent from Brooklyn and sad about Beauty. We were also coming to grips with how little what we got up to meant. Low Lords had long been like a version of Grand Masons. We had tools and ceremony. A sworn and sacred obligation. Scripture passed down to us from the sages of their age.

But that was back when alabastards seemed content to stay below. They took part in our pageants. We generally kept them in beef stock. We'd have above. They'd have below. We'd clash at the fringes sometimes.

It didn't help that the cavern that came with our farm was massive and far reaching. We were maybe twelve miles from Mammoth Cave and probably could have reached it underground. The previous clan had left us a detailed subterranean map of the region and the whole area was undershot with channels and rifts and passageways cut everywhere water could flow. Low Lords had worked for decades to seal off the local tourist caverns with rock slides and hardened barricades, and they'd mostly kept civilians safe. There was the odd guide gone missing or spelunker lost but never so many at once or so often to raise any sort of alarm.

Our cavern had stout steel doors on it with a reinforced surround that was coped tight against the rock. Scores of Low Lords through the years had scratched their names and their marks on the steel. The doors were held shut with a barrel bolt as big around as my forearm, and there was a lock in the hasp about the size of a cabbage. The key to it was big enough to club a man unconscious with.

"Here goes," Dad said as he turned the key with both hands. That locked worked like a dream and fell open.

It took three of us to draw the barrel bolt back, and then the doors parted of their own. The center seal released with a hiss.

That cave didn't smell dank at all. There was too much space and moving air for that. Dad found a service box as promised just inside on a post. It had a lone switch on the outer case. He threw it and lit the cavern. The ceiling arched out of sight, up in the gloom. That first chamber alone was big enough to hold our entire house. No trash anywhere. Not the first ottoman in sight.

There were six steel stairs down to the level floor. The place was so tidy it looked all but scoured. There were four ways out excluding the doors. One crack that would handle two men abreast. A crawl about three feet high. And a couple of spacious channels. One had no wear and so seemed a dead end.

I could well remember Cumberland with its cramped squeeze and crumbling rock. We'd battled alabastards there right up close and hand to hand. Here was some space in Kentucky where we could stand up and rattle around.

"So?" Clarice said.

She was talking to Dad. We all knew exactly what she meant. We'd shown up and come inside. Did we really need to press on? Was our sworn duty much worth doing?

Dad and Grady were from the same stock. We all forgot it sometimes, but they'd been raised and trained by Granddaddy Hoyt, and he'd been scrupulous and particular. You did what you were supposed to do, and you made damn sure you did it well.

"I'll take lead," Dad told Clarice. He pointed at one of the spacious channels. "Let's stay standing first."

We followed him in. Clarice on Dad's right shoulder with her ripper. Then Brody. Then Toppy. I brought up the rear in case anything fell in behind us. I heard the noise we made, but that was all. I felt tuned to alabastard racket. Every scuttling, sinusy sound those things had produced in my days under ground had gone into a memory log I consulted as we walked. I knew the right scrape or gurgle would grab me hard. I just wondered how I'd hold up.

The channel we'd taken lead us into a chamber about twice the size of the one we'd entered coming through the doors. There were rifts and branches off of it, and all of them got inspected, but the bulk of them narrowed and quit and a couple of the big ones were clotted with rock slides. Still no sign of alabastards, so we retraced and started fresh.

We tried the crack next. It snaked along for a good ways. I was leading on this one, ripper at the ready until we met with a curious blockade. Three tree stumps shoved into a spot, a constriction where the rock walls bent.

"Dead end," I said.

The root ends were on the far side. It was a keep out of here kind of thing.

We drew back again and tried the channel that had no wear and looked like it quit. It did, not twenty yards along, so there was only the crawl left for us.

Brody didn't want to go. He'd come to hate crawls. Me and Leigh Ann had snuck up on him in one and dragged him screaming by his ankles. He'd decided it had scarred him, and he knew just who to blame.

"Uh uh," he said outside the squeeze. He pointed my way. "You know."

"Then go to the house," Clarice told him.

"You're not my mother." Brody was going through a phase where he got that way pretty quick.

Dad wasn't much with Brody. Me neither, for that matter. And Clarice wasn't, in fact, his mother, so she kind of left him alone. Toppy gave us a chance to handle the kid and only stepped in once we didn't. She pulled Brody aside and said a thing to him. It was brief and didn't look particularly sharp, but Brody came away reformed.

He hit the crawl at speed. Disappeared. Came back.

"Y'all coming?"

We nodded. He slipped off again. We all paused to look Toppy's way.

"I'm going to answer all his girl questions. Even the weird, hard ones."

Then she crawled in after Brody. Dad said, "Luck to you," and we went in as well.

We came out in a sizable hollow. It was big enough to hold the five us with little room to spare. Then more crawling. Muddy this time. Then a cave stream and a chamber with a lone passage off it we decided to take. We'd found no trace of CFs. No claw marks. No spore. No musk we could smell.

"Girls have hair there?" A deal was a deal. Brody had questions. Toppy was handy.

She nodded. "Unless they shave it."

Brody looked more outraged than illuminated. "Why do that!?"

Toppy shrugged and led into the passage with Brody close behind her and talking. We all followed and tried to keep up. I was the last one in and the last one out. They were all standing and watching me climb from the crawl with peculiar looks on their faces.

"What?" I said.

Toppy pointed.

I thought I was dreaming again.

Beauty was parked on a ledge in a cage made of bones. Cow bones. Goat bones. Sheep bones. The spine of something that had walked erect. Maybe one of those wayward spelunkers or possibly an alabastard. That cage was fitted together like a puzzle. No door. No front. No back. She was down to three legs. Her left rear was gone, and her stump was slathered with poultice. The stinky stuff that Cracker Daddy had treated his bolt hole with.

She made her happy noise, seemed about as shocked as we were. Beauty stamped her front feet and all but whinnied.

Dad and Clarice feared a trap, but I didn't care. I called to her and climbed to get her. I found a weak spot in the bone work and pulled the whole damn cage apart. Beauty wiggled and yelped. I did much the same. She was a leg short but otherwise fine.

I laid her across my shoulders and carried her down to the cave floor. Clarice had her head on a swivel. She was clearly expecting trouble, but we all got sniffed and licked and warbled at, and no trouble ever came.

So it was back through the passage — five plus one now — and out through the crawl to the tidy cavern chamber. Then up the six steps and into the lit world through the cavern door.

Beauty rolled in the pasture grass. She yipped and barked. She ran in circles on three legs as well as she'd ever done on four.

Dad did some calculating on the way back to the house. She'd been lost to us for eight days. They didn't just patch her. They fed her and moved her.

"How'd they know to come here?" I wondered allowed. "What are they trying to tell us?"

They all took a stab. Toppy and Dad gave Cracker Daddy tactical chops and heroic stamina. Brody gave them some sort of sideways, subterranean elevator which the more he described it, sounded like a pneumatic alabastard tube. But Clarice was the one who, by my lights, came out with the proper answer.

"They're more than we've ever suspected," she said. "And probably worse than we've ever thought.

4

We had skirmishes only, never battles, and even the skirmishes were rare. Our CFs would reliably fall back before us and fail to draw us into mischief. No matter how far we pursued them, we always ended up alone.

I'm fairly certain I caught a solitary glimpse of Cracker Daddy. He was retiring along a passage just ahead of my headlamp beam. I identified him by his scarring — the X in puffy glazed tissue on his back. He turned once and looked my way before the darkness swallowed him up.

Chiefly we met with adolescents. They were nearly as tall as adults but a heck of a lot thinner. More bone than muscle. Coyote framed. It would have taken a dozen of them to do in a capable Low Lord. Marcy could probably have laid out three or four without even breaking a nail.

We couldn't help but notice their movements tended to be organized and regular. They'd flow and ebb in flanking order and make contentious exhibitions before us without actually risking harm. It was worse than a fight since the last thing we wanted to see from alabastards was regular battle tactics and a display of restraint. We'd long counted on them being animals that we could bait and master and with as much of a knack for strategy as house cats have for higher math.

We continued to do our cavern duty, just not every day. There was a farm to run and sheep to tend, nosy neighbors to lie to. Me and Dad learned to shear and supplied raw wool to Clarice and Toppy who figured out how to spin and weave it on the gear up in the barn. They made four-yard scarves at first and something they called hats for a while before they finally mastered the loom and began to refine their technique. We got a few lopsided sweaters — one sleeve to the elbow, one to the knee — but mostly regular stuff after that.

After maybe a year, they could turn out the kind of close stitched zippered top that quit at the wrists and the hip bones and kept cave chill off as well as anything I'd ever worn.

Brody took over the garden patch. It was the first thing we'd allowed him that was entirely his. Clarice drove him in to buy the seeds and the sets, and we only got past the garden gate when Brody decided to let us. He wouldn't tolerate one of us wandering in and plucking a tomato at will.

He cut Toppy more slack than the rest of us since she clued him in on girls. They'd moved well beyond elective grooming by then and were deep into relationship issues. Proper romantic etiquette. How best to listen to your partner. Somehow those were always the chats I was allowed to overhear. In time I realized that, while Brody was the student, the spillover was for me.

Let's face it, I was new to girls too. Toppy'd had a couple of boyfriends, and when she wanted to sting me, she talked about them at length. I especially disliked the Korean one, chiefly because I could never be Korean. Also, he was some kind of hard-body ninja which I was doubtful I could ever be as well.

I made up a girl to gall Toppy with, but she caught on and turned her on me. When I'd be wrong about something (like I often was) or short-tempered and impatient, Toppy would point towards the nearest doorway, "Go tell it to Haley," she'd say.

It was a big jump for me from no girl to Toppy all the time. But I like to think I grew up on the job. I had long been reliable and steady underground and only had to find the best possible way to export all that that topside. I knew I couldn't let me and Toppy ever get worse than bumpy. I'd seen what my parents went through, and I wasn't going there.

After a year or so, Dad joined and blessed us out in the far woods with just Brody and Clarice for attendants. There was a grove of white oaks with woods grass beneath them and a spring close by that some previous clan had deepened and tastefully rocked up.

We dipped our hands in it when the time came and drank from each other's cupped palms. Dad kept the wherefores and the notwithstandings and the albeits to a minimum.

Clarice had made Toppy a sheep-white gown. I had a rental suit for the occasion. Dad had let me carry the traditional hideous horn crown in my hand.

There were no photographs taken. There was only the moment. The sun behind Toppy. A breeze shifting the treetops. Quail somewhere close by. Then we ate the awful root cake just as The Great Book decreed, and me and Toppy got sent upstairs in mid-afternoon to go to be fruitful. They all started in on the fertility song, but none of them could remember the words.

For our part, we mostly talked and changed our clothes. Then we went back down and ate Brody's sweet corn and Clarice's tough stewed hen.

We'd been two years and a little on our Kentucky farm when Toppy gave birth to our daughter. Clarice midwifed. Me and Dad and Brody could hear the yelling from the yard. The racket raised questions, but we persuaded Brody to hold onto them for a month or three.

We named her Emily, after my mother. And Soo-jin, after Toppy's. Toppy started her straightaway on every niggling Great Book prescription. Coming to America meant for Toppy that she'd thrown over her past, had sacrificed it for the hope of a makeshift future. Toppy told me she didn't feel like one thing or another and was determined it'd be different for our daughter. Our girl would be a proper Low Lord with all her boxes ticked.

Toppy knew The Great Book upside down and sideways and was acquainted with rites of passage the rest of us had never heard of. I think we'd turned loose of most of them because they were hard to carry through. There were instructions for some kind of anointing accomplished with boar's blood and a blessing conducted in chant that involved the sap of a chestnut root and tea made from night soil. Worse still, it was supposed to be served up in an alabastard phallus chalice. That's not what they called it, but that's what it was — the dried and repurposed instrument of a "mature bull cavus ferinus."

"We don't do any of that," Dad told Toppy, and he imagined that would settle it. Hardly. Toppy had a daughter to bring up right and Scripture on her side.

It fell to me to wear her down and organize accommodations. So I walked Toppy deep in our woods and showed her our only chestnut tree. It was long dead and half rotted.

"A blight wiped them out. No sap. No how."

Then I explained what night soil was exactly and the chances of coming by a phallus. Toppy ended up letting us make do with oolong in a metal camping cup.

Beauty was her old self. She didn't appear to miss her leg. She ran the sheep and chased the chickens. She played in the yard with little Em. She was gray on her snout and cloudy-eyed but still agile and alert underground. She didn't seem to have any special feeling for the alabastards she saw. I feared time with them might have softened her, but she still snarled and showed her teeth. I felt certain she'd have been at the throat of a warrior if we'd ever come across one. But it was adolescents and smaller. One tap of my blade on rock and they went.

Em was eighteen months exactly when Toppy insisted we baptize her. We knew it was coming and should have been readier. We scrambled to throw the gear together and thought we could get by with substitutes. A litter instead of a gamadan. Our old, smelly karstula from Granddaddy's box. Em's puny, ceremonial groper made out of whatever we could find. Headlamps instead of pine knots. Pilot biscuits from the

Kroger. There were an awful lot of corners we would have been perfectly happy to cut.

Of course, Toppy got scriptural on us and put an end to all of that. It took time to prepare, so we invited Leigh Ann and Aldo to join us. They came down on the train with Marcy as well who was serving as chaperone.

"This one's not ready," she said of my sister.

Brody disagreed. He explained to Marcy a thing or two about girl biology.

We all worked to prep for Em's ceremony and had catch ups over dinner. Things were just as quiet in New York City, but Leigh Ann and Aldo — Marcy even — had a sense it was all just for show.

Of the army, Leigh Ann told us, "Smug sons-of-bitches." It turned out Sal was renting out barrack space at a Sal sort of rate.

Toppy made Em's Karstula. She butchered the sheep for the hide herself. Me and Dad worked on the gamadan. It would be a proper litter on the order of the specimen we'd lent out and never got back. Aldo and Leigh Ann found fire knots after a full day in the woods. We'd kept Marcy in the house making pilot biscuits to give the kids some peace, and they'd come back about half covered in pine straw and leaves.

Brody and Clarice manufactured a groper out of a bone they found in the back of the barn, that and post-hole digger steel. They turned it all into an elegant, kid-sized thing.

We waited two days for the moon to be right, and then draped Em in her new karstula and loaded her into the gamadan. It took Me and Aldo and Dad and Clarice to carry it out to the cavern. Leigh Ann and Brody brought the pine knots and a hot box we'd found in a shed. Marcy had the pilot biscuits. Toppy carried the toy-sized groper.

We threw the bolt at the cavern and opened the massive, steel doors. Dad started in on the prelude, a regular Jeffersonian thicket. Once he'd gotten to "As it is written," we paraded in through the doorway.

Just inside, we tried to light the fire knots, but they wouldn't take, so we laid them aside and hauled the Gamadan down the stairs in regular headlamp light.

Beauty growled straightaway. I nosed them up as well. Vague fungal/guano stink.

I don't know how they knew what we'd be up to. The longer I spent with those creatures, the less sure about them I became.

Aldo lit the hot box for ceremony's sake. We brought Em out of the gamadan and made her eat another biscuit. Then her mother placed her groper in her hands.

"We of the darkness," Dad started in, and we all switched off our lamps.

I could hear them for sure. Smell them even a little. Clammy breathing. Talon scrape. I never lowered my thumb.

"We welcome you unto us," Dad finally said, and we all switched our lamps back on.

They'd nearly filled the cavern. The walls and ceiling were thick with them, crouched and clinging to the stone. Adolescents and kidlings up high. Warriors crowding in down low. I decided it all felt less like a threat than a ceremonial obligation. We had business Great Book business to get up to, and they had a part as well.

I found Cracker Daddy back towards the far cavern wall. He was flanked by his lieutenants and his women friends, I guess. He made our sign (I tend to think of it now) – touched a talon to the spot on his neck I'd chose to leave unshot. Then he slipped into a passageway, and all his subjects followed. They retreated in good order, left like water down a drain.

Our daughter did the thing that she'd been carried in to do. She waved her puny groper, and she laughed.

44950428R00200

Made in the USA
San Bernardino, CA
27 January 2017